Soft Red Hills of Alabama

Soft Red Hills of Alabama

By: Samuel C. Knighton

Fundcraft Publishing Company
Collierville, TN

Copyright © 2006 by Samuel C. Knighton

All rights reserved. No part of this book may be reproduced in any form, except for the inclusion of brief quotations in review, without permission in writing from the author/publisher.

ISBN 1-59872-658-7

Printed by Fundcraft Publishing Company, InstantPublisher Division, Collierville, TN

Manufactured in the United States of America

DISCLAIMER
The story presented here is completely fiction and only lives in the mind of the author. Any reference to any person living or dead, any place, or event is not intentional and is absolutely coincidental.

FORWARD
**Everyone, no matter whether poor or famous,
has a story**

Most of us are so busy with our lives that the thought of living a "story" seems beyond belief. But, a few recognize it and even say that one of their life's ambitions is to actually write about themselves, but few actually do. Down deep, we either feel that no one would be interested in our mundane lives, or, we plainly do not want to share the good and bad things that we've experienced over our lifetime.

But, no matter our social standing, whether rich or poor, we all have interesting things to tell and, this story is one of those.

*   *   *   *

Olabe Mae grew up in a very poor family in southern Alabama. Through her talent and strength, coupled with timing and just plain good luck, rose to become one of the most popular country western stars the world had seen in many years.

She was the epitome of fame and fortune and lived with her family on a high-fenced and guarded massive estate outside of Nashville. She had people to take care of her every want and need. Her music fueled her life and took care of her family. Her life couldn't have been better.

Bill Renwick was Olabe Mae's husband. They had two children, Robert, and Alexia. All competed for her attention and affection, which often made Olabe Mae escape into her music.

But, regardless of status or social standing, a sudden unexplainable tragedy can cause catastrophic change in a person's life, and just such an event changed Olabe Mae's life forever.

*   *   *   *

Olabe Mae was preparing for a concert at the Phillips Arena in Atlanta. Her life was good. She was extremely popular with a huge fan-base and her concert had been sold out for weeks. Her body was filled with anticipation, adrenaline, and excitement.

Back home, her husband, Bill, drove his Jeep Cherokee taking Robert and Alexia to a soccer tournament and excitement was high. Unbeknown to him, or anyone, destiny was coming in the opposite direction.

Two teenage kids had stolen a car and were racing towards Nashville. They were suddenly slowed by a plodding, huge dump-truck loaded with crushed stone. In their impatience, they recklessly passed the truck, but then saw Bill's oncoming car just as they crested a hill. They swerved in front of the truck to avoid the oncoming car which caused the truck to skid to the left and hit Bill's vehicle head-on. The Cherokee was mangled beyond recognition and all it's occupants were killed instantly.

In the matter of a fraction of a second, Olabe Mae's life had changed forever.

Severe depression followed and washed over her very soul.

Finally, one day, her depression lifted a little. Olabe Mae felt an unexplainable calling from the soft red hills of Alabama to come home. Come home to her mother, to the house she was born in, and to her Alabama roots.

CHAPTER 1

Life Can Change Forever in a Microsecond

"Where's that stupid helicopter?" Olabe shouted as she paced back and forth.

Olabe Mae was one of the most popular performers to come onto the country music scene in years. Her strong, high-pitched voice sang her way into the hearts of her fans across every state with her first number one hit; Country Girls. It was followed by nine more number one singles along with numerous CDs. Olabe had been touring the country giving concerts to sellout crowds with front row seats now exceeding one thousand dollars each. Her popularity had even sparked fans around the world, with a huge following in Japan.

She was appropriately thin, but not without a lot of work. Her house had a special exercise room that was filled with all the latest equipment. She had long hair that was bleached to blonde, but her hair stylist always allowed just a tinge of natural auburn color to lightly show through. She had green eyes and was naturally beautiful. For traveling today, she wore a thin electric blue blouse and a pair of skin-tight Levis.

Olabe lived in a mansion estate about twenty miles south of Nashville. It was very private. Her property consisted of almost 400 acres that was completely fenced. The house sat on top of a hill which provided a wonderful panoramic view of the valley below. She was in her huge bedroom suite waiting.

"Helicopter 460 bravo. This is Nashville Center," a pleasant female voice sounded in the pilot's headphones.

"460 bravo," he responded.

"We have you at twenty one miles south of the airport."

"We are following Interstate 65 and request permission to drop to fifteen hundred feet at the Rapid Reach Road interchange. Our final destination is OM alpha," the pilot said into his microphone. OM alpha was the code name used for Olabe Mae's heliport.

"Permission granted 460."

"I thought the chopper wasn't coming until five o'clock this afternoon," Olabe's husband, Bill Renwick, said as he helped their two children get their gear ready for the soccer game in the early afternoon.

"Carl called me this morning and told me there was a change in plans. They want me to sing the national anthem with some Atlanta celeb and she wants to rehearse it," Olabe responded sharply.

Carl Strom was Olabe's agent. He had signed her when she was just breaking into country music and had managed her career all through her rapid rise to stardom.

"You're going to miss our game, Mom," Alexia whined as she clomped by the bedroom door in her purple and green uniform with one shoe on. "Do you know where my other shoe is, Dad?"

"You know, Olabe," Bill said as he sat on the bed watching his beautiful wife nervously pace back and forth by the massive wall of windows of their bedroom.

"You haven't been to one of the kids' games yet. They were counting on you coming to this one. It's going to be their first tournament game."

Suddenly, Olabe stomped right over to where Bill was sitting, snorting with rage.

"Bill Renwick!" she shouted. "Don't you dare try to throw a guilt trip on me. You know full well there is no way I can go to their game today."

"But, you promised, Mom," Robert said as he walked into the bedroom followed by Alexia. "You said you could come to at least part of it before you had to go."

Robert was their oldest child. He was twelve last June. He had light, sandy hair that was totally unmanageable, or at least as unmanageable as a twelve year old boy cared it to be. He was a typical pre-teen boy. His voice was starting to crack when he talked and his sister constantly made fun of him. A little acne was starting to plague him too. He liked playing sports, and especially liked playing soccer. He was probably just an average player, but always tried his very best. Robert was usually quiet and reserved and was a pretty average student in school. He hated country music and was often chastised for playing his stereo too loud. But, mostly, his reprimands came from his choice of playing rap music that was so popular with the kids in his grade.

Alexia, on the other hand, was a complete opposite of Robert and a year younger. She was outgoing and excelled at sports. She was a "straight A" student and liked by her teachers and most all of her classmates. She had blonde hair with just the hint of an auburn tinge, like her mother. Alexia was extremely competitive and very well coordinated which made her an excellent soccer player. She was rapidly maturing and turning into a beautiful young woman. She loved country music and often sang with her mother in their music room, just for fun. But, Alexia's greatest gift, much to the consternation of her brother, was she had lots of natural talent and intelligence and hardly ever needed to practice nor study very much.

"It may seem like a little thing to you, Olabe, but to these kids, this game is pretty important," Bill added as he watched the two children go to their rooms to pack the rest of their soccer equipment.

"Helicopter is coming," Olabe's maid, Jasmine said as she ran into the bedroom. "Should be here is another few minutes. See it out there?" She pointed out the window towards a small little dot in the sky.

"Don't think I'm done with you, Bill Renwick," Olabe snorted with fire in her eyes. "You've been on the gravy train now for more than fifteen years. You're a 'stay at home' dad and I bring home the bacon. Your job is to do what all 'stay at home' folks do. Your job is to take care of the kids. You truck them to where ever they have to go. Is that clear? Not me. I'm not ever going to sit out there in the hot sun while they run back and forth all over some weed patch while sweaty parents slobber around me, telling me how much they love my music. Hah."

"But, they're your fans, Olabe,"

"Fans, huh? Ever see the way some of those men try to look down my blouse when they come near me? Ever wonder what sort of evil thoughts are going through their little pea brains? Now, I've got to get out of here. If you need me for anything, and let me emphasize how big of a crisis it will have to be, call Carl on his cell.

He'll be with me all during this concert in Atlanta."

Olabe turned and walked right out the bedroom door and down the stairs. Bill opened one of the glass sliding doors from the bedroom to the deck and walked outside. He stood and watched the helicopter land on their green asphalt heliport. He watched Olabe run from their garage to the waiting chopper. She was as beautiful as ever. Her long, blonde hair surrounded her, puffing upward from the prop wash from the whirling blades of the helicopter. He watched her tight fitting Levis hug her as she stepped up into the cabin and shut the door.

"Love you," he whispered and waved, but Olabe neither waved nor looked back.

"Come on, Dad," Robert shouted at his father. "Let's go."

"Alright," Bill said as he came inside and shut the sliding door. "Where's your sister?"

"I'm coming, Dad," Alexia shouted as she bounded down the stairs with Jackie, their black lab barking behind her. "Jackie's coming, too. Right, Dad?"

"I suppose so. Come on now, you guys. You sure you have everything?"

The two kids assured their father that they had thought of everything, but experience had taught him to check for himself.

"Don't suppose you need these, Alex?" he asked as he gave her two plastic shin guards.

"Oh. Thanks, Dad. Guess I forgot."

They ran excitedly through the garage until they came to a yellow Jeep Cherokee. Doors opened, kids, gear, and the dog got in. Doors slammed. Bill started the engine and pushed the garage door opener.

Soon, they turned onto Wilson Pike blacktop that took them south through Clovercroft. The Jeep turned right onto Clovercroft Road towards Mudsink. The big outdoor sports arena at Mudsink was about ten miles from their house and usually took about fifteen minutes.

"Turn the radio on, Dad," Alexia shouted from the back seat.

Suddenly, there was a flash of something speeding directly towards the Cherokee. Bill swerved. There was a horrendous crash. And then, silence.

*   *   *   *

"You okay, back there, Miss Olabe?' the copilot said into his microphone.

"I'm fine," she reported.

Carl filled a glass of Merlot and handed it to her.

"Here. This will help take the edge off."

"How do you do it, Carl?" Olabe asked as she reached for the glass and took a small sip. "How can you tell?"

"Well. After almost twenty years of working with you, guess it's second nature. Besides, it's part of my job."

"Bill and I had a big tiff just before you got here. Guess I should say, I had a fight with Bill. He never fights. Boy, do I ever hate that. I sure wish he would yell back sometimes."

Carl smiled and could still feel the sharp edge in Olabe's voice.

"Funny," Olabe said as she finished the wine. "It always seems to happen right before I leave. Either he wants to be lovey-dovey or the kids want me to go watch them play some stupid game. Today, it was a soccer game. Originally, I had told them I could watch the first part. You know, that was before you called and told me about singing the national anthem."

"You should have told me, Olabe," Carl said as he poured a little more wine into her glass. "I could have easily told them you couldn't make it."

"Actually, Carl. It was a godsend. There was no way I wanted to go to that stupid game anyway."

Carl watched Olabe's anger fade away. It was wonderful how a little wine could relieve the tension and he had seen it happen many times over during Olabe's career.

"Airport coming up," the copilot said. "We'll have you on the ground in a few minutes."

The helicopter touched down softly and the pilot immediately shut the engine down. By the time Olabe and Carl had unbuckled their seatbelts and the door was opened, the main rotor had stopped turning. A white Cadillac limo pulled up right next to the helicopter steps, a man in a blue uniform jumped out and opened the door for Olabe.

"Afternoon, Miss Olabe," the man said as he tipped his hat.

Olabe smiled but didn't say anything. She got in first, with Carl stepping in after her. The door was shut and the limo raced off towards the Philips Arena. The afternoon traffic was terrible. Travel was slow and bumper to bumper.

"Don't worry, Olabe," Carl said as he noticed her fidgeting. "There's plenty of time."

Olabe's face formed a quick smile, but Carl could tell that she wasn't convinced.

When the limo arrived at 1 Philips Drive it drove right up to the building and a huge garage door opened. It moved inside and the door immediately closed behind them.

"See?" Carl said as he looked at his watch. "Lots of time."

Olabe had done two other concerts at the Philips Arena, here in Atlanta, always to sellout crowds.

"What's the audience look like for tonight?" she asked Carl as they walked along now with four other people dressed in magenta blazers with the arena logo on them.

"Full house, as always," he responded.

Olabe was introduced to Mary Belle Evans, the young woman that she was to sing the national anthem with. She was some sort of local celebrity, probably about twenty-one, and a pretty, petite little thing. She was so nervous that she floundered around when they first went out onto the massive stage. But, thankfully, when the lights came up and the prerecorded music started, she changed. Her body movements became fluid and easy. She looked confident and professional. Stage hands handed microphones to her and Olabe and showed them the switch to turn them on.

There was a pause as the sound system went silent, and then, the music of the prelude to the national anthem boomed across the massive overhead speakers.

"Oh say can you see," they both sang together as the sound board operators adjusted slide controls to maximize the effect.

It only took two practice times before everyone seemed to feel satisfied.

Olabe was led to her dressing room to rest for a while before it was time to shower, get her hair done, and get dressed for tonight's performance. She hated these dead times because there was nothing to do. Many performers needed a small rest to rejuvenate right before going on stage, but Olabe was not one of them.

Later, she calmly waited behind the towering curtains in the dim light while Mary Belle paced back and forth. The musicians had taken their places and were about ready. The murmur of a multitude of voices ebbed and flowed from the overfilled massive Philips arena.

Standing room only, Olabe thought to herself and smiled. She loved being on stage. It was her adrenalin rush and her reason for being.

A hush came over the crowd. Then, a drum roll started as the main curtains rose in the dim light. That was Olabe and Mary Belle's signal to step out onto the stage and take their positions.

"Ooohhh say can you see," the two voices blended while everyone in the audience stood and tried their best to sing the very difficult song with them.

When it was over, the applause was deafening and thunderous. Mary Belle smiled and waved as she was introduced to the audience.

Suddenly, the stage lights lit to full illumination and a deep male voice boomed across the packed arena.

"Ladies and Gentlemen. I have the pleasure to introduce," he shouted as the multitude started clapping, whistling, and yelling. "Miss Olabe Mae."

The whole arena erupted into an explosion of noise. It was a combination of thousands of hands clapping with thousands of watts being transmitted through the Philips Arena's massive sound system. The spotlight came up and Olabe stepped into the brilliant circle of light.

Olabe sang all her old hits and the crowd roared its approval and sang along. She sang a few of the songs on her new CD and each one brought the house down. After three encores, it was over. Olabe was exhausted, but the adrenalin was still smoking through her veins.

By the time she was in her hotel suite she had calmed down some and sat on the large couch while Carl poured her a tall glass of dark red wine. He walked over and handed the glass to her.

"Great concert, as always, Olabe," he smiled. "I think this was your best yet."

"Where do we go from here, Carl?" she asked and took a big sip of wine.

"Chicago on the 24th of this month. Then, Omaha, Los Angeles, Dallas, and finally, Las Vegas."

"Well. Six down and six to go."

"You sure you're okay?" Carl asked as he walked to the door in response to a gentle knock.

"I'm fine, Carl. You worry too much. Besides, it sure keeps the money flowing in."

"That it does, my lady. That it does," Carl smiled as he opened the door.

"Room service." a young man said as he pushed a cart with numerous plates covered with silver domes.

Carl said he would take it from there and handed the bellman a generous tip. He closed the door and pushed the cart over to the table.

"Dinner is served," he said as he held the chair for Olabe.

Dinner was prime rib, mashed potatoes, and mixed vegetables. Very similar to what one would expect to eat in one of the meeting rooms of the hotel, except it was probably three times more expensive.

When they had both finished, Carl stood and put all the dishes back on the little cart.

"Guess you had better get some sleep. The limo will be here tomorrow morning at eight to get us out to the airport by nine. Should have you back at your house before eleven. Want me to call you in the morning?"

"No, thanks," Olabe said as she followed Carl to the door. "Good night."

Carl bid her good night, pushed the cart out into the hallway, and shut Olabe's door.

She turned, walked towards her bed, kicked off her boots, and pealed off her tight jeans. It felt wonderful to relieve the tightness and pressure of those designer pants. She went into the bathroom, removed the rest of her clothes, and turned on the shower.

Olabe smiled as she stood in the shower and let the prickly hot water pour over her for a long time. She had always felt that Carl had something for her and would jump at the chance, if she ever even hinted at it. But, she never had. Even though she had spent many nights far away from home with him in hundreds of hotel rooms, she had always remained true to her one love, and that was Bill. But, Bill could be so exasperating sometimes she thought to herself as she soaped up for the third time.

Finally, Olabe was in bed and the hours of stress and the physical demands of her concert all took their toll. She was asleep in a few minutes.

Suddenly, the phone on the night stand rang out.

Olabe's mind solidified enough to recognize that it was the telephone and decided to ignore it. Whatever it was, could wait until morning.

The problem was, it kept on ringing. Finally, she reached out her hand and picked up the receiver.

"Hello? She said in an irritated, sleepy voice.

In just a few seconds, Olabe's world, as she knew it, had changed forever. Bill, Robert, Alexia, and Jackie had all been killed instantly.

      *   *   *   *

It was a cold, rainy day in Nashville. The wind gusted and the man that stood next to Olabe tried his best to hold his umbrella over her.

She heard the words, "ashes to ashes and dust to dust," but none of it registered in her brain at all. In fact, the only thing she was aware of at all was the way her right, high-heeled shoe pinched her little toe.

CHAPTER 2
Coming Home

Olabe's mind cleared a little. Her brain told her that the television was blaring and irritating her mind, but so what. She felt hot, but didn't care. Her nose told her that she smelled of sweat, but she didn't have the energy to care. She just wanted to stop thinking anything at all. She wanted to die.

Suddenly, the bedroom door flew open and her maid, Jasmine, ran in. Quickly, she turned off the television and opened the drapes.

"Miss Olabe. My gracious, but how long you been up here? You didn't eat nothin' I fixed you for Saturday. I know, because it's still on the table down there in the kitchen."

Jasmine came over to the bed and pulled back the comforter. Olabe was curled up in the fetal position with her eyes shut.

"Phew! Miss Olabe, you stink. We've got to get you out that bed and into the shower. Here, I'll help you."

Olabe cracked her eyes open and looked at Jasmine with a blank stare. Her brain didn't want to engage or even tell who it was standing over her.

"Miss Olabe, you get up now. We've got to get those smelly clothes off and you into the shower. Come on, now. It'll make you feel better."

Olabe's brain told her that she didn't want to feel better. She didn't want to feel anything at all.

But Jasmine was persistent. She kept tugging and pulling until she had Olabe standing up like a little child. She pulled off her clothes and noticed that they were the same ones that she had worn to the funeral. Jasmine ran into the bathroom, turned on the shower, and then came back. Olabe was still standing right where she left her, with the same blank stare.

"Come on, now, Miss Olabe," Jasmine said as she pulled her by the hand. "A nice warm shower will make you feel better."

Jasmine pulled and coaxed until she had Olabe into the shower stall. She handed her a washcloth and shut the glass door. She went back out into the bedroom, pulled off the sheets, and picked up Olabe's clothes. She went back into the bathroom and shoved her load down the laundry chute. Jasmine turned and stared. She could see through the glass door that Olabe was still standing exactly as she had left her. The water from the shower head was pouring down over her body, but she didn't seem to notice it at all.

"Miss Olabe. Here's the shampoo. Now wash your hair."

As long as Jasmine gave orders, Olabe's brain seemed to engage enough to do whatever she was asked to do. Jasmine helped her dry off and get dressed. She held her hand as she led her downstairs and had her sit in a big leather chair while she looked in the refrigerator to see what might appeal to her. She found cups of chocolate pudding and took one out. She went over to Olabe and leaned on the arm of the chair while she spoon-fed her. And, surprisingly enough, Olabe ate it.

Over the course of the next week, the schedule was the same. Jasmine came at eight in the morning, she got Olabe up, and into the shower. She helped her dress and come downstairs. She spoon-fed her, just like a small child, and had her sit in the big leather chair while she did laundry and cleaned the house. In the late afternoon, Jasmine led Olabe back up to the master bedroom and helped her get ready for bed, and only then, after everything was done, Jasmine went home to her husband. Every morning was the same. When she came back to Olabe's master bedroom, she was always just as she left her. Curled up, in the fetal position, in bed.

Olabe's physician came one afternoon in response to Jasmine's urgent request. He examined her and tried to get her to respond. His diagnosis was deep clinical depression resulting from severe trauma. He gave Jasmine some antidepressant pills, but told her to watch closely whenever she gave them to her and watch for signs of suicidal symptoms. If that happened, she was to call him immediately and never let her out of her sight. After the doctor left, Jasmine decided to never give the pills to Olabe. She took them out and put them in her car. That gave her the idea to protect Olabe from anything in pill form, just in case she got some crazy ideas. Jasmine grabbed a plastic garbage bag from the laundry room and rushed around to all the bathrooms in the house and cleaned out each medicine cabinet. She took the garbage bag out and put it into her car.

The first week was the worst. Olabe responded little. She did follow Jasmine's orders, but virtually nothing else. Olabe was always very trim and had little body fat, but even that had pretty much disappeared. She looked terrible. Her eyes appeared dark and sunken in. Jasmine shuddered every time she helped her get undressed to take a shower as she noticed her emaciated body getting even thinner.

But, Jasmine thought she noticed a slight improvement during the second week. Olabe ate a little better, but not much. Her approach was to offer lots of little meals during the day and eat with her. That seemed to help the most. Olabe even would answer questions with a word or two.

The third and fourth week were sometimes better and then, often followed by a complete reversal. Just when Jasmine thought they had turned the corner and she could see real improvement, she would find Olabe in the fetal position in bed and virtually unresponsive.

Jasmine worked and worried about Olabe. Her husband told her that she needed help with her work, and that Olabe could certainly afford it. But, not only was Jasmine Olabe's personal maid, she was also a very close friend, and friends don't leave friends to strangers. Jasmine continued her grueling schedule which was taking its toll on her.

One afternoon after working all morning just to get Olabe out of bed, Jasmine was down in the laundry room loading the washer.

Dear Lord, she prayed to herself. *Why do you allow people to suffer so much? If you are such a forgiving God, why do you let things happen like this?*

Jasmine had extreme faith, but this situation was testing it to the fullest. Fortunately, God had seen to it to provide her with such a good and understanding man. Her husband was her rock and her solace was coming home and just having him hold her. They didn't need to talk at all. She just needed another human being to care. And, he did.

Days turned into weeks and weeks turned into a month. Nothing seemed to change very much. Jasmine worked into a regular routine and fortunately for her, it had become manageable. Her husband even accompanied her, on occasion, and was a great help.

It was a little past midnight on Wednesday and it was raining outside. The temperature was mild, but the wind was gusting now and then. Suddenly, the heavy fog that had cloaked Olabe's brain faded away and she came fully alert and aware. She looked around her bedroom for a few seconds.

"What's going on?" she asked herself out loud.

She jumped out of bed with newly found energy and ambition, almost as if she were being driven by some irresistible force. She went into the shower and felt the hot water prickle her skin. She washed her hair and scrubbed her body. She avoided looking in the mirror as she dried off, dressed, and finally, only looked at herself as she brushed her long hair. A thought raced through her mind as she wondered who it was in the mirror starring back at her.

Olabe was driven now. She went to her huge walk-in closet, pulled down two suitcases, and took them out and laid them on her bed. She filled one with underwear and t-shirts. The other was filled with jeans, casual shirts, and blouses. She filled her overnight case with deodorant and other necessary toiletries. The bags were closed and the latches snapped shut. Olabe dragged each suitcase down the stairs one at time, not because they were so heavy, but mainly because she didn't seem to have much strength. She took them into the laundry room and set them side by side.

She went back upstairs and into her music room. She turned on the lights, now completely focused on her mission. The room was surrounded on three sides by floor-to-ceiling windows. There were musical instruments all around setting on stands. There was a complete professional sound board and recording equipment. Olabe didn't see any of it. She went straight to one corner of the room and stood by the wall. She keyed a number into a keypad on the wall hidden by the drapes that looked like the keypad for an electronic thermostat or even a security system. She pushed the "enter" key and there was a dull "thump" in the floor. A panel of hardwood flooring popped up. Olabe reached down and pulled it up which revealed a sunken built-in safe. Olabe knelt down and quickly entered a number onto its keypad. She pulled the heavy door open. Inside were lots of folders and papers. But, she knew exactly what she was looking for. She pulled out five banded stacks of twenty dollar bills. Each contained one thousand dollars. Olabe shut the door of the safe and then the hardwood floor panel. She replaced the throw rug, shut off the lights, and ran out of the room and back down to the laundry room. She pulled off a few bills and stuffed them into her pocket, opened one of the suitcases, and put the stacks of money inside.

Olabe then dragged each suitcase down the long hallway and opened the door to the huge six car garage. There was a black Cadillac Escalade, a huge, orange colored pickup truck, a red Ferrari, a vacant space, a green CJ-7 Jeep, and, at the far end, a yellow BMW convertible. She took the two bags and overnight case to the little yellow car and opened the trunk. Olabe had never put anything into the trunk before and was astounded at how little it was. In fact, she could only get one suitcase and her overnight case into it. She shut the trunk lid, went to the passenger's side, and opened the door. Somehow, she managed to cram the second bag onto the seat and was just able to get the door shut. She ran around to the driver's side and was about to reach for the door handle when she stopped short. Olabe ran back to the trunk, opened it, opened the suitcase, and pulled out one of the stacks of twenties. She then ran back to the house and into the kitchen. She rummaged through a drawer, found a pad of paper and pen, and quickly scrawled a note:

> *Jasmine-*
> *I've found myself and have to go away. Don't worry at all. Thank you so very much for everything you did. Here's a little something for all your trouble.*
> *I love you,*
> *O.M.*

Olabe went back out to the garage, got into her car, and started the engine. The garage door behind the yellow BMW rose and she backed out. The door shut behind her.

Soon, the little yellow car was racing southward on Interstate 65. Olabe fumbled with the radio. Not to listen to, but more for company and just noise. Every station she found seemed to be playing country songs, but after all, this was Nashville country. She found a station with someone talking, but she soon discovered that it was a hellfire and brimstone preacher expounding on the wickedness of the world. Olabe quickly changed the station. Finally, she found a talk radio station and blankly listened to two men talking about the importance of the Amazon rain forests. She fought back the dark blanket that kept trying to smother her mind.

The miles went by, but Olabe didn't noticed them at all. She just kept the little yellow car going south. She noticed a huge billboard coming up on the right side that said, "Welcome to Alabama."

After driving for more than two hours, Olabe's mind was suddenly startled to full attention by a small, blinking light on the dash panel. The flashing light was in the shape of a little gas pump which caused her eyes to move instantly to the gas gauge. It showed that she still had a about an eighth of a tank. She was nearing the outskirts of Huntsville.

She went up an off ramp and into a very large Rebel Fast Gas station. There were no cars anywhere, but all the lights were on. Olabe drove up to a gas pump, stopped, and shut the engine off. She then realized that she had no idea how or where to put gas in her car. Finally, she got out of the car and walked into the brightly lit building that looked like a well stocked mini-mart. The only person inside was a young man behind the counter.

"Can I help you?" he asked brightly and smiled. He jumped up and came over to the counter. "You all need gas?"

"I'm so sorry to bother you," Olabe said. "But, I'm completely helpless here. I've never put gas in my car before and don't know even where it goes."

The southern gentleman culture of the young man rose to the occasion. It was always an honor, or more directly, a duty for any southern man to help a lady in distress.

"I'll be happy to help you," he said as he locked the drawers of the two cash registers and came around the counter. "Come on. We'll figure it out."

Olabe followed the young man out to where her car was. He looked the back fender over.

"Here's the door, but there must be a release somewhere inside. Mind if I take a look?"

"Not at all," Olabe said as she opened the door for him.

"Here it is," he said proudly as he pulled up a lever with a gas pump emblem on it which caused the door on the back fender to pop open.

Within a few seconds he had the gas cap off and the hose nozzle in place.

"Cash or charge?"

"Cash."

When the automatic holder on the nozzle snapped, he took the hose out and put it back into its holder. He then replaced the cap and shut the fuel door. They walked back into the store now chatting like old friends.

He went around the counter and turned towards Olabe and said almost apologetically, "that's going to be fifty eight dollars and ninety cents. Your car takes premium, you know."

"Do you have any coffee?" Olabe asked as she put three twenties on the counter.

"I was just making a fresh pot when you came in," the young man said. "Let's see if it's ready.

He came around the counter and went over to a coffee center. The coffee was done and he poured some into a paper cup for Olabe.

"Won't you join me?" she asked as she went over, pulled out a chair and sat by a small table.

"Sure," he said as he quickly poured a cup for himself, came over to where Olabe was sitting, and sat down.

"What's your name?" Olabe asked.

"Ron," he said with a big smile.

"Hi Ron. I'm Olabe," she said as she reached out her right hand to shake hands.

"I know," Ron said as he immediately looked down at his shoes while his neck and face turned a bright shade of crimson. "My wife, Marlene, and I are big fans. We've got all your CDs. We even went down to Birmingham once and camped all night to get tickets for one of your concerts."

"Was it worth it?" she asked and took a sip of coffee.

"Worth it? Why, Miss Olabe, if we could afford it, we would go to all of your concerts. You were wonderful."

Olabe was outright embarrassed. She had many fans often tell her she was good or how much they had enjoyed her concerts. But, here was a young man that probably didn't make enough money to even pay the rent telling her that he and his wife truly loved her music.

"Do you have any children?"

"A little girl," he said proudly and dug out his wallet. He showed her a photograph. "This is her. Her name is Savannah."

"Cute," Olabe said as she examined the photo.

Olabe had an idea. She reached into her pocket and pulled out some money. She put four twenties on the table and pushed them towards Ron.

"I'm sorry I don't have any photos with me, Ron. But, here. Take this. I want you to take your wife out for dinner sometime."

Ron was astonished. His eyes filled with tears which wasn't very manly. Especially, for a young southern man.

"I can't take that, Miss Olabe," he almost whispered.

"Yes, you can," she said firmly. She picked up the bills and put them into his hand.

"I don't know what to say, Miss Olabe."

"Just say that you'll take Marlene out for dinner."

"You don't know what this means to me."

Olabe smiled and signed a paper napkin for Ron. She stood up and Ron immediately got up, too. She put her arms around him and hugged him. Olabe waved to him as she went back out to her little yellow car.

Again, the miles went by without registering at all in Olabe's mind. She constantly fought the black blanket of depression and occupied her mind by reciting the multiplication tables. She had to change the radio station as the one she had on before was fading as she drove south.

She had been driving for quite a while when she noticed that the sky ahead looked like a huge dome of illumination. A sign proclaimed that the next five exits were for Montgomery. Olabe turned off of the next interchange and went into another gas station.

This time, she put the gas in herself. It wasn't easy, but she did it. Olabe went inside, paid for the gas, and used the restroom. She bought a cup of coffee and took it out to the car. Within a few minutes, she was back on the highway, now looking for 231 to Dothan. The sign came up, she turned right, and headed south again. She noticed the clock on the radio said that it was a little after five and it was just barely starting to get daylight.

Olabe's route took her south through Pine Lever, Macedonia, Meeksville, Friendship, and Troy. She turned east on Alabama 10 which took her through Brundidge, Clip, and Blue Springs. She saw a sign pointing to the right for Highway 105 to Clopton. The little yellow car turned and accelerated going south again. It was now almost full daylight. Olabe kept going until she found the turnoff for a small, blacktop road. She turned left, went a few more miles, and then turned right onto a gravel road. Her route continued for another mile. There it was. She recognized the opening for a little lane to the right. She turned and drove up the long lane towards an old house that looked very dilapidated and uninhabited. Olabe suddenly felt a pang of worry as she shut the engine off.

She sat for a few seconds and then, noticed that the screen door seemed to be opening. An old woman stepped out onto the porch. Was this her mother, Jewel? She looked so old and wrinkled. How long had it been since she had seen her mother? Then, Olabe remembered. The last time she saw her was more than fifteen years ago at her daddy's funeral. She felt a heavy pang of guilt shoot through her.

"Mama?" Olabe said as she stepped out of the car. "Is that you?"

"Olabe? "Oh, dear God. Olabe? Is that you?"

The two women rushed towards each other. They threw their arms around each other and their eyes filled with tears.

"Can I stay here for a while, Mama?" Olabe finally managed to whisper.

"This is your home, Olabe. Of course you can stay. Come in the house now and have some coffee."

Over the course of the next week Jewel watched Olabe carefully. She saw the darkness of depression take her very soul to the brink. Olabe spent most of her time sitting on the porch and just staring off into the distance. She ate so little that Jewel worried that she was starving herself.

On Tuesday afternoon, Olabe sat in her rocker and stared. She didn't have shoes nor socks on. She wore a pink summer blouse and a yellow skirt covered with pastel flowers. Her stare was the same as always.

All morning Jewel thought and prayed for guidance to help her daughter. It was like living with a complete stranger. Even though she hadn't seen Olabe for a long while, she still loved her and she still was her daughter. Finally, after lunch Jewel decided to act.

"Olabe," Jewel said as she came up to the rocker. "Olabe. Now, listen to me, Olabe. I need you to come out to the garden this afternoon and help me. Do you hear me?"

Olabe's expression didn't change and it appeared as though she hadn't heard her mother at all.

Jewel's garden was her life sustaining gift from God. It was huge compared to most vegetable gardens. It always produced two crops; one for its produce and the other for seeds for replanting. Right next to the garden was a large orchard. It had apple, peach, and pear along with four pecan trees. All in all, Jewel grew, harvested, and canned huge amounts of food every year. It even produced excess so that when her neighbors butchered a steer or pig, she could trade for a ham, bacon, or some smoked meat.

"Olabe," Jewel said louder and put her hand on her daughter's thin, bony shoulder. "Come on now. I need you to help me."

Slowly, Olabe turned her head and looked at Jewel with staring, expressionless eyes that couldn't quite seem to focus. She stood up and reached out for her mother's hand. Jewel led the way to the garden and Olabe followed along behind like a little puppy.

Olabe followed her mother's orders and seemed to do whatever she was instructed to do, but no more. It was as if her mind was turned off. Jewel was perplexed and didn't know what to do. She kept telling her daughter to do small chores, and Olabe did them almost as if she were a small child.

Jewel was down on her hands and knees one afternoon picking black-eyed peas and Olabe was standing next to her. She noticed that Olabe was scrunching the soft, red Alabama earth between her toes, just like she did when she was a child. Somehow, that seemed to give Jewel hope.

Time passed slowly and Olabe seemed to improve a little. Her depressions didn't seem to be quite so deep anymore, nor as often. They didn't seem to last for days on end either, but now, only lasted a day or not even that. She would have good days and talk like any other person. But then, without warning, there would be darkness and silence. Jewel worried.

One late afternoon, Jewel and Olabe sat out on the porch in their rockers when suddenly, a funny noise seemed to be coming from Olabe's car. She got up, walked to it, and opened the door. She seemed to be talking on something inside.

"What in the world was that?" Jewel asked when she came back up on the porch.

"What was what, Mama?"

"Who were you talking to in your car out there?"

"Oh, Mama. You're funny," Olabe chuckled which warmed Jewel's heart. This was the first time since Olabe's arrived that she even hinted of laughing.

"Well. What was it?

"It was my cell phone, Mama. I was talking to my business manager up in Nashville."

"A telephone in your car?" Jewel said a little astonished. She naturally knew what a telephone was, but didn't have one, and had little use for one. But, she had even talked on one on occasion at the little store down in Clopton. She remembered she had called Olabe and her sister to tell them about their father's death which now seemed so long ago.

"It's actually a cell phone, Mama. I just keep it plugged into the cigarette lighter in my car to keep the battery charged. You can make calls from anywhere. Even out in your garden."

"Why, whatever for?"

Both women laughed and it felt good to hear Olabe feeling better.

CHAPTER 3
We Need a Truck

It was a hot Alabama evening. Not a whisper of breeze even rustled the huge pecan tree that grew near the house. The two women sat on the porch in their rockers while Jewel sipped her cup of evening tea and watched Olabe out of the corner of her eye. Olabe's depression had seemed a little better today, Jewel noticed. Not much, but maybe just a little. Instead of picking at her supper tonight, Olabe had actually eaten a fair amount and even talked a little. But, what Jewel noticed most was that she had actually asked for a cup of tea tonight. All the previous evenings while they sat out on the porch before bed, Jewel had tea and Olabe just sat and stared.

"Mama?" Olabe broke the silence which almost startled Jewel.

"Yes?"

"I've been thinking."

"About what, dear?" Jewel asked as she sat her cup on the table and gave her full attention.

"I've been thinking that we need a truck."

"A truck? Whatever for?"

"Well, my BMW is useless if we want to haul anything or take anyone with us."

Jewel thought carefully. Jewel had no real experience with vehicles of any kind. When her husband was alive, he had a truck and she had ridden in it many times. Although she didn't feel the need for a truck, nor the need of Olabe's little yellow car either, she did like Olabe's new found interest.

"What would you do with your car?"

"Just trade it in, Mama. I don't know and don't care. It's pretty useless down here in the hills."

Jewel liked to see Olabe thinking out loud again and wanted to inspire her to continue on, but was unsure how.

"Won't have to be a new one. Just a pretty new one, so it will be dependable."

"Gracious, Olabe," Jewel's practical side began to show. "We don't have the money for a truck or even money to put gas in it."

"Money?" Olabe said as she jumped up and walked to the porch railing. "Don't worry about money, Mama. I've got more than enough."

Jewel had no idea what she meant by "enough." No one ever seemed to have enough money. She had little idea what Olabe had done with her life, except that she was a singer and actually had some of her songs played on the radio. But, because her house had no electricity, Jewel had never actually heard any. Some years back, she remembered, folks around had told her about Olabe "making it big." But, she had no idea what that actually meant.

"Where are the car dealers around here, Mama?"

"Olabe, I have no idea. I've never been to one."

She remained by the porch railing for a while silently thinking. Finally, she turned around and faced her mother.

"Mama, how far away from here have you been?"

That statement turned in Jewel's mind. She was born less than a mile from her farm and had lived right around here all of her life.

"I've been to Montgomery once," she almost whispered. "I went with your father up there when we were first married when he took the examination for his trade."

Olabe felt a tinge of guilt as she heard her mother utter those few words. She, on the other hand, had traveled all over the United States, Canada, Europe, and even Japan giving concerts. Yet this was the first time the thought of who her mother really was entered her mind. Olabe had even done a concert in London and shook hands with the Queen. She had an audience with the Pope when her concert tour played Rome. And, yet her mother had spent all her life right here, never going anywhere, except one trip to Montgomery.

"Didn't you ever want to go anywhere, Mama?" Olabe asked as she moved her rocker closer to her mother's chair and sat down.

"Oh, I suppose I did back when I was young. Most of the girls I knew dreamed about going everywhere. But, most, just like me, never did and ended up right around here."

Olabe was silent for a long while and Jewel was afraid that the little progress she saw tonight had regressed and could only hope she had said the right things.

"Now, Olabe. What about this truck you've got your mind set on?" Jewel asked to break the excruciating silence.

Olabe sat for a while and then started rocking a little. A dog barked off in the distance. Nightfall had come and it was now completely dark. Dark, except for the beautiful display of millions of stars overhead.

Suddenly, Olabe jumped up.

"Mama? Let's drive up to Montgomery tomorrow. We'll get an early start, way before breakfast. We'll find us a truck and maybe, how about we buy you a new dress?"

The thought of going to such a big city scared Jewel. But, she could tell that Olabe had her mind already made up and she liked the new found fire in her voice. But, what would she wear? She only had an old blue dress that she had kept special for funerals and weddings. The last time she wore it was more than two years ago when they buried Jonathan Bates. Jewel rocked and worried.

"Well, Mama? What do you think? Shall we go get us a truck tomorrow?"

"I guess so. If you've got your mind set on it."

Jewel worried through much of the night. She was torn between two forces. First, going to a big city scared her, and second, she was afraid that something wouldn't go right and give Olabe a set back in her depression. Jewel wished that Olabe would talk to her about what happened to her up in Nashville. She only knew that there had been an accident. But, that's all she knew, and that was only from a neighbor that told her she had heard it on the radio. Sleep came in spurts followed by long periods of laying awake and worrying.

Olabe got up before daylight, built a fire in the wood stove, and made coffee. She took a cup out onto the porch and sat it on the table. She then walked out to her car and picked up her cell phone. Olabe scanned down through the electronic phonebook until she found what she was looking for and pressed "dial."

"Good morning," a sleepy male voice said.
"Good morning, Carl. I didn't wake you, did I?"
There was a long pause, and then, she heard someone shouting in the phone.
"Olabe? Olabe? Is that you?"
"It's me alright, Carl," she responded and smiled a little.

Carl Strom was Olabe's agent and general manager. He had been there since the beginning of her skyrocketing career as a country singer. Carl was not only her agent and manager, but a good friend, too. She trusted him completely. His company had been instrumental in forming the companies and organizations that she owned. They had made lots of money together over the years and his company still managed and paid all her bills.

"How have you been? We've all been worried about you. Where are you?'

They talked for a few minutes and Olabe told him of her ending up at her mother's house near Clopton, Alabama, living in the backwoods with an outhouse and no electricity.

"Wow, Olabe. Must be sort of like camping."
"Kind of. Now Carl, the reason I called is, I need your help."
"Of course. Anything."
"Well, I want to buy a truck and I also want some money. You know, a bank account where I can get cash when I need it."
"Certainly, Olabe. Just tell me where you want the account and we'll take care of everything."
"We want to go up to Montgomery this morning and look for a truck. And Carl, I want to get rid of my Beamer. Do you think it can be used as a trade in or something?"

Carl thought a few minutes and digested the new challenges.
"Carl? You still there?"
"I'm here. Just thinking. Okay. Now here's what we can do. At nine o'clock this morning, I'll have our people call the Southern National Bank in Montgomery. We've done lots of business with them and I know Bill Weeks, the president, pretty well. We'll have an account set up for you and have fifty thousand dollars transferred into it. That should be enough for a start. We'll set it up so as the account draws down it will be able to transfer more from here, whenever you need it."

"So, how do I go about buying a truck?" Olabe asked. She had never bought a vehicle in her life. When she wanted a new car, or more likely whenever her husband had thought she needed one, it just showed up. Her husband had always taken care of those things before.

"Here's what you do," Carl said now fully awake. "You go to any dealer you want in Montgomery. Tell them you will only talk to the manger. When you decide on a truck, have the manager call Bill Weeks at the bank there in Montgomery and he will handle everything."

"Sorry about bothering you so early, Carl," Olabe apologized as she noticed that it was just now becoming daylight.

"That's what I'm here for. Oh. One other thing. We don't want to trade your BMW in. I'll have the bank take it for now and we'll get it sent up here to Nashville where it will bring a good price."

"But, how will I get it to the bank, Carl? Mama doesn't drive."

"Don't worry about a thing, Olabe. Weeks will work out all the details with the dealer."

They talked for a few minutes more and Carl softly asked if she had thought anything about when she might return to her career.

"Your fans love you, Olabe. Your CDs are still selling at a fantastic rate and everything else, too. Your clothing line is exploding."

"I can't," was all Olabe could say as tears filled her eyes. "I can't."

It was just quarter after six when Jewel finally stepped into the passenger side of Olabe's little yellow convertible. Olabe started the engine, put the selector in "D" and zoomed down the lane.

Jewel was a little frightened. She certainly had ridden in cars before and her husband's truck, but never with Olabe. And never this fast. She felt pressure and a tingling sensation in her gut whenever Olabe accelerated. They went through Clio and Brundidge. They turned north on Highway 231 and the little car raced toward Montgomery. The farms and scenery flew by. Jewel was a little dizzy. She had never been this fast in all her life and was afraid to look at the speedometer or ask how fast they were going. She stared straight ahead and said nothing.

"What's the matter, Mama? You haven't said a word for almost an hour."

"We're going too fast," Jewel finally managed to say. "I think the wind is taking the words right out of my brain."

Olabe laughed and put on her sunglasses but didn't slow down at all. She pushed a button on the side of her arm rest and Jewel watched her window go up. Almost like magic.

The trip from Clopton to Montgomery was a little over eighty-six miles and took about two hours. They were coming into the suburbs of Montgomery when Olabe pointed to a building coming up on the right side of the road.

"Looks like a restaurant over there, Mama. Hungry?"

Jewel's stomach was too tied up in knots to even think about being hungry. But, the thought of being able to get out of this race car and stand up was very appealing.

Olabe turned into the parking lot and shut off the engine.

"What do you think, Mama? Look okay to you?"

"Looks alright," Jewel said but remembered that she could count on her fingers the number of times she had eaten in a restaurant before. "They must have coffee."

"Coffee? I'm starved. Let's have a real breakfast."

Jewel smiled to herself as she reveled in Olabe's new found enthusiasm. Her legs complained as she stood up after being cooped up in that awful little car.

The restaurant looked clean and very pleasant. It must have been a pretty popular place because there were lots of people eating and the parking lot was practically full. The hostess greeted them, showed them to a table, and handed menus to both of them.

"Coffee?" a young teenage girl dressed in a magenta uniform with "Carla" on her name tag asked.

"Sure," Olabe said and pushed her cup towards the girl.

"The waitress will be along in a little bit," the young girl said as she filled both their cups with smoking hot coffee.

"Hot!" Jewel exclaimed as she took a sip of her coffee.

Olabe smiled and opened her menu.

"Gracious," Jewel whispered as she looked at her menu. "Olabe. Do you know that they charge a dollar for a cup of coffee? And, look at these prices. Good gracious. I've never seen such a thing."

"It's fine, Mama. Don't worry at all. We're out to have a fine time today and we're going to spend whatever we want to."

"Good morning, ladies," a blonde, well worn, middle aged woman said with "Gladys" on her name tag. "What can I get for you all this morning?"

"I'm going to have biscuits with sausage gravy," Olabe said as she closed her menu and handed it back to Gladys.

"Guess I'll have the same," Jewel responded not sure if she could even eat a bite, but was more than happy that Olabe's appetite seemed to be improving.

They talked for a few minutes when Gladys came over and refilled their coffee cups.

"Hope you don't have to pay by the cup," Jewel found herself sputtering.

"No, ma'am," Gladys smiled. "Just awful what prices are these days, ain't it."

"By the way, Gladys," Olabe spoke up which caused the waitress to turn around. "We're looking for an honest car dealer who sells trucks. Might you know where to look here in Montgomery?"

Gladys frowned, crossed her arms and said, "Most of them crazy places are a nightmare to go to. I just hate buying a car." She continued to frown and then, a huge smile crossed her face. "Hold on just a minute. I think I know just the right person to help."

Gladys walked over to a table a ways off and talked to the lone gentleman sitting there drinking a cup of coffee. She pointed at Jewel and Olabe, and then continued to talk. Finally, the man stood up, took his cup of coffee, and walked towards their table. He looked to be about sixty. He was well dressed in blue slacks with a yellow polo shirt. His sandy colored hair was immaculately trimmed and his brown eyes looked warm and friendly.

"Good mornin', ladies. My name is Jack Timmons." He reached out his hand and shook both Jewel's and Olabe's hands. "Gladys over there said you all might be lookin' for a truck."

Olabe nodded.

"Well, I have a Dodge dealership not too far from here and I would consider it a great honor if I could lay to rest some of those ugly rumors about car dealers and such. May I sit down?"

Olabe pointed to the vacant chair. Jack put his coffee cup down and sat down.

"Now. First, let's lay all these business matters aside and enjoy a nice breakfast. Where all do you folks come from?"

Before Olabe could answer, Gladys had returned.

"You all want breakfast brought over here, Jack?"

"Yes, Gladys. If you don't mind. Have these ladies already ordered?"

"They have," Gladys said. "You all want the usual?"

Jack laughed. "Thought only bar folks asked questions like that. But, yes. Guess I'll have the usual. Some nice grits with lots of butter."

Gladys was just about ready to leave when Olabe spoke up.

"Gladys, I think Mama and I would like small bowls of grits to go along with our biscuits and gravy, but better make those half-orders."

Gladys smiled and walked away.

"Grits are good for the soul," Jack said as he took a sip of coffee. "Now, where all did you say you're from?'

"We live down near Clopton," Olabe said.

"Ain't that 'but ninety miles, or so, south of here? Seems like I've heard of it."

"It's just a little town," Jewel added and put more sugar in her coffee.

The three talked for a little while getting to know each other better. Jack told them how his daddy had started the dealership right after World War 2 and how he came to work for him as a mechanic-trainee after he had graduated from college.

"Funny," Jack said. "Back then, I certainly didn't think learning to be a mechanic was much fun. I would have much rather been a salesman, or such. But, my daddy wanted me to learn everything from the bottom up. Mainly, I washed and got cars ready for customers. Being young, I was impatient, and all. Finally, one day, I went up to my daddy's office and told him that I quit. I remember how he just sat there and smiled, but didn't say much. He asked what I planned to do and I told him. I said that I was going to work for the Ford dealer."

"That must have caused a stir," Olabe said and smiled.

"Did at that. But he let me go my own way. Well, I worked for that company for almost five years and was doing alright, I guess. Then, I got a call one day from my mama at the hospital. Daddy had a heart attack and was in pretty bad shape. By the time I got to the hospital, he was gone."

"Good gracious," Jewel said as she remembered getting the call about her husband, Henry.

"Well, guess it was time for me to grow up some, and fast. I'm an only child you see, and there was only one thing to do. That was to jump right in, take over my father's business, and take care of my mama. Well, that's all history now. We sure had some rough years back then keeping everything going, but somehow, and with God's help, we did it."

Gladys brought a huge tray of plates and each one was heaped with food. Jewel had to keep pinching herself to make sure she wasn't dreaming it all.

"Love grits, don't you all," Jack said as he spooned in a huge helping.

The grits were wonderful and the biscuits and gravy were too, but Jewel thought that her biscuits were maybe just a little better. But, of course, she didn't say anything.

Everyone enjoyed themselves. The food was too much and Olabe couldn't finish either her grits or her biscuits and gravy. But Jewel did. Not only was everything good, but at these prices, she was going to make sure she ate everything on her plate. But what made her the happiest was the fact that Olabe's appetite was improving.

Gladys came over and picked up the empty dishes. She put two bills on the table. One for the two women and one for Jack. Jack immediately picked them both up.

"Let me have the honor of buying breakfast," he smiled broadly. "You know, most every day I sit over there and eat by myself, but, today, I've had a nice visit with you two."

Olabe smiled and Jewel looked suspicious. Jack paid the bill and they all went outside.

"Now, ladies, if you'll just follow me. I'm driving that white car over there," he said as he pointed at the biggest, whitest, car Jewel had ever seen. The only one that could match it was the one that McBride's funeral home used.

Jack walked over to his car and got in. He was a little taken aback when he saw a little yellow convertible drive up behind him and noticed that Olabe waved out the window to him.

"What in the world," he murmured to himself as he started the engine and drove out of the parking lot onto the street making sure the little yellow car was right behind him.

Olabe followed Jack's white Dodge Magnum through traffic. It turned out to be a little farther to the dealership than she expected, but it wasn't bad. She just worried that if she had to stop at a traffic light, he might get too far ahead of her and she wouldn't be able to find him. But everything worked out just fine and soon she followed him into a huge Dodge dealership. Jack drove around the lot that was filled with cars of every make and color until he parked in a space behind the large glass building. He got out and motioned to Olabe to park next to his car.

"Come on in," he motioned and held the door for Olabe and Jewel.

They were greeted by a large suite of offices. But, of course, neither Jewel nor Olabe had ever been in a car dealership before, so neither knew what to expect at all.

Jack led the way. He opened a beautiful mahogany door that led into his office. The lighting was subdued, yet his desk was lighted from spotlights from high above in the ceiling. The carpeting was a deep, thick, dark blue. Instead of going around behind his desk, Jack motioned for the ladies to come over to a table and sit down.

"Now, ladies," he smiled, "let's see what you might be looking for in a truck."

"I don't think a new one would be quite right," Olabe said, which surprised Jack a little. After all, she was driving an almost new yellow BMW convertible.

"Oh? Why not new?" he asked and sat back in his chair.

"It wouldn't fit in," Olabe said as she folded her arms.

"We don't want to look like we're showing off to our neighbors," Jewel said which Olabe had never given even the hint of a thought to.

"Now, I understand. What you want is something that's almost new, but has enough wear so it looks used."

Olabe and Jewel nodded.

"Pickups come in lots of styles and colors," Jack said and noticed Olabe frown. His years in the business and his senses told him that she was not aware of much when it came to buying a vehicle. "First, there are full size ones like the Dodge Ram here," he opened a brochure and pointed out a picture of a red truck. "Here's a smaller one. It's called a Dakota."

Both women looked at the pictures. Olabe told Jack that she wanted one with a back seat. It didn't have to be big, just room enough to take another person or two now and then.

"That's called a crew cab and comes in a few models, too, " he said. "But let's see what we might have in stock, so you can see in person what they look like." Jack picked up the phone and touched the keys on the key pad.

Olabe was relieved, but determined. Jewel was just happy to watch Olabe coming out of her depression.

"Hello, Charlie. Jack. I've got some nice ladies here that are in need of an almost new truck."

Jack listened and made some notes on his little pad.

"Here's the thing, my friend. What we need here is a mid-size, with small crew cab."

Jack scratched out the notes he had made and drew a little picture of a dog on his pad as he listened.

"Uh huh. Well, now those three sound about right. Will you have all three of them brought up to the wash stalls and give me a buzz when you've got 'em there?"

Jack hung up the phone and stood up.

"That was my general manager on the phone there. He said we've got three trucks that are close to what you might like and will bring them up so we all can take a look at them."

"I never knew there were so many choices," Olabe said out loud honestly. "Why does it have to be so complicated? All I want is- just a truck, after all."

"Most folks are just the opposite," Jack laughed. "They want all kinds of choices and variations. Keeps us hopping just to keep up.

The phone buzzed and Jack picked it up. He talked for a few minutes, hung up, and came back over to the table.

"Well, they've got two of them where we can go look at them. Turns out the one I thought might fit the bill best has already been sold."

They followed Jack out the door, through the maze of offices, and out across the huge service shop. Finally, they reached a large open room with huge windows which made it virtually glow from all the light. The floor was wet and hoses were neatly rolled up at one end. There, stood two trucks.

The first truck was a Ford. It was bright red and had big tires.

"Now this one is an F-150 Ford," Jack said as he walked over and opened the door so the ladies could look inside. "It's a last year's model, but only has four thousand miles on it. It's got jump seats in back behind the front seats, there."

Olabe climbed up on the running board and had to virtually crawl up into the cab. It seemed huge and not what she was looking for. Jewel thought it was too big and didn't like the red color.

"This one over here," Jack pointed as they walked to the next truck. "This is a Chevrolet Silverado. It's two model years old, but really, only about fourteen months old. It has low mileage and a full crew cab."

The truck was lower because of the more normal sized tires. Olabe was able to get right in with little trouble. She thought the silver color was alright, but wasn't thrilled with it.

Olabe climbed out and as she stepped back down onto the wet floor, her eye caught another truck across the shop that was up on the service rack It was black and seemed smaller.

"What about one like that," Olabe pointed out.

"That's a new Dakota," Jack said. "It's one we sold a while back and is back having the oil changed."

"I like that, don't you Mama?"

Jewel shook her head that she approved. Certainly better than the two monsters they had just looked at.

"Those are the most popular vehicle we sell," Jack said. "We can hardly keep them in stock."

He walked over to the phone that hung on the wall. He punched in a few numbers, talked to someone for a few minutes, and then came back to where Olabe and Jewel were standing.

"Now I know what you said about wanting a used truck and all, but I think we may have something that might just fit the bill. Charlie is having one of the boys bring it up here right away."

Jack led the conversation for a little while and told the two women about how his dad borrowed a little money from his grandfather when he got out of the Army. He bought four cars and put them in the front yard of grandfather's house.

"That was right over there," he pointed. "Sure would never know it now. Back that way was the farm. None of these businesses were there then, just farm land. Guess that's what they call progress."

Soon, the big overhead door opened and a very cute, small, blue truck drove in.

"I like it," Olabe said to Jewel almost immediately.

"We just got this one in," Jack said as he held the door so Olabe could get in.

Olabe liked it right away. It was just the right size and it actually had a small back seat. The color was dark blue and wouldn't stand out, so she knew her mother would like it. The seats were blue too. Olabe was just looking over the gauges when she noticed her mother get in the passenger side and shut the door.

"I like this one, Olabe," Jewel whispered.

"So do I, Mama. It's brand new, but I love the color and it won't stand out."

Jack had dealer license plates put on so they could drive the little blue truck around for a while.

"I really like it, Mama. I think we should buy it, don't you?"

"Gracious, Olabe. I don't know what it costs, but I'm sure it will scare me half to death if I ever knew."

"Don't worry about it, Mama," Olabe said as she turned back into the dealership, drove around to where Jack was standing, and stopped.

"We love it," she smiled as she stepped out while Jack held the door for first her and then ran around to help Jewel.

They went back into Jack's office and sat back by the table.

"Now, how do you want to handle the financing?" Jack asked confident that he had just sold a new truck, and not a stripped down model either. This was the top of the line in the mid-size series.

"I would like you to call Bill Weeks at the Southern National Bank," Olabe said confidently. "He will take care of all the financial arrangements."

"Why, of course," Jack smiled as he walked over to his desk and opened his little desk phone directory.

"Hello, darlin'. Jack Timmons at Southern Dodge. I was wonderin' if I might speak to Bill Weeks for a minute or two?"

Jack smiled and signified he was on hold.

"Bill! How are you? We've got to get together here soon and play a round over at the country club."

Jack chatted for a few minutes about business and family. Finally, he got around to discussing Olabe.

"Well, now Bill. It seems that I'm being visited by two fine southern women this morning, by the name of Miss Jewel and Miss Olabe. I'm embarrassed to say it, but I didn't get their last names."

"Uh huh. Yes. Certainly Bill. No. No. You don't have to worry about a thing. Yes, I can take care of everything. Sure. We'll hold the BMW for you. Yes, it is really a cute one. So, you think you might be interested in it, yourself, huh? Mid-life crisis coming on there, Bill?" Jack laughed and continued to chat for a few more minutes.

"That was certainly easy," he said as he came back to the table. Ol' Bill will take care of everything, even taking your convertible. Now, I'm going to step out for a few minutes and talk to Charlie so he can do everything necessary to get your truck ready. We'll have you on your way in just a little while. Oh, before I forget it. Could I have the key to your BMW?"

Olabe took the key out of her purse and handed it to Jack. He smiled warmly and thanked her.

They sat there for a few minutes looking around the huge room. There were deer heads mounted on the walls and big fish. There were citations and awards everywhere. There was even a photograph of Jack shaking hands with Lee Iacocca, the famous former CEO of Chrysler. Both men were smiling.

"Well, Mama," Olabe said. "What do you think?"

Jewel was perplexed. On the one hand, she was overjoyed that Olabe seemed to have found herself. She ate a good breakfast, something Jewel had been trying to get her to do for the last three months. But, on the other hand, weren't they buying a truck? That was scary business. How much did it cost and where was the money coming from? Who were all these people on the phone that seemed to be right there to help Olabe whenever she called?

Jack came back in the room. He helped Jewel up from her chair and then held the chair for Olabe. Truly, he was a southern gentleman of first class.

"Looks like everything is ready ladies. Your truck is right outside the door. The license plates are temporary and the regular ones will be sent to your house within a week or two. Be sure to have them put on as soon as you can. The law around here don't like these temporary ones."

Jack shook hands first with Jewel and then with Olabe. Today, he had really done his job. He loved selling cars and trucks, which he rarely did anymore. But, today was special. Not only was he able to have breakfast with two lovely ladies and sell them a new truck, but to be with a famous country star, Miss Olabe Mae, and her mother, Jewel, well, that's what made life all worth while. Jack knew who Olabe was and never showed it at all. He had dealt with many celebrities over the years and knew the importance of keeping their identities anonymous.

Olabe and Jewel drove away in their new, blue Dodge Dakota truck. Within a few blocks, Olabe spotted a large shopping mall, turned into the parking lot, and stopped.

"Come on, Mama," she said as she got out of the truck. "We're going in and buy ourselves new dresses."

Jewel's head was spinning. Olabe was spending money like water. But, where was the money? She hadn't seen even one dollar.

It took most of the afternoon to convince Jewel that she needed something new, but Olabe prevailed. After trying on at least fifteen things, Jewel finally consented to a beautiful gray dress. She loved the way it fit her and the feel of the almost silk-like fabric. She was in the dressing room and had just put her old dress on when she happened to see the price tag attached to the sleeve.

"One hundred-fifty-nine dollars!" she exclaimed and felt sick to her stomach.

"What was that, Mama?"

Jewel came out of the dressing room and handed the dress to Olabe.

"I can't believe the price," Jewel whispered. "Put that back and let's get out of here."

"Nothing doing, Mama. That dress looks wonderful on you and I say we're going to get it."

Jewel just stood there as Olabe took the dress to the sales counter. She chatted with the sales clerk and handed her some sort of plastic card. Within a few minutes Olabe came back carrying a plastic dress bag with the gray dress inside.

They got into the new truck and Olabe hung the dress bag on the hanger on the inside of the cab. She started the engine and drove out of the parking lot.

After driving back towards home for more than an hour, Jewel couldn't stand it any longer.

"What was that plastic thing you gave the clerk, Olabe?" she asked and continued to stare straight ahead.

"Plastic thing? You mean my credit card?" Olabe laughed then realized that her mother probably had never seen nor heard of a credit card. "You use it like cash, Mama. Instead of carrying cash around, you just use a credit card. They send you a bill at the end of the month."

Olabe didn't explain it any further than that. In fact, she had no idea where the bill went or even how it got paid. Somewhere, somehow, one of her businesses paid it.

Jewel seemed relieved, but concerned that Olabe had spent far too much money today and especially, on that dress. Things got back to normal and the two chatted for the next hour as they drove home.

"Olabe, let's go over and see the Thompson family tomorrow afternoon," Jewel said. She knew that she was pushing her luck a little, but she wanted to keep Olabe's mind going with any weapon she could use. "They haven't seen you for a long time, and I'd like to see how Rachael is getting along. I think we should cook up something to take with us, too."

CHAPTER 4
Meeting the Neighbors

As Olabe and Jewel drove up the long driveway they watched kids of all ages coming out of everywhere. Olabe stopped the truck near the porch of the dilapidated shack whose siding lacked any tinge of paint.

"Hello" Jewel called out as she stepped out of the truck.

"Why, hello, Miss Jewel," a rather pretty, but very thin woman called out as she came onto the porch and let the screen door slam behind her.

Olabe got out and walked around and stood by her mother.

"Rachael, I would like to introduce you to my youngest daughter, Olabe."

The woman came to the edge of the porch and then, stepped down the two almost not-existent steps. She walked up to Olabe with her hand extended.

"Well, hello, Miss Olabe. I'm very happy to meet you."

Olabe grasped Rachael's hand and smiled. Rachael's hand was rough with heavy calluses, probably from years of overwork, Olabe thought as her brain quickly scanned her new acquaintance. Rachael appeared older than she probably was. She was just about Olabe's height, but her shoulders were much more rounded and her eyes were dark and sunken. Still, they had a twinkle that seemed to light up her face when they met Olabe's eyes. Rachael's dress looked old and patched, but surprisingly clean. She didn't have shoes on.

"That big one over there," Rachael pointed. "That's my oldest, David. He'll be nineteen pretty soon in another month or two."

David smiled shyly and looked down as his neck turned a slight tinge of red. He looked almost full grown, although still pretty much looked like a kid. He wore an old blue shirt that was patched everywhere. His overalls were worn so thin that Olabe could see both of his knees sticking out. He had red hair that he constantly tried in vain to keep out of his eyes. His eyes were blue and shown true and warm as they locked with Olabe's for a few seconds.

"Hello, ma'am," he managed to mumble.

"Hello, David," Olabe said and smiled warmly.

"That'ne up there on the porch is Elizabeth Ann. She's a senior in high school and is a big help to me."

"Oh, Mama," Elizabeth Ann shrugged. "Hello, Miss Olabe. Nice of you to come and see us all."

Elizabeth Ann was seventeen, going on thirty. She looked almost as tired and worn out as her mother. Her shoulders were rounded and slumped. Her auburn hair was tied back in a tight bun which caused her thin face to seem even thinner. Her eyes had dark circles around them. Her dress, like her mother's, was nothing more than a patchwork of pieces of cloth, but it, too, like her mother's was very clean.

"Very glad to meet you, Elizabeth Ann," Olabe said as she walked up to the porch and reached up to shake her hand.

Another young girl came out of the house and stood on the porch by her mother.

"This'ne' here, she be Ellen May and is just nine months younger than Elizabeth Ann," Rachael said.

"I help Mama, too. As much as I can, anyway," Ellen May said with a smile that showed a perfect set of beautiful white teeth. Her flaxen blond hair shown and her blue eyes sparkled as she put her arm around Rachael.

"Ellen May, I'm sure you are a wonderful help to your mother and I'm very happy to meet you."

"That'un runnin' over there," Rachael pointed to a younger boy as he ran from the barn up to where David was standing, "he be Barton John."

Barton looked like any young boy. He was short and uncoordinated. His reddish blond hair was in complete disarray as was his shirt and pants.

"Those twouns over there," Rachael pointed at two little boys running up the driveway to see who was visiting them. "They be William and Obadiah."

Olabe smiled and waved. Out of the corner of her eye, she noticed a little one hiding behind her mother's skirt and noticed that every time she peeked up at Olabe, she would quickly look away and hide when Olabe smiled down at her.

"This little one, here," Rachael tried to scoot the little girl around from behind her. "She's awful shy and all."

"She be Liza Jane," William called out breathlessly from running. "She'en don't talk much."

Olabe bent down and saw a little face peak around her mother's skirt and then quickly look away.

Just then a man appeared in the doorway and somehow managed to get himself out on the porch as he struggled with his crutches.

"Here, Papa," Ellen May said as she rushed to hold the door open. "I'll hold the door for you."

"Thank you, honey," the man said as he hobbled over to the little crowd that had gathered. "Hello, Miss Jewel. Haven't seen you in quite a while."

"It has been quite a while," Jewel said as she smiled up to the man. "I brought my youngest daughter, Olabe, over to meet your family. She's living with me now."

The man struggled to get his crutches situated to leave his right hand free. He reached out his hand to Olabe. "Miss Olabe, welcome. I'm sure you all don't remember me, but my name is Raaf and I'm the father of this here rag tag group you all see in front of you."

Olabe shook Raaf's hand and told him how impressed she was with his brood.

Raaf also looked much older than he probably was. Olabe wondered what was wrong. Must have been some sort of accident because his disability didn't seen congenital. His hair was reddish brown, quite long, but neatly combed. His clothes looked like patches held together by a network of thread.

For a few minutes everyone chatted and all seemed to talk at once, but quieted down immediately when Raaf held up his hand.

"We're all very happy to have you all come over to visit, Miss Jewel and Miss Olabe," Raaf said. "Can't you all come up on the porch here and sit a while?"

"Well, Raaf," Jewel said and she stepped up onto the porch. "I was telling Olabe this morning that it looked like such a good day to go a visiting. Well, you know how it is when us women get to talking. We were in the house for lunch and started cooking and talking and pretty soon we had cooked up so much we didn't know what to do. I told Olabe the only thing missing was the wonderful biscuits that Rachael, here, is so famous for. Well, one thing led to another and pretty soon we loaded up the truck and came on up here to see you folks. Now, we trucked along a ham, sweet potatoes, baked corn pone, and three pies."

"Now, Miss Jewel, it all sounds wonderful," Raaf said as he tried to stretch out his right leg. "But, you'ns all know how we feels 'bout charity."

"Charity?" Jewel scoffed. "This ain't no charity. It be a trade, you ol' fool. We plan to take supper with you all and trade some of this here food we brought up here by eatin' our fill of Rachael's biscuits."

"Well, Lordy be," Rachael said wringing her hands. "You know you all are always welcome, Miss Jewel. And, it just so happens that I've got a double batch of biscuits in the warming oven rising right now."

"Alright, kids," Jewel commanded. "Fetch them vitals from the truck out there, and bring them inside."

Like an army of ants, all six of the older children worked together and carried everything inside. Liza Jane clung to her mother's skirt as they went inside. She almost looked like a tiny puppy cowering near its mother for protection. Olabe was drawn to Liza Jane and watched her peak out of her mother's protective skirt and stare at her, but as soon as Olabe made eye contact, Liza Jane would immediately look away.

Elizabeth Ann and Ellen May were busy setting the table with plates and glasses that Olabe first thought might have come from the dump. All were chipped and none matched. She also noticed that two places offered a full set of knife, fork, and spoon while the others only had a spoon or fork. Olabe assumed the full sets were for Raaf and Rachael, but was soon surprised to learn that they were for she and her mother.

"Ain't got 'nough to go all 'round," Ellen May said as she noticed Olabe looking at the place settings. "But, we'uns don't need full sets anyway. We always share."

Olabe smiled and continued helping get tablespoons into the food dishes.

Everyone was called to the table. The kids chattered while coming to the table, but as soon as they were all seated, they became silent. They all folded their hands and were ready for prayer. Olabe watched, amazed.

"Lord," Raaf said softly in his deep, resonant voice. "Lord, we ask you to bless all of us here seated at this poor table. We thank you for bringing Miss Jewel and Miss Olabe to visit with us today and for all the vitals they brung with them."

"And the pie," a meek voice squeaked out.

Everyone smiled as they looked at the source. It was Obadiah who sat solemn and stoic as a stick, with hands still clasped in good prayer form.

"And, the pie," Raaf said as he did his best to keep from breaking out into laughter. "We ask your blessing today and also ask you to watch over all of us. Amen."

No sooner had the "Amen" been said by all than the dishes were passed. Conversations sprung up here and there, but mainly the noise was just silverware on dishes.

Olabe noticed how each person took such modest portions.

"Liza Jane?" Olabe said softly and looked at her seated on her mother's lap. "Think you could come over here and help me figure out what's best to put on your mama's biscuits?"

Liza Jane dug deep into her mother's arms.

"She don't cotton up to strangers, much," William said as he shoved half a biscuit into his mouth.

"Which preserve do you think would go best, Liza Jane? Apple or peach?" Olabe pressed on as she smiled and waited for Liza Jane to respond.

Slowly, Liza Jane sat up a little and pointed towards the bottle of peach preserve.

"Don't talk none, either," Obadiah reported.

"Think you could help me put some on a biscuit?" Olabe asked Liza Jane softly.

Time stood still, but the clatter of silverware on dishes continued. Slowly, Liza Jane moved over a little and held out her hands indicating that it would be alright if Olabe picked her up.

Rachael was a little shocked at her daughter's newfound willingness, but was impressed. She put her hands under Liza Jane's arms and moved her over to Olabe's outstretched hands.

"Now," Olabe said softly to the top of Liza Jane's head. "Let's get some peach on this biscuit. Can you help me?"

Proudly, Liza Jane tore the biscuit in half and pointed at the peach jar. Olabe responded and brought it within her reach. She handed a spoon to Liza Jane who immediately pushed it into the sweet peach preserve that Jewel had made. Liza Jane plopped a more than generous amount on one of the half biscuits. She put the spoon back into the jar and plunged her fingers into her mouth to lick the little preserve that had stuck to her.

"Let's show all those kids how much you and I can eat, shall we Liza Jane? They all think they can eat more than you and I together."

Liza Jane shoved the whole half biscuit into her mouth which made her little cheeks stick out like a chipmunk.

"No she can't," William and Obadiah shouted in unison taking up the challenge. "Pass them sweet 'taters and we'll show you."

"Don't be greedy, boys," Raaf and Rachael said almost together.

"You let them boys eat all they want," Jewel said immediately. "You too, Raaf. And, Rachael, have some more ham."

Rachael and Raaf exchanged glances and seemed to mentally agree that seconds were acceptable. Soon, everyone had seconds and some even enjoyed third helpings.

Olabe kept feeding Liza Jane about as fast as she could swallow and wondered when the last time she actually had a full tummy.

"Let's not forget the pie," Obadiah reminded everyone. "I want some of that'n apple, there."

Everyone laughed as Jewel dished up a piece for him.

Finally, the children had enough and David and Barton asked if they could be excused to go start the evening chores. Elizabeth Ann and Ellen May immediately started picking up the dishes and taking them to the sink. Jewel, Raaf, Rachael, and Olabe with Liza Jane on her lap stayed at the table and talked. The conversation ranged from the children's progress in school to how wonderful all the food was. Olabe reminded everyone, especially Rachael, that her biscuits were the best she had ever tasted.

"Oh my, Miss Olabe," Rachael said. "I hope your arm ain't broke from holdin' Liza Jane for so long there."

"She's just fine," Olabe said softly and continued to hold Liza Jane close to her breast and rocked her gently.

"Probably time to get her into bed anyway," Rachael said as she stood up and offered to take Liza Jane from Olabe.

"Here, let me help you," Olabe said as she stood and didn't offer her little burden to Rachael.

"Alright, then. The bedroom is over this way."

Olabe followed Rachael to a tiny little room with no door. Inside, Olabe noticed there was barely room for the small bed and crib. She assumed that Elizabeth Ann and Ellen May slept in the bed and Liza Jane in the tiny crib.

"Here, lay her on the bed thar while I get her nightgown."

Olabe laid Liza Jane on the bed and began getting her dress off.

"Can't believe how she made up to you like that, Miss Olabe. Liza Jane usually don't make up to no one, let alone a perfect stranger, and all."

Olabe pulled the little dress over the sleeping Liza Jane's head and was astounded at what she saw. The little girl was nothing more than a tiny little skeleton. She looked so thin and frail that Olabe thought she could count each rib, if she wanted to.

"Here's her nightgown," Rachael said as she handed the little garment to Olabe.

With expert fingers, she slid the nightgown over Liza Jane's head and buttoned the two buttons. She picked the tiny child up and moved her to the crib where she laid her down softly and pulled the thin, well-worn blanket over her body. The feeling only a mother knows of a helpless child next to her breast lingered with Olabe as she stood up.

"You have any babies, Miss Olabe?" Rachael asked innocently which took her completely by surprise.

Time stood still as Olabe's mind rocketed back to when her two children were babies and her eyes filled with tears. The two women talked for a while and had within seconds, developed a strong bond between them. They stood in silence for a few more seconds. Finally, they walked back out into the main room of the house where the two girls were just finishing washing the dishes and Jewel and Raaf were enjoying cups of coffee at the table and talking.

No one seemed to notice as Olabe and Rachael came back from putting Liza Jane to bed. No one, except Jewel.

Jewel finally announced that it was time to go and smiled internally at the new bond that had developed between Olabe and Rachael. Jewel didn't know why, but she certainly approved and was relieved that finally, Olabe seemed to be coming out of her shell. If even a little.

The short trip home was quiet. Olabe said nothing and Jewel could feel that her mind was churning. Even as a little girl, Olabe would suddenly become quiet, even for days at a time, as she mentally sorted and went over things that bothered her until she made a decision of action. Jewel knew that it would all come out pretty soon and that she would tell her.

"Let's sit on the porch for a while, Mama," Olabe said as the two walked towards the house.

They climbed the two steps and each sat down in their rockers. The evening was wonderful, as only a deep, southern Alabama evening could be. The night creatures chirped and in the distance an ol' dog barked. Jewel rocked and listened. Olabe remained silent.

"Mama?" Olabe broke the silence.

"Yes?"

"The Thompsons. All of them. They look sickly."

Jewel thought for a while before answering.

"Can't say I've ever noticed. Guess I've knowed them most all my life and never thought much about it. They've always been just who they are- the Thompsons."

"But, surely you've noticed that their eyes are sunken in."

"Well, Olabe, I know they ain't starvin', if that's what you mean. They, like all the rest of us here sure ain't wallerin' in rich food, but the good Lord takes care of us and provides, no matter how meager it is. We all seem to get along somehow."

"You should have seen it," Olabe continued almost as if she hadn't heard her mother's previous comment. "I was helping Rachael get Liza Jane ready for bed and when I took off her clothes, I couldn't believe what I saw."

Ah. Here it is. Our Lord in Heaven has softened Olabe's heart and done it with a little child, Jewel thought to herself, but said nothing.

"She's nothing but a tiny skeleton covered in skin," Olabe said as she rocked a little in her chair.

"Always been a sickly little thing," Jewel responded hoping to keep Olabe talking.

"What's wrong with her, Mama? What did the doctor say?"

"Doctor? Don't think she's ever been taken to no doctor. None that I know of anyway."

"You mean they have a sickly child and they don't try to get medical help?" Olabe scoffed and turned toward her mother.

"None of us have that kind of money. Besides, don't need no doctorin' less we break a bone or something."

"How about you, Mama? When's the last time you went to a doctor?"

Suddenly, Jewel felt a little uncomfortable. Here they were talking about their neighbors and now, the conversation had turned on her.

"Only one time, I guess. Right after your sister was born, I just couldn't seem to get the energy to get out of bed and take up my responsibilities. Your daddy insisted that he take me to see a doctor over in Ozark."

"Did he help?"

"Nope. He told me it was all in my head and tried to give me some pills to get my energy back. Never took none of those ol' pills and made up my mind that if it was all in my head, to just get over it. Never laid around since that day. Never told anyone how I felt any days after that, especially your daddy."

"Mama. That's called postpartum depression. It's a well known thing, these days. I felt it for a while after Alexia was born."

"Don't know any of them fancy words for it, but just knowed how I felt."

"You mean you've never been to a doctor after that?"

"No reason to. I always been pretty fit and have been able to do all the doctorin' I've ever needed. myself."

The two women continued to sit and rock for a long while. Finally, Jewel said she could hardly keep her eyes open, got up, and went to bed. She laid in bed for a while waiting for sleep to come and wondered how long Olabe would stay out there on the porch and brood.

CHAPTER 5
Settling Up

The next morning came and Jewel found that Olabe was already up and had the coffee made. The two talked about everything under the sun except going to meet the Thompson family yesterday.

Over the next few days Jewel noticed that Olabe seemed to have pulled herself out of a "thinking brood" and was pretty much back to her old self.

It was a hot Alabama afternoon and the two ladies were out in the garden picking green beans when they noticed an old truck driving down the road kicking up a huge cloud of dust. Neither made mention of it until it turned and came up the lane towards the house.

"Well, I'll be," Jewel said and started towards the house. "It's Jimmy Wade Betterund."

"Who's Jimmy Wade Betterund, Mama?"

"He's the man that works our land and I'll bet he's here to settle up for last year's crops. I've been expecting him for almost a month, now."

Olabe came up alongside her mother and stood watching as the old truck wheezed to a stop and was almost immediately hidden in a cloud of dust for a few seconds.

"Sure is a hot one," the man said as he stepped out of the truck and slammed the door twice before it stayed shut and walked over to where the two women were standing. "Miss Jewel."

"Hello, Jimmy Wade," Jewel said. "Don't know if you remember my youngest daughter? This is Olabe Mae."

Jimmy Wade was a very tall and slender man. His face was ruddy from too many years in the hot Alabama sun. He had pure white hair that seemed to blow in every direction. He was wearing a tattered white shirt and a pair of tan slacks. His gait was long and gangly as he came over to shake Olabe's hand.

"Why, Miss Olabe Mae. I 'member when you was just a lil' chil'," Jimmy Wade smiled as he took Olabe's hand in his and held it a second or two too long for her liking.

Years of training in the music business had taught Olabe well. Especially, about lecherous old men and Jimmy Wade, here, was a perfect example. She felt his eyes scan her body as he mentally undressed her. She saw his gray eyes flit around as he tried to peer down the cleavage of her tight summer blouse. She hated the way his tongue darted across his thin lips and could imagine the terrible thoughts that were racing through his mind. All in all, and in a few seconds, Olabe had developed a huge dislike for Jimmy Wade Betterund.

"Would you like to come up on the porch, Jimmy Wade?" Jewel asked. "Olabe would you fetch us all cold glasses of water?"

"Ah, yes. That would be wonderful Miss Olabe. Cold water would certainly take the edge off this here hot afternoon."

Jimmy Wade followed the two women up onto the porch. Olabe went inside while Jewel sat down and pointed to Olabe's rocker for Jimmy Wade. He took his hat off in a typical southern swoop which freed his long white locks to blow in the light breeze.

Soon, Olabe returned with three glasses of water. She handed one to her mother and another to Jimmy Wade. She again watched the telltale movements of his eyes.

"Oh, Miss Olabe, that sure does hit the spot," Jimmy Wade said as he downed the full glass in just a few gulps and held the cool glass up to his forehead.

Olabe faked a friendly smile, turned around, and looked off down the lane pretending not to be interested in anything other than her cool glass of water.

"Now then, Miss Jewel. I'm sorry to be so late this year to get your papers to you, but seems like everyone 'round here needs me to do their farmin', don't you know."

Jewel nodded and Olabe continued to look disinterested.

"Crops were not very good again this year and fuel and wages rose at an alarmin' rate. So, I'm 'fraid there ain't too much left," Jimmy Wade said as he handed Jewel a small packet of papers.

Jewel opened them and studied the first page carefully.

"Well, I was sure hoping it would be more than that," she almost whispered so no one would hear, but it caught Olabe's attention.

"I know, Miss Jewel," Jimmy Wade continued to drawl on. "But, prices were down and the cost of seed this year was just somethin' awful. Don't rightly know how they 'xpect us farmers to make a go of it, no how."

Jewel nodded, but said nothing. She took the folder and walked into the house.

The hot afternoon breeze picked up and fluffed Olabe's hair. Suddenly, she was aware that someone was standing too close to her.

"Sure is a hot one, ain't it," Jimmy Wade said which made Olabe almost whirl around and met him virtually nose to nose.

"Not too warm," she managed to say and immediately moved back to give them more space.

Thank goodness the screen door opened and Jewel came back out onto the porch.

"Well, ladies," Jimmy Wade drawled and tried to lock his eyes with Olabe's, but she immediately looked away. "Time for this ol' farm boy to get movin'. Got lots more stops to make before I can call it a day."

He put his hat back on and walked back to his truck in a long, gangly gait. After a little struggle from the truck, it's motor finally came to life, he drove down the lane, and out onto the road.

"I sure dislike that man, Mama," Olabe said as she sat down in her rocker. "Did you see the way he looked at me?"

"Ol' Jimmy Wade?" Jewel said as she sat in her rocker. "Why, he's 'bout as harmless as an ol' fly. I'm sure he didn't mean nothin'. He probably was just curious 'cause he hadn't seen you in years."

Olabe rocked and stewed. She had always hated the way some men looked at her, but over the years of performing, she had learned to manage it. But, this Jimmy Wade was different. Without really knowing why, she had developed a real dislike for him.

The next morning, Jewel asked Olabe if she would take her to Skipperville to the little store as she wanted to get a few things she had been putting off until her annual settlement came. So, after the dishes were done they started out. Jewel noticed that Olabe was still quiet and brooding, but just blamed it on her meeting Jimmy Wade yesterday.

The store reminded Olabe of an old country store she saw in the movies. They sold everything from groceries to kerosene. Jewel went about her business and examined the things she was interested in very carefully. Meanwhile, Olabe walked around and browsed.

"Mama?" Olabe asked as she came over to where her mother was looking over the different colors of thread. "Nothing is priced. How do you know what anything costs here?"

Jewel looked up. "They look up the prices when they add things up. Most folks don't use money here anyway. It just goes onto your bill."

"Well, you have to pay for it sometime, Mama."

"Sure you do. But, most of us don't have to worry about it directly. You see, it's just deducted from our bank accounts over there in Ozark."

"What? You mean they can just charge you anything they want for things and have an open door to your bank account?" Olabe snorted in disgust.

"Oh, Olabe. It's not as bad as all that. Here, now. When Miss Helen works up my bill for today, she will give me a copy of it so I know how much things were."

"I'm shocked," Olabe said as she carried a bag of material and sewing supplies for her mother out to the truck. "Who ever came up with this idea?"

"Why, Jimmy Wade Betterund, Olabe. It makes our lives easier, for all of us."

Both women boarded the truck, Olabe started the engine, and drove off. Her gut churned worse than before. It appeared that this awful man, Jimmy Wade Betterund, had his fingers in most everything around. Her mind worked over all the possibilities she could think of during the short ride back to her mother's house.

For the next few days, Olabe still brooded and seemed lost in her thoughts. She went through all the motions of helping her mother with her huge garden, picking the vegetables and fruit, canning the produce, preparing the meals, and even sitting on the porch in their rockers sipping cups of tea in the evenings. But, Jewel could tell that Olabe's mind still was working full force and she hoped that she would soon tell her what was bothering her so much. Maybe, she would tell her about what happened with her husband and two kids, too. Jewel hoped she would.

It was nearing ten o'clock the next morning and Jewel and Olabe were busy in the garden picking the last of the green beans. All the plants in Jewel's garden had produced in overabundance and all the beans and peas were no exception.

"Whew, Mama, it sure is going to be hot today," Olabe said as she straightened up and mopped her brow with a hankie. "I'll bet it's ninety already."

"Probably so. At least we can sit on the porch this afternoon and snap these ol' beans and then can them in the mornin'."

"Think I'll go up and get us some cool water, Mama. That alright with you?"

"Yes, Olabe. That's fine. I'll just keep at this ol' last row here."

Olabe started up towards the house. Her mind was still on how much she distrusted that ol' Jimmy Wade Betterund. The path took her past the outhouse and then to the porch. Olabe climbed the two steps, walked across the porch, and opened the screen door.

Suddenly, a thought solidified in her mind.

I know Mama would skin me alive, but I don't care, she thought. *I've got to know.*

Olabe went straight into her mother's bedroom and into the small closet. There on the floor was her target. It was an old cardboard box. It was where she had seen her mother put the folder Jimmy Wade Betterund gave her and she had to see it. Carefully, she lifted the lid and looked inside. There, right on the top of lots of papers and receipts was the folder. She slowly opened it and looked at the first page which was handwritten. It appeared to be some sort of annual business summary for her mother. Olabe slowly read and absorbed the words and numbers:

Jewel Bostwell
340 acres
Junction Road, Clopton, Alabama

Sale of peanuts and cotton grown on 340 acres owned by Miss Jewel	$19,900
Expenses: seed, fertilizer, labor, equipment, and hauling	<u>10,700</u>
Profit	$9,200
Jimmy Wade's half	-4,600
Property taxes paid by me for Miss Jewel	-900
Income tax preparation and filing for Miss Jewel	-600
Management fee	-500
Settlement for goods bought at the Skipperville store	<u>-1,200</u>
Total charged off to Miss Jewel	-$7,800
Profit deposited in Miss Jewel's account at Ozark Bank	$1,400

Olabe put the paper down. She was stunned, mad, and astounded.

"My mother lived on one thousand four hundred dollars last year!" she almost shouted out loud, but got a grip on her voice and held it to a hoarse whisper. "My God. That's so little it wouldn't even be considered poverty level. There's something wrong here and I've got to find out what it is. And, when I do, that low-life cracker is going to pay."

Quickly, she looked through the next few papers while her fingers trembled with new found anger. She found the receipts for the taxes paid on her mother's land and her federal tax return. She put all the papers back and put the lid back on the box. Olabe was fuming. But, she knew she had to get a grip on her temper and not show any emotion to her mother until she had decided what to do, and, that wasn't going to be easy.

"Did you forget about my glass of water?" Jewel smiled as she looked up.

"Oh, Mama. I just plainly forgot. I'm sorry. Do you want me to go back and get some for you? I was so hot and drank so quickly, I just forgot that I told you I would bring a glass back for you."

"Don't worry, dear. I'm fine. In fact, looks like we're just about done. Let's go back to the house. I'll get a drink while you wash these beans."

As the two women walked back up the path toward the house Olabe almost blurted out that she had to make a quick run to Clopton before lunch.

"I want to get some gas for the truck and I need to charge the battery in my cell phone before I can call my business manager in Nashville today. Think I will do that right now before lunch. Will that be alright with you, Mama?"

"Yes, that's fine. But, why can't we have lunch first and then go later this afternoon? I could talk to Sarah there at the store while you make your call."

"I was supposed to call him before noon today, Mama," Olabe said as she tried in impress on her mother her urgency. "I'll be right back. Want me to pick up anything while I'm at the store?"

"Don't think so. I'll start on these beans and work on them until you get back. Then, we'll figure out something for lunch."

By that time Olabe was already in the truck, had the engine started, and waving to her mother as she drove down the lane toward the road.

The trip to Skipperville only took about fifteen minutes or so which hardly gave Olabe much time to formulate a real plan of action, but her mind was at work, full speed.

She drove into the parking lot of the local gas station and got her cell phone out of the glove compartment. She plugged the charger cord into the cigarette lighter and the other end into her phone to make sure it wouldn't go dead while she was talking. She opened the phone and pushed the phonebook button. She paged down with her thumb until she found the number she was looking for and pushed it.

"Megastar Agency," a pleasant female voice answered.

"Yes, hello," Olabe said as her brain scanned the voice she had just heard and found the right name. "Jeanette? Is that you? This is Olabe Mae."

Jeanette worked the reception desk for Megastar for years and Olabe remembered her life as being almost like one of her country songs; married the wrong man, married too young, got pregnant right away, thought she could change her man, found him cheating on her, and he left her with a bucket load of credit card debt.

"Why, Miss Mae. We've been wondering about you and worried actually."

"Could I possibly talk to Carl?" Olabe asked and hoped her agent could help her.

"You certainly may. Just a moment and I'll get him on the phone for you. Nice talking to you and hope you are well."

Jeanette was gone and her phone played some unknown, elevator music to let her know she was still connected.

"Olabe Mae," Carl's voice boomed into the phone. "My gracious, but we've been worried about you. Are you alright? Are you well?"

Olabe answered all of Carl's questions. Then, she got to the real reason for her call.

"Carl, I think the person that's working my mother's land is cheating her and I want to find out if it's true."

"Hmmmm. Now, that's really out of the area of my knowledge, Miss Olabe. What do you want me to do?"

"Can you get our lawyer on the phone?"

"Sure. But, Miss Olabe, John specializes in contracts and show business. I'm not sure what he knows about farming things."

"I know, Carl. But, maybe he can at least point me in the right direction to find out who can help."

"You know I'll do everything I can. Now, hold tight for a minute or two while I see if John is in his office."

Olabe waited. John Dunn was the resident attorney for the Megastar Agency and she had worked with him many times. He was a man in his mid-forties, friendly, and always impeccably dressed. He was married and had two daughters that should be in high school by now, Olabe thought, as she continued to wait.

"Olabe? You still there," Carl's voice interrupted the silence.

"Yes. I'm here."

"Good. Now wait a minute while Jeanette tries to get John connected with us."

"Hello?" a male voice said.

"John? Is that you?" Carl asked.

"Yes, it's me."

"Olabe? Can you hear John?"

"Yes, I can."

After a few formalities and friendly talk, Olabe got down to business.

"So you see, John, I want to know if my suspicions about this Jimmy Wade Betterund are true or if I'm just going a little crazy."

"Well, Miss Olabe," John finally said. "What your asking is certainly out my field of expertise, what ever that is." He laughed and was joined by Carl. "But, now wait a minute. Maybe I do know just who the right person for this task might be."

"Oh? Who's that, John?" Carl asked.

"Well. Whenever we've had need for legal services in Alabama there is a firm in Birmingham that we've often used. I've been down there a few times and as I remember, one of the senior partners......let me think....what was his name? Yes. I have it. David Becker. That's who it is. Anyway, I've enjoyed a drink or two with ol' Becker and I believe he is an agriculture specialist, in regards to law, anyway."

A muffled conversation took place for a few seconds and then, John was back on the phone.

"My secretary is trying to find the phone number right now. I don't know if he's still practicing law by now, though. It was more than five years ago when I saw him last and he looked then like a man that should be enjoying life and let the younger people on his staff do the cases."

Again, Olabe, Carl, and John talked for a while in friendly conversation.

"Oh? Just a minute," John interrupted. "Katherine says she's got Becker on the phone and we'll try to get him patched in."

Finally, a deep, very southern sounding, slow voice said, "Hello? Becker here."

John talked for a little while and introduced David Becker to Carl and then finally, to Olabe.

"Now," John said. "Miss Olabe, tell Mr. Becker here what all you've told us so far and let's see what he thinks."

"Please, Miss Olabe. Call me David."

Olabe, again, went through the whole story. She wanted to make sure she left nothing out and was sure she had said the same things twice. Maybe more than twice.

"Well, for goodness sakes," David drawled slowly.

"Do you think there is anything to it, Mr. Becker?" Olabe finally asked quietly.

"David, Miss Olabe. David. And, yes, I certainly think there is something to it. Something, indeed."

"Can you help me, then?"

The older man laughed softly and finally managed to say, "Well, Miss Olabe, I am what some folks 'round here, call retired."

"Oh. Could you recommend someone else, then?"

"I didn't say that I was actually retired. It's just that some folks think that way. I will be happy to look over whatever you have and we can take it from there. By the way, I have a new associate that could probably be of great help. He's new to our firm, but very dedicated, and he's my grandson."

"That would be wonderful, David. Please work out how to get paid with Carl. He's my agent and will get any bills paid."

"Oh, let's not worry 'bout that just yet. Let's see if we can catch an ol' weasel before he robs another chicken house."

They all chuckled and Olabe was beginning to like David Becker a lot, even though she hadn't even met him yet.

"Now, Miss Olabe. Here's what I need you to do. And, I need you to do it right away. Get those papers and any other documents you think I might need up here to me as fast as you can. FedEx them to me in the next day or two, if you have a place nearby that can do that for you."

"I don't know, David. I'm calling you from Skipperville and one thing is for sure; they don't have a FedEx office."

David laughed and laughed. His laugh was very contagious and pretty soon everyone on the conference call was laughing right along with him.

"Miss Olabe," David finally managed to say. "I know that area very well and if you're in Skipperville, why you're just a hop, skip, and a jump from the end of civilization, as we know it."

"Actually, I'm living on a farm near Clopton."

"Good gracious, but you really are at the end of the world, aren't you. Now, let's get our plans straight. Can you go home, get those papers, get over to Ozark, and ship them up here to me this afternoon?"

Olabe's heart sunk. How in the world could she ever get that box out of her mother's closet and get them to Ozark without her mother finding out about it?

"Just a minute, Miss Olabe," David interrupted her thoughts. "Maybe Ozark isn't the best place to ship them from. Never know 'bout small towns. You know, who knows who and we sure don't want any news sneakin' out that could get back to our culprit."

"How about Dothan?" Olabe asked. "It's a pretty big town. I've driven my truck down there a few times."

"You are right 'bout that. Do you think you can get down there and get that package off to me with no one recognizing you?"

"Sure, David. I just wear old clothes, and if someone asks me if I'm who they think I am, I always tell them that I hear that all the time and just look like her, that's all."

David chuckled.

"I don't think I can get away today, though. Not without my mama thinking that something was up."

"She doesn't suspect anything, Miss Olabe?"

"I don't think so. She talks about this man as an old friend of the family. I think he's a crook and a dirty old man besides."

"Well, let's not hang him 'fore I see those papers now, Miss Olabe."

She agreed and told everyone how much she appreciated their help. She was a little relieved in knowing that she was actually doing something. Maybe not what she wanted, which was probably to get a gun, jam it in the stomach of old Jimmy Wade, and force him to confess. But she was doing something.

She filled the gas tank and paid for it with cash, as she always did. She then drove back the eight and a half miles to her mother's farm while she tried to work on a plan to get away soon without her mother suspecting anything.

"You weren't gone long," Jewel said when Olabe came up onto the porch from the truck. "I wish you wouldn't drive so fast. Especially on these ol' back roads."

Olabe smiled, moved her rocker closer to the old table now filled with the beans they had picked in the morning, and began working on them with her mother.

Jewel carried the conversation noting to herself that Olabe seemed to be far away in her thoughts again. Jewel tried to sound her out a little.

"Must be a serious problem that's troubling you so much," Jewel said as she snapped another pod.

"What? Oh, well....." Olabe stammered as she tried to get her brain back to reality and to what her mother had just said. "I guess, I must confess, Mama. It's the Thompson family."

"The Thompsons? Why are they so troubling for you, Olabe?"

"Well. It's that they all seem so sickly, and all." Olabe said and suddenly noticed her southern accent had worked its way back into her vocabulary and speech mannerism.

"They seem all right to me, and I've knowed them all my life."

"I guess it's mostly Liza Jane," Olabe said as she shifted herself in the chair to get better situated to the task at hand.

"Yes. She always been a tiny little thing. Borned early, she was. Always seemed to never quite catch up."

"Well, I'll admit it. I'm worried about her. She's so small and the part that really bothers me is, she doesn't even try to talk."

"Yes, dear, I understand. But, what could we really do?"

"Well. For one thing," Olabe straightened in the chair. "We could take her to a real doctor."

"We've talked about that before. They can't afford to put money out for anything like that."

"I know, Mama. You've told me that. But, I can afford it and I want to do something."

"Raaf Thompson and Rachael are proud folks, Olabe. You can't go bargin' in when they ain't asking for no help. We can only be ready to offer if something comes up and they ask us to help."

"Pushaw," Olabe snorted and rocked faster. At least she had diverted her mother's attention away from what was really bothering her and that was trying to figure a way to get that box of papers sent off to Birmingham by talking about Liza Jane. But, now that made another problem surface, and that was Liza Jane. Olabe was truly worried about her and now those thoughts clouded her mind.

The two women continued to work throughout the afternoon. They talked now and then, but mostly it was Jewel asking a question and Olabe brooding and only answering now and then.

Morning came and it was already warm. It was going to be another hot and humid southern Alabama day. Olabe stewed and fretted. Her only relief came from all the work they had to do. They canned all the beans from yesterday which was time consuming and hot work. But, the good thing was, it burned up lots of hours.

After working most of the morning, Jewel suggested that they sit out on the porch in the afternoon and cool off a while. The two ladies sat, rocked, and sipped cool well water from their glasses and mainly talked about the weather.

A car slowed at their lane and turned in, which immediately caught Jewel's attention.

"Why, it's Margaret Bane's car I think."

"Who's she, Mama?"

"Oh, she's a lady that heads up the women's group at church over there by Skipperville."

The car drove up near the porch and stopped, inundated by a cloud of dust. A small, very well dressed, quite elderly lady stepped out and quickly walked up onto the porch.

"Good afternoon, Jewel," the older lady said. "My, but it sure is warm this afternoon."

"Hello, Mrs. Bane. Don't know if you remember my youngest daughter or not, but this is Olabe."

Olabe stood, smiled, and came over to shake Mrs. Bane's hand.

"Yes, I do remember you. You and your sister were always so cute when your mama and papa would bring you to church every Sunday."

Olabe offered Mrs. Bane her rocker and stood leaning against the porch railing.

"What brings you way out here, Mrs. Bane," Jewel asked as she put her glass on the table. "Especially on such a hot day as this."

"Well, I'm glad you asked, Miss Jewel. It's my duty you know, as leader of the women's group at church to make sure everyone, especially those that, well, are not attending services all that often, are aware of our annual meeting tomorrow."

Jewel brightened up. Church had always been such an important part of most all her life, but since her husband died she had no way to get there. Now and then, she accepted rides from her neighbors, but she didn't want to be a burden, so she refused most Sundays. When Olabe came to stay, she had hoped that she and Olabe would start going. But, Olabe was dead set against it. She offered to take Jewel often, but refused to step inside any church herself.

"Mama?" Olabe smiled as an idea immediately formed in her searching brain. "What a great idea. I can take you there. I'm sure you'll have a wonderful time."

"Yes, Jewel. Please say you'll come. We've missed you and will welcome your ideas. Won't you be coming with her, Miss Olabe?"

"No, thank you, Mrs. Bane. But, I will be happy to bring Mama over and pick her up when the meeting is over. What time will it all take place?"

"The main meeting will start promptly at ten o'clock, but most folks try and get there about a half-hour early, you know. We'll break right at twelve for lunch and then, start again at one. We'll go until three or so which will be followed by a short, half-hour prayer meeting led by our Reverend Chillson."

"Oh, Mrs. Bane," Olabe smiled and she beamed as she remembered many years ago and how active her mother had been in her church. "It all sounds exciting. You must go, Mama. I'll take you and come and get you when it's over."

Jewel sputtered and worried about being a burden and after all, what would Olabe do all day, if she wasn't going to the meeting with her?

"You're welcome to attend with your mother," Mrs. Bane said to Olabe. "Lunch will be provided, too."

"Thank you for the kind offer, Mrs. Bane. I really mean that. But, I've got to go over to Ozark and do some things tomorrow, but I will be very happy to bring my mama."

"Now, you're sure I won't interfere with your plans, Olabe?" Jewel continued to worry.

"Not in the least, Mama." Olabe reassured her mother and felt relieved that her problem of getting time to get those papers shipped to Birmingham had just been solved.

"Well, I had better be getting along," Mrs. Bane said as she stood up. "Got lots of others to see this afternoon. We'll be looking for you tomorrow, Jewel."

"I guess so," Jewel smiled and could hardly contain her joy. The only thing better would be if Olabe had decided to go with her.

Olabe was more talkative the rest of the afternoon and asked many questions about the little church and the people.

Jewel loved that church and answered all of Olabe's questions. The two women talked a long time about when the girls were young. Olabe smiled to herself as she saw the excitement in her mother's eyes and heard it in her voice. Besides, this would give her almost six hours to get those papers and get them shipped to David Becker in Birmingham.

The night dragged for Olabe. Her sleep came in short spurts filled with dreams. Dreams of Liza Jane and how badly she wanted to find out what was really wrong and then, help her.

Jewel woke early and smelled coffee. "Good morning, she said as she walked out into the kitchen to find the cook stove hot and coffee boiling. Olabe was sitting at the table. "You're up early this morning."

"I love the early morning, Mama. Everything is uncomplicated and fresh," Olabe said as she took a slip of hot coffee.

"By the way, Olabe. While you're out shopping today, could you stop somewhere and get some flowers for me. I want to plant them on your papa's grave after the prayer service today."

"Sure, Mama. What would you like me to get?"

"I don't rightly know. Ask the person at the flower shop. They know what grows best in the cemeteries around here."

Finally, it was time to get going. Jewel seemed to take forever to get ready and Olabe paced back and forth on the porch.

"Better hurry up, Mama. You don't want to be late, you know."

"I hurried as fast as I could," Jewel said as she came out the door and gently let the screen door close behind her. "It's been so long since I've been to church, I couldn't decided whether to wear the new gray dress you bought me or my old blue one. But, when I finally decided on the blue one and put it on, I found that some of the seams were ripped, so I couldn't wear that ol' thing."

"What you need, Mama, is another new dress. Why don't we go shopping for one this weekend. That way you'll have two good dresses to wear on occasions like this one today."

Olabe started the truck while Jewel got in the passenger's side and shut the door. Olabe drove down the lane and out onto the road.

"You don't have to drive so fast," Jewel complained. "I'd much rather get there in one piece than not get there at all."

Olabe didn't answer, but smiled a little to herself as she noticed that she was only going thirty five miles per hour.

In the distance they could see the little country church partially hidden in a grove of pecan trees. There was a large conglomeration of virtually every form of car and old truck imaginable. Olabe slowed, negotiated the driveway, and came to a stop near a large gathering of women about her mother's age.

"Why, there's Mrs. Willet," Jewel exclaimed excitedly as she opened the truck door. "Marjean," she called out and waved. A woman acknowledged and waved back. Jewel turned back to Olabe and said, "Wish you were coming with me. Don't forget, now. I'll be ready at three-thirty. Bring the flowers." She stepped out, slammed the truck door, waved to Olabe, and was immediately inundated with a flood of women.

Olabe drove out of the church driveway and back onto the road. She drove back home and didn't waste any time. She skidded to a stop in a cloud of dust right by the porch. Olabe jumped out of the truck, rushed inside the old house, and went right to the little closet in her mother's bedroom. There, was the prized file box. She picked it up and carried it back out to the truck and put it on the floor on the passenger's side. Her stomach now burned with anxiety as she started the engine and drove down the lane. Olabe's course took her down Highway 10 in the opposite direction of Skipperville, as she didn't want to run the risk of going past the little church again, although, she thought that by now everyone would be inside and would never notice her going by. Nevertheless, she didn't want to run the risk. As she came to Graball, she turned south on 431 which would take her to Dothan, Alabama.

As Olabe came into the outskirts of Dothan she realized that she had no idea what she was looking for. The only thing she knew was that she needed to find FedEx.

When in doubt, pull into a gas station and ask, she thought to herself as she signaled a right turn and drove into a large Rebel Fast Gas facility.

Olabe walked in and was relieved to find that she was the only person other than a young man behind the counter.

"Hello," the young man said as he came over to the counter. "What can I do for you? You need gas or something?"

"Oh, no thanks. Just need some help, I guess."

The young man smiled and Olabe noticed his front teeth were so decayed they were almost not there. But, he seemed friendly enough.

"I've got a bunch of papers and such that I need to ship up to Birmingham by FedEx," she said. "Would you have any idea where I can do that around here?"

"I'm pretty sure there's such a place not too far from here," he said as he came around the counter and walked over past the bank of coffee, pop, and candy machines. "Hey, Harvey," he called out. "You all know where a lady, here, can send something up to Birmingham by FedEx?"

Olabe heard someone talking from an office area, but was not able to understand what was being said.

"Ol' Harvey says there's a Pak 'n Ship, or somethin' like 'nat, over on Schuler Street," he said as he pointed off in an unknown direction like she would know where he was talking about.

"Schuler Street?" Olabe asked and looked helpless even though she tried not to.

"Yep. Schuler Street. Here. I'll draw a map for you," the young man said as he got a sheet of paper and a ball point pen. "Now. Here's were we all are, right now. You all go on down that street right out there 'til you comes to a stop light. First light you comes to. Then, turn left. Afterwards of turnin' left, you goes 'bout a block or two and you'll come to Schuler Street. Turn left onto ol' Schuler and go another block or two like you are coming back this here way and you'll spot a little strip mall on the right hand side. Think there's a liquor store and such in there. But, you all will see the shippin' store in 'moungst rest of them stores. Looks like they will be able to help you out, most likely."

She thanked the young man and hurried out to the truck and set out to follow his map. It was farther to the stop light than she figured, but nonetheless, did as his instructions said. Within a few minutes of turning and driving she saw a little strip mall on the right side of the street and, in the middle of the stores, a sign said "You Bring and We Ship."

48

Olabe left the box inside the truck and walked into the store. A girl sat behind the counter reading a paperback book that looked like she was hardly old enough to be in high school, let alone working at a job. The girl looked up.

"Anything I can hep you for?"

"I've got a bunch of papers and old family photos that I want to overnight up to my uncle in Birmingham," Olabe lied a little. "I'll need a box to put them in, too."

"Don't see no papers," the girl said as she slowly got up and came over to the counter.

"They're in the truck," Olabe pointed out towards her truck. "Didn't know if you all did that sort of thing before I brought everything in."

"Yup. That's what we all do here. Best you haul all that stuff in here so's we can figure out what size box you all gonna need."

Olabe went outside and opened the passenger side door of her truck. She took the cover off of her mother's file box and dumped the contents onto the seat. She picked up all the papers, forms, and tax returns and took them back inside the store to find the young girl had gone back and sat down.

"Here's what I want to ship," Olabe said as she plunked the stack on the counter.

The young girl got back up and walked slowly over.

"Looks like you all gonna need a ten inch deep by ten inch wide by twelve inch long."

"Great," Olabe said.

"Only one problem," the girl said. "Ain't got no ten by ten by twelve."

"What? What can we do?"

"Well. We got a twelve by twelve by twelve. That should work out alright."

Olabe was perplexed, but kept her cool. She couldn't see what such a little difference could make anyway. All she needed was a box to ship her papers in. It didn't matter if it was big enough to ship her truck. She just needed a box.

"You all want to try that size box?" the young girl asked. "Or, you'ns wants to go somewheres else?"

"No. That one will be just fine."

"Costs more."

"I don't care. It will be fine."

Slowly, the young girl came around the counter and went over to a stack of different size boxes that were flattened. She rummaged around until she found what she was looking for.

"Here we go," she said and handed the flat cardboard to Olabe.

"How do you make a box out of this?" Olabe asked as she looked over the cardboard and noticed the astonished look on the young girl's face.

"I'll shows yah. Here. Push these sides together. See? It makes a box. Then, fold these two flappers down and I'll gets the tape. We're a gonna have you a box here in no time."

Soon, the box was together and filled. The top flaps were taped.

"Here," the young girl said as she handed Olabe a form. "You all gots to fill out the who you are part and the who you gonna send this here box to."

Olabe wrote her mother's name on the "Ship from" part of the form and found the address David Becker had given her and wrote it on the "Ship to" part. She handed the form to the girl.

She took the form, pulled off the label, and stuck it onto the box. She then took the box and put it on the scale.

"Uh oh," she murmured. "It's gonna be pretty expensive."

She looked on two charts and then added some numbers on a little calculator.

"Gonna be twenty eight dollars and seventy nine cents. You all still wanna ship it anyways?"

"Yes. That's just fine," Olabe said as she took out a ten and a twenty dollar bill and handed them to the girl. "You just keep the change for all your help."

The young girl again looked surprised. "For that price you all could almost drive up to Birmingham and drop it off. Must be mighty important papers, there."

"No. Not really. My old aunt died and we're just getting her papers and things together and sending them up to her brother."

"Well, if that's what it all is, you don't have to ship it overnight, you know. It would be lots cheaper to send it by mail and all."

"That's alright. They gave me the money and we've already got it ready," Olabe said without going into the "who" gave her the money.

"Was you all close to her?"

"Who?" Olabe said without thinking.

"You aunt. You know the one who just died and all."

The girl looked at Olabe like she thought she had just lost her mind.

"Not really. I only saw her on holidays and even then, not very often."

"It's a pity and all. Families not being close anymore. Take me. I never see my two sisters no more and we only live a few miles apart."

"Guess that's what we get for our modern lives," Olabe smiled and started for the door.

"Here. You all forgot your receipt."

"Oh. Thanks."

Olabe was relieved. The papers were now on their way to David Becker. She had to get home and put her mother's file box back into the closet. But, on the way home she realized that the empty box was no where near as heavy as it was almost filled with papers.

When she got back home, she searched around the house and finally saw the round rag rug at the end of her bed. She rolled it up and then folded it over. It just fit in the file box. The box wasn't quite as heavy as before, but it wasn't empty either. For now, Olabe was satisfied.

She got back into the truck and drove back onto the road. She drove through Skipperville and was relieved that even though the parking lot of the church was filled, there were no people outside the building. Olabe continued down Highway 105 and on into Ozark. She drove around for a while looking for a flower shop and finally saw the sign of "Fancie's Flowers" on her left. She parked and ran across the street.

A bell tinkled as she opened the door and the aroma of lots of flowers filled the air.

"Be right with you," a voice called out from in back.

Olabe looked around at various vases and saw a huge cooler full of roses and other cut flowers.

"Sorry to keep you all waiting," a middle aged lady said as she came around the counter from a back room. She was carrying a huge bouquet of yellow and orange flowers. "It's for the Parmalee funeral," she said as if Olabe would know who the deceased person was. "Now, what can I do for you?"

"I'm looking for some flowers to plant on my daddy's grave," Olabe responded. "I'm sorry about being so dumb about it, but I don't even know what kind of flowers people plant on graves."

"Oh, don't worry 'bout that," the lady laughed. "But, to tell the truth, I don't have anything you could use, lest your daddy was just freshly buried and you all wanted some fresh, cut flowers. I only carry house plants otherwise. You know, just to supplement sales."

"My daddy has been gone a long time. Do you have any idea where I might find something that would work?"

"Well, let me think on it for a while," the lady said as she went over to the counter and looked through the Ozark phonebook. "You might try Elmer's Garden Supply. He's always got plants and flowers and such."

"Can you tell me how to get there? I don't live around here and wanted to make sure to plant some flowers before I leave."

"I could tell," the lady smiled.

"Tell? Tell what?"

"Tell you ain't from here."

"Why, how would you know that?"

"Your boots."

"My boots? How can you tell anything from my boots?"

"Too nice for being from 'round here. Ain't no red clay on 'em."

Olabe's mind raced. She had to convince this woman that she was no one out of the ordinary.

"Guess you're right about that," Olabe said using her best Alabama drawl. "Actually, I live up past Clopton and my best ol' uncle bought these for me when he was up in Birmingham. I only wear them for good."

The lady smiled and thought, *Now don't that just figure? A Clopton hillbilly can't ever cover it up. Even with them expensive boots.*

Actually, she was a very nice, friendly person, and gave Olabe directions on how to get to Elmer's Garden Supply.

Olabe parked in Elmer's parking lot. There were plants and potted trees everywhere. There was a building, of sorts, that looked like it might be a store so she went in. She looked around at pots and plants. There were things everywhere. There were big bags of dirt and fertilizer. Finally, a little old man with a ragged blue shirt came around a stack of white pots.

"Good afternoon, Miss," he said politely. "What all can I do for you this fine day?"

Olabe explained what she was looking for.

"Well," he drawled thoughtfully. "Guess I've got lots of perennials that might work out. You all gots any preference on 'em?"

"Not really. Just something that blooms a lot that we can plant on my daddy's grave."

"Oh. Now that's a different story all together," the old man said as his blue, friendly eyes locked with Olabe's. "Now what you all need first is pots. Cement pots to put flowers in."

"Why on earth do I need cement pots? I just want to plant flowers."

"Well, now I'll tell you," The man said as his white hair puffed upward as he walked under a ceiling fan. "Now, most of them fellers that take care of graveyards don't take the time to watch out for no planted flowers. They'll just mow 'em down in nothing flat. If'n you all plants the flowers in cement pots, they can't chop 'em up."

"Oh. I see," Olabe smiled as she let the friendly, southern charm of the old man sink in.

"Now, I gots all you need right over here. You'll need two pots, a bag of gravel, and two of dirt."

He pushed a small flatbed cart and stacked things on it as he talked. He told Olabe to put the gravel in the bottom of the pot so water could run through which would prevent root rot. He showed her lots of plants and helped her pick out some hardy ones that she thought her mother would like. Finally, after she paid him, he helped her, or rather practically loaded her truck for her.

"Thank you much," he smiled and waved. "Hope you can manage everything alright."

Olabe looked at her watch and noticed it was a quarter after three. She had spent lots more time at the garden center than she thought and it was about ten miles to Skipperville.

The miles sped by and soon she turned into the church parking lot. People were standing around everywhere. She looked for a place to park when she saw her mother.

"Olabe!" Jewel called out. "Olabe! Here I am. Wait a minute and I'll be right there."

Olabe smiled and watched her mother wave goodbye to three of her old friends and then, turned and walked to the truck.

"Hope you weren't waiting long, dear," Jewel said as she got in and shut the door. "The prayer service ran over a little bit."

"No, Mama. It worked out fine. I just got here."

"Now, drive over there and down that little road. The cemetery is right over there behind the church."

Jewel was very pleased with the flowers and even the cement pots after Olabe told her what the man said at Elmer's Garden Supply. Even though the pots took both of them to get them off the truck and onto the ground, they somehow managed it.

They worked and planted. When it was all done, Jewel stood up and admired the grave of her beloved husband.

"Seems like only yesterday when we were all here. And then, it all seemed like a dream," Jewel said as tears welled up in her eyes.

Olabe felt a pang of guilt rifle through her body. She was at the funeral, of course, but left right afterward to do a concert in Dallas. This was her first time back to visit her father's grave since. She had never seen the headstone, but did remember her business manager telling her that she had paid for it. It was a beautiful rose colored stone with the name of her father, his birth date, and his death date. Jewel's name was engraved along with her birth date. Their marriage date was also carved within a wedding ring between the two names.

Suddenly, Olabe felt tears looming. She missed her daddy. Memories flowed through her and she thought about how much she loved him.

The two women stood silently as tears flowed and a gentle breeze played with Olabe's hair. Time passed but they still stood there a while longer.

Finally, Olabe said, "Let's go, Mama."

CHAPTER 6
Let's Catch a Varmint

Olabe was up earlier than usual and put the tea kettle on the stove to boil.

"You're sure up early this morning," Jewel said as she came into the kitchen.

"Good morning, Mama. Remember, today is the day I have to go up to Birmingham to meet the people that help manage my business affairs."

"Oh, yes," Jewel said as she got a box of tea bags out of the cupboard and set them by the stove. "Will you be gone all day?"

"Probably, Mama," feeling a little guilty for not asking her mother to go along with her, but this was not a meeting she wanted to share with her just yet. "These meetings usually take forever and are almost always very boring."

The water in the tea kettle was now boiling so Olabe slid it away from the heat, pulled off the cover and placed three tea bags in to steep.

"Well," Jewel said, "sure glad I won't have to face that wild mess up there in the city. Cities always make my head spin."

Olabe smiled and nodded as she poured them each a cup of tea. She smiled inwardly, too, as she thought to herself that her mother had probably never been more than 90 miles away from home in all her life.

Jewel continued to ramble on as they sipped their tea while Olabe's mind raced over a million questions she wanted to ask in today's meeting.

Trying her best to keep her anxiety from her mother, Olabe slowly stood, picked up her now empty cup, and put it into the dry sink.

"Well, Mama, guess I'd better get going. It's a long drive up there to Birmingham."

It was a few minutes after six when she hugged Jewel and walked out to the truck. Her stomach was churning as she drove down the little driveway and she had a three and a half-hour drive ahead of her. She turned on the radio and scanned for an all-talk station as she still couldn't stand to listen to music at all.

The only give-away feature in Olabe's attire now was her sunglasses. Other than that, she had reverted back to being pure country. Her jeans were tight and pressed, but not designer. Her blouse came from Minnie's Southern Woman's shop in Dothan instead of being tailor made for her. She wore cowboy boots and drove a pickup truck.

The miles rolled by smoothly. The morning was cool so she had the windows down and loved the feeling of the wind blowing through her hair. The radio provided the mindless noise she wanted as she let her mind drift into "blank." Mile after mile went by and the warm Alabama sun began to heat the air until she noticed it was now very hot and humid as she turned off the Interstate toward downtown Birmingham.

Traffic moved at an absolute crawl. Olabe finally had to relent and turn on the air conditioner full blast. Finally, she saw the Southern National Bank building coming up on the right with its high-rise parking garage attached next door. As she drove inside the garage the temperature must have dropped twenty degrees which caused her windshield to fog over. Olabe slammed on her brakes, reached for the switch to turn off the air conditioner, and turn on the defroster. She drove up to an area where cars were stopping and uniformed parking attendants were getting in allowing the driver to walk the short distance to a double door and into the elevator lobby.

"Mornin', miss," a uniformed, very sharply dressed, young man said as he opened the door of Olabe's truck and held out his hand to help her out.

He gave her a receipt, stepped into the truck, and rapidly drove away smiling to himself at the strikingly beautiful, "Alabama peach." *Little mature*, he thought to himself as he wove his way around the parking building until he slid into an open space. "Sure nice body, for an old lady, though," he murmured and then laughed out loud. "Must be getting desperate," he continued laughing as he flipped the keys into the air and caught them on the fly.

Olabe stood waiting in the lobby with six elevators on each side of the narrow room. Finally, a door opened and she, along with three smartly dressed men and one woman, stepped in. The middle-aged man nearest the button console called out, "floors?"

Voices responded for the fourth and ninth floors.

"Ma'am?" he asked as he smiled warmly at Olabe.

"Oh, I'm sorry. Seven, please."

When the elevator silently stopped at the seventh floor Olabe found herself facing a huge glass lobby with the names; "Griggs, Becker, Tummalson, Brown, and Thomas, Attorneys at Law."

She opened the door and walked in feeling the deep, expensive carpet beneath her feet.

"May I help you, ma'am?" a young woman sitting behind a huge desk asked. She looked like someone that should be in Hollywood going to an expensive restaurant rather than a person sitting behind a desk. Her auburn hair glowed in the warm light from a ceiling fixture which also caused her green eyes to sparkle as she talked. Her dark brown suit fit perfectly. She seemed warm and friendly, but her eyes silently scanned and caused her to wonder why this country bumpkin was standing in the most prestigious law office in all of Alabama.

"I'm here to meet Mr. Becker for a ten o'clock meeting," Olabe said firmly, but professionally to let this "greeter" person know she was used to dealing with all sorts of self-important people throughout her career.

The woman picked up the phone and was about to ask for Mr. Becker's office secretary when he burst through the huge wooden doors that led to the inner-sanctum of offices.

"Miss Mae," the elderly man exclaimed. "I'm David Becker. Welcome."

"Good morning," Olabe smiled and grasped David Becker's outstretched hand.

She followed Becker through a maze of offices, copy machines, and a large number of cubicles with women clicking non-stop on their computer keyboards. She noticed that the man she was following looked to be about six feet tall with long, flowing white hair. His face was ruddy from years of living, but warm and friendly. Olabe laughed to herself as she visualized him in old overalls and a flannel shirt rather that the expensive blue suit he was wearing, and most likely, handmade dark blue shoes.

Becker held the door open to a large office that was dimly lighted except for the center table that glowed from a suspended overhead set of bright lights.

"May I offer you some coffee, Ms. Mae?" he drawled. "I'm about to have some."

Silently, the door opened and, almost by magic, a young woman floated in carrying two china cups and an urn of coffee. She set them on the table and disappeared. Becker poured the coffee and Olabe's nose delighted in the warm, wonderfully aromatic aroma of the brew.

Becker made small talk with his warm, slow, and deep southern drawl. He told her funny little stories with all the southern charm and warmth of anyone's favorite grandfather. He was a senior partner and had pretty much retired unless he was called in to look over an "interesting" case from time to time.

"Now, then, Ms. Mae," he drawled and set his cup on the table. "I'm sure you want to get down to business and not waste your time with my rambling stories."

Olabe smiled and told him she had all the time in the world and loved his stories.

"Let's get our business out of the way first, Ms. Mae, and then take a nice leisurely lunch. Would that be alright with you?"

"Yes, it would be very nice. But, first, Mr. Becker, please call me Olabe."

"Why certainly, and then, you must call me David."

They both agreed and David wove a long story of his interest in the law and agriculture. He brought out a large stack of papers and set them on the table.

"Don't be frightened, Ms. Mae, I mean Olabe. We won't look at more than just a few things here. Most of this is just legal dirt for us lawyers."

Olabe smiled and moved her chair closer to the table.

"Now, I've had the opportunity to review your mama's last year's tax return and I guess there is no other way to say it other than things just don't add up. Add up isn't the correct phrase, I'm afraid. The arithmetic is just fine. It's the numbers that I'm troubled with," Becker said slowly in his soft, deep, Alabamian drawl. His eyes caught her's for an instant and he noticed a glimmer of fire as she drew her chair closer to the table.

"I suspected something was wrong. I didn't trust him right from the start. Call it woman's intuition or just plain mistrust."

"Well, Ms. Olabe, it looks like your feelings were very accurate. Now, let me explain how I arrived at my conclusion here."

The acid in Olabe's stomach churned as feelings of contempt grew. She knew there was more about Betterund she disliked. More than his mental undressing her and his leering smile. She had grown used to that long ago in her music career. There was something about Betterund that didn't make her afraid, exactly. But, she knew in her heart that he was a deceitful, untrustworthy person that was somehow taking advantage of her mother.

"We have to begin by looking over some things about the mill at Skipperville. Will that be alright with you?"

"Yes, but what does that have to do with anything. I thought I was here to discuss my mother's income situation and taxes."

"Well, yes, that's true. But, after a long discussion with your business manager and attorney along with a little analysis of the returns and such that you sent up here, I did a little work along another line on my own.

"A few days ago, I took a little drive down thata way to see an old friend of mine that lives in Ozark. His name is Will Jespers and we grew up as friends all through high school. We sat on his porch, drank a little whiskey, and smoked a few fine cigars. He has owned a real estate business down there for as many years as I've been a lawyer, and that's so many that I've lost count.

"Anyway, we talked about everything under the sun and I eased the course of conversation around to that ol' mill. I lied a little, but not much, and told him I had a client that might be interested in looking at it for a little investment, if it was for sale.

"Well, wouldn't you know it? He smiled and poured me another little snort and told me it might just be my lucky day. The owner lived up in Montgomery and it had been in his family for generations. He was now eighty-three and wanted to retire, and yes, it could be for sale at the right price.

"We continued to talk well into the evening and decided to have dinner together. I booked a room at a local motel so I could drive back in the morning.

"I told him I was sure my client could be very interested, but told him any deal would have to be in strictest confidence to insure confidentiality of my client and that if we could reach an agreement, it would be purchased through a blind trust.

"I told him I would need to see all the books for at least five years back, to insure at least a history of modest return, and he said he would see to it. He kept his word and within a few hours, handed me the ledgers.

"I've gone through them completely, Olabe. And, they are very interesting."

David's eyes sparkled. He wouldn't have made a very good poker player, because his smile and little tuft of white hair that slid downward on his forehead gave away his secret that he was holding four aces.

"You won't believe what I've found."

Olabe sat silently on the edge of her chair staring into David's warm, gray eyes. She waited breathlessly as she tried desperately to rein in her anxiety, but couldn't help wringing her hands together on her lap.

"You see, Ms. Olabe, it's the practice all over the south for farmers to bring their produce to a mill during harvest time. Most farmers have no way of storing anything. Besides, they need the money their crops will bring and that's where the mill comes in. Mills keep track of the amount each farmer brings in, or in your mama's case, the amount brought in off her land by Betterund's men. That way, Betterund has a record of how much was produced on each farm he worked so he can share the proceeds with each respective land owner. And, it also creates the total amount the mill owes him. So you see, it's very helpful to all."

Olabe nodded her understanding, but wished Becker would get to the heart of the matter. She wanted to know how someone could lie and cheat her mother.

"So," David drawled softly onward, "I took the production numbers your mama's farm generated times the going rate for peanuts per hundred pounds and arrived at the gross dollar amount the mill paid Betterund for what he grew on your mama's farm. See here? It's a pretty sizable amount."

Olabe studied the number and frowned.

"How can that be right, David? I know the total income on her last year's tax return showed she earned far less than that."

"Yes. You're most certainly right. But, the common way of share cropping is for the land owner to give the use of the land and pay the taxes on the land. The renter provides the seed, fertilizer, fuel, and other expenses, but charges them off the top of the gross income. What's left is then shared equally between them. Looks like Betterund deducted everything off, including his share before he divided what was left in half."

"So, he cheated Mama, didn't he David?" Olabe almost shouted as she stood up and pounded the table.

"I fear so. Not only that, looks like he's done it for years. Now, if you say he farms for lots of folks like your mama, I would say the dollar figure will amount to a pretty big number."

"How much do you figure it amounts to, David?"

"Looks like, over five or more years, probably somewhere nearing a hundred thousand dollars or so," David said as he adjusted his glasses watching Olabe's reaction.

"And, you think he cheated the others, too?"

"Probably, Ms. Olabe. Bad folks like this usually aren't content with trimming money off just one."

Alright, David," Olabe said firmly and sat back down. "What do we have to do to get that ol' awful man?"

"Well, now, Ms. Olabe, we have to remember one thing, here. We want to win the war, so let's plan our strategy slowly to make sure we get our possum fully treed before we bring out our shootin' guns."

"I hate things that take time," Olabe said as she looked David squarely in the eyes.

He smiled warmly, reached out and grasped her hand.

"We just want to make sure we do everything just right before we spring our little trap. For a while, we will need complete secrecy."

Olabe's brain wanted nothing more than to rush home, get the law on Betterund, and beat the living daylights out of him herself.

"We must keep this little secret between just you and me for a while. Do you understand?"

Slowly, Olabe let the words sink in. She was finally able to overcome her strong urge for action and she nodded her head that she understood.

"Fine. Now, here's what we must do. We need to get one of your blind trusts to buy that little ol' mill down there in Skipperville. We need those books in our possession. I know Will still has them because he promised me that he would keep them in his office safe for a few weeks just in case my buyer might want to see them."

David reached for the telephone and pawed through some papers until he found the number he was looking for.

"Hello? Well, good afternoon to you, Miss Katherine. I hope your day is going well," David drawled in his slow, deep, and soft southern voice. "My name is David Becker and I would like to talk to your Mr. John Dunn for a few minutes."

There was a pause and David smiled reassuringly at Olabe.

"John! David Becker here. Yes....., yes. I'm here in my office with Ms. Mae right now. Yes..." David laughed. "Now, John, Ms. Mae agrees that we should buy that little ol' mill and that we should do it through one of her blind trust accounts like you suggested. I can take care of all the details for you. All I need to know is how to transfer the deed and, of course, where to get the money."

Olabe knew that the John he was talking to was Megastar Agency's attorney, John Dunn, in Nashville. John was the one that told her about David Becker and that he was the best, most mature, and experienced agricultural attorney in Alabama. Olabe was glad he had, too. She liked David and he gave her assurance.

David talked over some of the details he thought would close the deal filling Olabe in on the fly.

"Alright, John. You'll have the cash transferred to the Southern First Bank this afternoon? Fine. Fine. Yes. That's the same building where my office is located. Yes. I plan to go down there in a little while and get a Cashier's Check so when I meet their agent, I'll be ready. Money talks, don't you know?"

David laughed and continued talking.

When David finally put the phone back in it's cradle, he turned to Olabe and said, "Well, the first part of our plan is all set. Now, let's get ol' Will on the phone and push our little plan along, shall we?"

He winked at Olabe as he touched the keys on the phone and waited.

"Hello. Will Jespers, please." There was a small pause of silence. "Will. It's David, here. Yes, I know. Don't hear from me in a long while, and then twice in a few days."

David laughed and made small talk. He was an expert at making people feel at ease and reveled in it. He told little stories and cackled over his own punch lines. She could just visualize the person on the other end of the line, probably about David's age, probably pretty successful, and probably just a little tattered from age. He probably had his feet up on his desk and was thoroughly enjoying bantering back and forth with his beloved friend.

"Now, Will, I talked to my client and they are not only interested in that little ol' mill over there in Skipperville, but ready to make an offer."

David listened for a few seconds and winked again at Olabe.

"Well, now we think the half a million asking price is a little high and off the mark, but not by a whole lot."

Again, David listened.

"Yes, I remember. But, Will, the land is probably worth about a hundred-fifty thousand. The ol' building certainly can't be worth much at all. I do remember that the equipment was in pretty good shape, though."

David listened and made little comments now and then.

"Here's something we can all get excited about, Will. My client is ready to offer two hundred fifty thousand in cash and assume the debt. That's a total of four hundred sixty thousand. Pretty close to the asking price wouldn't you say?"

David laughed and listened.

"Yes, Will. Cashier's Check and a guarantee for the mill's note at the bank in Dothan which will be paid in full in thirty days from the date of purchase."

David gave the "thumbs up" sign to Olabe and continued to chat for another few minutes.

"Fine, Will. Yes, I can meet you on Wednesday in Montgomery to close the deal with your man. Fine. Don't forget to bring all the books with you. I know, but the whole deal hinges on having them. Good. Tell Kate hello for me. Yes. Alright. See you then. Bye, Will."

Olabe couldn't help herself. She jumped up, rushed over, and threw her arms around David. She was almost overwhelmed at finally doing something.

David hugged her back and chuckled softly. "Looks like you're going to be the new owner of a mill if everything goes 'cordin' to our little plan, Ms. Olabe. Now, how about the lunch I promised?"

"That sounds wonderful, David. I'd like that very much."

"Miss Olabe and I are going to take a little lunch, Miss Marlow," David said to his secretary who looked up from her computer screen and smiled warmly.

As they walked away, Olabe felt Miss Marlow's eyes scan and carefully evaluate her. She smiled to herself and even loved the little tinge of jealousy Miss Marlow must have been feeling right about now.

They boarded the elevator and sped to the ground floor. They walked out of the lobby and onto the busy sidewalk.

"Let's walk this way," David said has he motioned to the right. Olabe fell in step and put her arm through David's.

"Hah, ho," he chuckled. "We should have done this when we left the office. That would have really made those office secretaries' tongues wag."

Olabe smiled slyly and walked along with a man over twice her age, but who looked as distinguished as the President of the United States.

He guided her into a small, but very intimate restaurant. The aroma was inviting as Olabe realized it was past one o'clock and she was hungry. David, the perfect southern gentleman, helped Olabe with her chair and made sure she was settled before he sat down.

He ordered for both of them and completely entertained Olabe with his stories and antidotes of his law practice and odd cases.

"As I grew older, I must have become more eccentric. Seems like all the really odd cases are thrown my way. Makes one wonder just how odd I've really become."

Both laughed as David's sense of humor rippled and flowed like a babbling, southern stream as it chuckled and splashed it's way through the Alabama hillside.

Lunch was served and was elegant to say the least.

"Why, my gracious," David drawled and smiled widely. "Ms. Olabe, I believe you inhaled everything but the plate."

"Guess I was starved. Everything was wonderful, David," Olabe said as she put her cloth napkin on her empty plate.

"Too bad it wasn't supper," David continued his warm and casual conversation. "Seems this would have been a wonderful time to enjoy a glass of port. Something to toast our new business venture."

"Oh, my," Olabe exclaimed as she glanced at her watch. "It's well after two, David. I had better get going. I've got a long drive ahead of me."

He paid the bill and they walked out into the hot Alabama afternoon sunshine.

"Drive carefully, now. And remember, secrecy is key here. Not a word to anyone until I contact you."

"Yes, David. I remember. I have to tell you the waiting will be a real struggle for me. I've always been an action person. You know, act first and think about it later."

David chuckled. "But, this time, you've got to remember to hold those horses."

"I will."

"Now, I'll call you on your cell phone near the end of next week."

"Oh, David. I'm afraid I won't hear it. I have to keep it plugged into the truck's lighter to keep the battery charged."

David thought a minute and frowned. "Don't your mama even have electricity?" He knew the answer when he saw tears well up in Olabe's eyes. "Now, don't fret, Ms. Olabe. Here's what we'll do. Set your cell to vibrate so no one will hear it ring. I'll make sure to call early in the morning. That way, all you have to do is check for voice mail now and then each day."

"Wish it was today and we were ready to go get that ol' boy," Olabe said with vengeance in her voice and it was at that instant she realized her southern Alabama accent had crept back into her voice. The hillbilly accent she had worked so hard to overcome all those years. But, it was that accent that won her fame and fortune in the country music world.

"I'll be callin' near the end of the week, next week," David said, reassuring his snorting charge who was ready to bolt at any instant.

Olabe thanked David for all his help and patience while he escorted her back to the parking garage. The garage attendant brought the truck to the waiting area, jumped out, and held the door open so Olabe could get in.

The long drive back was boring and hot. Olabe tried her best to get interested in a talk-radio station, but her mind kept coming back to that awful man that had cheated her mother for so many years. The more she thought about it the faster she drove. Her mind suddenly came back to reality and she noticed she was doing over eighty miles per hour. She immediately let her foot off the gas and nudged the brake until she was back going just the speed limit. She quickly scanned her mirror to make sure no squad cars were following her. Relieved, she told herself that she had to pay more attention and stop thinking about Betterund. She set the speed control and told herself to do as David told her. *Get a grip!*

It was almost six o'clock when she turned into the little lane that led up to her mother's house. As she stopped the truck she noticed that Mama was sitting in her rocker on the porch sipping a cup of tea.

"Hello, Olabe," she said and stood up. "I was beginning to worry. You know Birmingham is a long drive."

Olabe really strained to suppress the urge to rush over, hug her mother, and tell her everything, but somehow, she managed to keep her composure.

"Hello, Mama. You're right. It was a long drive. Any tea left?"

"Kettle is still on the stove," Jewel said and sat back down.

Olabe went into the kitchen, threw her purse on the table, and poured herself a cup of tea. She walked back out to the porch and sunk down on the second rocker, took a deep breath, and tried to relax as she took a long sip of the lukewarm liquid. She kicked her boots off and then took her stockings off and let her feet feel the soft, late afternoon sun.

"Good thing we live way out here," Jewel said with a twinkle in her eye. "Next, you'll be peelin' off the rest of those clothes just like when you were a little girl."

"Wish I could, Mama. Sometimes, I wish I was a little girl again running around without a care in the world." Olabe took another sip of her tea and looked glassy-eyed into the distance.

Jewel didn't reply. She just continued to rock and watch. Her thoughts went back to when Olabe first showed up. She remembered how depressed and skinny she was and how the warm, red hills of Alabama had softly and silently caressed her troubled daughter back to health.

Over the next few days, Jewel noticed that Olabe seemed distant again and just a little irritable. Nothing too apparent, but something that only a mother could notice.

Olabe's thoughts were in another world. Her gut was in constant turmoil as she anxiously waited for David Becker to put a call on her voice mail. She checked her cell phone three times a day, but nothing so far. She tried in vain not to look too suspicious as she found need to look for things in the truck, but that was pretty unconvincing after the first day so she stopped making up excuses and just went and looked when she could no longer overcome the need. Jewel watched, but didn't say anything.

Finally, Thursday morning David called. He told Olabe that he needed to meet with her mother and one more family, if that would be possible. He would drive down to Ozark tomorrow and stay at a motel and asked if Olabe would pick him up at the motel on Saturday morning.

"Don't want no unfamiliar car roamin' 'round down there and raise any suspicions," David said. "Remember, Miss Olabe. Secrecy is the word."

That night, after supper, Jewel and Olabe were tired after a long day's work of canning green beans. They sat out on the porch in their rockers and sipped tea listening to the night sounds.

Finally, Olabe could hold back no longer.

"Mama?"

"What is it, child?"

"Mama. I've got something that's been bothering me for a while and I think I need to tell you."

Jewel rocked and listened.

"What I've got to say may make you mad, but I have to tell you anyway."

"Olabe, dear. Don't you know that you are my daughter? And, as my daughter, don't you know that whatever it is, may make me angry for a little while. But, it has nothing to do with the love I have for you."

"Well, Mama, you probably aren't going to like this at all."

Having said that, Olabe began the story of her dislike of Jimmy Wade Betterund and her suspicion about him after finding her mothers tax return folder. She told her mother how she had sent them to a law firm in Birmingham that was associated with the legal branch of her businesses. She told about meeting David Becker, the attorney, and how Betterund had apparently swindled her mother out of thousands of dollars over the last five years.

When she finished, she sat back and waited for the tirade that was surely to follow. But, nothing happened. Jewel rocked slowly and remained silent for a long while.

"Olabe?" Her mother finally interrupted the long silence.

"Yes, Mama?"

"First, dear child. I'm not mad at you for any reason. So, rest your heart and be at peace. At first, when you told me you had gone through my old tax records, I'll admit I was a little miffed. But, after your explanation I resolved any temper quite quickly."

"Oh, Mama. Thank you, so much. I certainly never meant to hurt you, in any way."

"Yes, child. You know, I've always sort of suspected that ol' Jimmy Wade was doing me wrong for a long time, but never did anything about it."

"Why, Mama? Why didn't you find out about what was going on?"

"Well, honey. When your papa died more than fifteen years ago, my world fell to pieces in the matter of one day. You and your sister had both left home by this time, if you remember. Your daddy left for work that awful October morning, just like he did every other day of his life, it seemed. I even remember the soft rain making little red puddles on the lane as he drove away. It was before dinner time, they told me, and he was wiring an electrical panel for a new bank building, down there in Dothan, you know. Somehow, somebody turned on the main power and your papa was electrocuted." Jewel was sobbing now.

Jewel rocked silently for a little while and then wiped her eyes and blew her nose softly.

"After the funeral, people promised to stay close and help, but as with all families, everyone had their own lives to live.

"I know, Mama. It was just like that when my family was taken away from me."

"Yes, I imagine it was, dear. Soon, the visits became fewer and less often, until most stopped coming all together. Oh, I saw folks and friends at church, and all. But, other than asking how I was doing, that was pretty much it.

"Back when I was a little girl, I lived with my mama and papa along with seven brothers and sisters. Then, Henry came along. When he and I married, I moved in with him and his family until we could afford this place. Soon, your sister and you were born and we had our own family to look after. Even when you and Rebecca June left home, I still had Henry. When he was taken away from me, I had no one."

"I'm sorry, Mama," Olabe sniffed, stood up, and came over and put her hand on Jewel's shoulder. "I'm so sorry."

"All I could do, for a long while, was drag myself out of bed each morning, milk ol' Bessie, and go to the cemetery. Those three things sapped all my living energy each day, for many days. Then, one day, Jimmy Wade Betterund drove up in his ol' beat up truck. He told me how sorry he was that Henry had passed on and wanted to help. He said he would farm the land on shares and deposit my share in the bank for me. He even said he would pay the taxes on the land, out of my share, of course, and file my income taxes. I could even buy anything I needed from his store and they would just deduct it from my bank account. I didn't have to think about anything. At the time, I thought he was a godsend, Olabe. A true godsend. I wanted to and did trust him completely. How little did I know."

"You are certainly right about that, Mama."

"So, Olabe. What can be done?"

"A lot of things, Mama. Mr. Becker said that we probably won't be able to get any of the money back because people like Betterund usually don't own anything."

"But, doesn't he have big equipment? You know like tractors and combines and such?"

"Mr. Becker says people like that lease them and don't actually own anything. That way if they run into trouble, there is nothing to take. He said that they siphon off the money and put it into blind accounts so no one will ever know where it is, including the government."

"But, can't he be arrested?"

"You bet he can, Mama. And, Mr. Becker said that Alabama has a law to protect widows and disabled folks from predators like Betterund. He said the law was passed right after the Civil War to protect poor folks from the northern carpetbaggers and, although it's not used very often, it's still on the books and has real stiff penalties."

Olabe then told her mother all the rest she remembered from her trip to Birmingham and her meeting with David Becker.

"Well, I want him stopped," Jewel said firmly. "Now, what do we have to do from here on?"

"Mr. Becker wanted to know if you knew anyone else that Betterund does the farming for."

"Let me see, now," Jewel pondered. "I know for certain he does the work for Thompson's down the road there." As she continued to run the list of neighbors over in her head she counted each one on her fingers. "Olabe, I know of nine more so far for sure and I'm pretty sure there are at least four or five more on the other side of Clopton."

"Are there any of those families that you can trust, Mama, so we can borrow their tax records to make sure Betterund is cheating more than just you?"

"Well, certainly. If I ask for their confidence, I know I can trust most folks around here. But, I know the Thompson family certainly know how to keep a secret. Most folks around here see them often at church and still don't know that their Liza Jane don't talk none. That's how good they can keep a secret."

"Mama? Didn't you tell me that Raaf worked for Betterund when he got injured?"

"Yes, he did. The way I remember it happened was when Raaf was working with a crew that was pitching peanut vines that had fallen down into the path of the combine so it would pick them up. The story goes that Jimmy Wade was driving a tractor with a wagon alongside the combine to unload the peanuts while it was working. That way, it didn't have to stop for anything. I guess Raaf somehow tripped and fell. He was right in front of the tractor that Jimmy Wade was driving and I guess he ran right over him. He was hurt terrible bad."

"Did they get him to the hospital?"

"No. Jimmy Wade told Rachael that Raaf told him that he didn't want to go to no hospital, so they took him home, instead.

"He was in terrible bad shape. His right leg was broken and something happened to both of his hips, too."

"Did the doctor come out to their house, then?"

"They sent for an ol' vet. Jimmy Wade told Rachael that he was better than any ol' doctor."

Now Olabe was certain that she not only wanted this Jimmy Wade devil stopped, she wanted him crucified.

CHAPTER 7
Springing the Trap

It was Saturday morning and Olabe was on her way to Ozark. The sun was out already and it promised to be another hot day. She passed the little intersection that went to Asbury and roared past the crossroad that led to Beamon.

Olabe suddenly realized that she was so tense, she was gritting her teeth. She just happened to glance down at the speedometer.

"Whoa," she said out loud to herself as she saw the needle pointing right at seventy miles per hour. "Better hold it down." She took her foot off the gas and let the truck slow until it was rolling along at a little more that fifty-five. "Sure don't need a speeding ticket."

Olabe drove into the parking lot of the Crimson Edge Motel, parked, and walked towards the coffee shop. She was to meet David Becker there and bring him back to meet her mother and then, possibly take him to meet the Thompson family.

"Good morning, Miss Olabe," David said warmly as he stood up from the booth. "Come and sit for a while and we'll take some breakfast together."

Food was about the last thing on Olabe's mind this morning, but there was something about David's gentle personality that enticed her to order a bowl of grits with butter and a cup of coffee.

"Grits are what makes us southern folks stay alive," David's eyes twinkled as the waitress put a bowl down for David and one for Olabe. "My Mama used to pour in a little bacon grease, too, but my doctor would have a massive coronary, if I ever told him that."

Olabe's anxiety eased off a little as the effect of warm grits and coffee began to sooth the savage beast that raged inside her. It was also David's friendly and warm southern gentlemanly personality that was most effective.

Suddenly, a young man impeccably dressed in a green polo shirt and tan slacks rushed up to their table.

"Morning, Grandpa," he said with a sheepish grin. "Sorry I'm late. Guess I stayed up a little late last night watching television."

"May I introduce my grandson, Miss Olabe?" David smiled back. "This is Richard Becker, the newest member of our firm."

Richard gasped a little as he reached out and shook Olabe's hand. This was the first big star he had ever met in his life and struggled to act casual. His face began to turn a brilliant shade of beet-red. He felt warm and uncomfortable.

"Good morning, Miss Olabe. I've been, that is, I still am, I mean, I'm a big fan of yours."

"Well, Richard," David said as he buttered a piece of toast. "Close your mouth and sit down and have some breakfast with us."

Richard immediately sat by his grandfather, like a well trained puppy.

"Maybe I'll just have a cup of tea and a fruit cup."

"Good gracious," David said in a mock-concerned voice. "That surely ain't enough substance to even see you through half the morning." David looked up and winked at the waitress who was standing ready to write. "Bring this growing boy a nice big bowl of grits, with lots of butter, and some good crisp bacon."

"Grandpa," Richard said in a startled voice. "Just think of all that bad cholesterol."

"Well, yes, Richard. Suppose we should think about it a minute or two, but I don't want you passin' out from lack of nourishment."

The waitress smiled and poured Richard a steaming cup of coffee. She added the grits and bacon to her order book and walked towards the kitchen window.

"Should have tea," Richard grumbled quietly. "Better for you, you know."

David laughed and said, "Richard, my boy, most of it is in the genes. Might just as well enjoy life a little, don't you think?"

The waitress was back in a few minutes and sat a bowl of grits and a plate of bacon in front of Richard. There must have been a full quarter pound of mostly melted butter on top of the grits. Without even looking up, Richard dove in.

"Good gracious, Richard. I don't believe you even took one breath while downing your breakfast."

Everyone laughed, but again, Richards face and neck turned a warm shade of red.

David paid the bill and they walked out into the warm, Alabama sunshine. Richard sat in the back and David climbed into the front passenger's seat.

David and Olabe chatted all the way back to Clopton while Richard remained quiet and watched the beautiful scenery go by. Occasionally, they would pass an old, dilapidated shack that looked like it would fall down any time, but there were four or five little kids running around the yard and probably their mother was out in the back yard hanging up wash on a homemade clothesline tied between two pecan trees.

Olabe turned into her mother's lane, drove up to the house, and stopped.

David stepped out of the truck and walked towards the porch.

"Well, well. You must be Miss Jewel," David said as he came up onto the porch and extended his hand to shake Jewel's. "Sure is a hot one, today."

By that time Olabe and Richard were up on the porch, too.

"And, Miss Jewel, this is my grandson, Richard. I'm so proud of him, and all. I know he don't look it, but he's not only graduated from the University of Alabama, but he's even gone back and got his law degree, too. And, of course, the best part is he's our newest employee down at our law firm."

Jewel stepped forward to welcome Richard who was noticeably embarrassed by his grandfather's glowing remarks.

"Miss Jewel," David continued on without any regard to Richard's fragile constitution. "You know, the best part is, he's just as common and nice a boy as you could ever meet. Besides all that, his interest in the law centers right 'round agriculture. Why, he couldn't make me any prouder, if he was the President of all these here United States. Well, might have to make an exception, if that were to ever happen."

"Oh, Grandpa, you're embarrassing me to no end."

They all laughed and sat down,

"Wouldn't you like a nice cool drink of water from the pump?" Jewel asked David.

"I surly would, Miss Jewel, that would be very nice," he responded and fanned himself with his hat.

Jewel jumped up and ran into the house. Within a few minutes, she returned carrying a tray with four glasses of water. She first handed one to David, another to Richard and Olabe. She then took hers and sat down.

"Ah. Now that just hits the right spot, Miss Jewel. There just ain't nothin' as refreshin' as a cool drink of well water on a hot day, such as this one."

Olabe could see that David's wonderful sense of "down home" personality had set Jewel's mind at ease immediately. But, in one sense, it all took time. Olabe wanted to get right to the crux of the matter, but not David. He wanted to talk and visit. He told them about growing up on a farm outside Birmingham and then joining the Navy. When he got out of the service he told about going to graduate school to get his law degree and his father thought it was a complete waste of time and worried that he would never be able to support a family. To make matters worse, he found a wonderful woman, got married, and they had their only child while he was still in school and living on a part-time job. He told about his daughter, Tracy, and what a joy she had been to their lives.

"She sure should have been a lawyer," David said with a big grin. "When she was eleven or twelve, she would argue with me over any little thing."

"Mom still does," Richard joined in quietly and everyone laughed.

They talked and joked for a while and David settled into what Olabe would have expected her grandfather might have been. The trouble was, both of her grandfathers were long buried before Olabe was born.

"Guess it's probably time we look into this sticky business before us," David said. "Richard, would you all just run out there to the truck and fetch my satchel?"

Without saying a word, Richard jumped up and trotted to the truck. He returned immediately, like a dog learning to play fetch, with his grandfather's black, very well worn briefcase.

David opened the case and rummaged through some papers.

"Richard, why don't you all get started and tell Miss Jewel and Miss Olabe what you all discovered.

"Well," Richard said, "after studying the mill records and then looking over your tax returns and receipts, Miss Jewel, it appears that our perpetrator has absconded away with well over...."

"He done what?" Jewel interrupted. " And who done it?"

"Sorry, Miss Jewel," David smiled. "Let me translate for you. What Richard is trying to say, and all, is that our good ol' boy, Jimmy Wade Betterund, done took away, cheated, from you a lot of money. 'Pears that over the past five years that, to put it mildly, he got away with more than $100,000."

Jewel gasped and put her hand up to cover her mouth.

"How many years has he all been doin' the farmin' for you, Miss Jewel?" David asked as he shuffled through his chaotic arrangement of papers.

"Let me see," Jewel's face frowned. "Most onto fifteen years, I supposed."

"Good gracious. Let's hope his ol' cheating habits came on just over the past five years."

It all made Olabe's blood boil and she began to pace.

"What do we have to do to put a stop to him?" Jewel asked firmly and stood up.

"First, Miss Jewel, it's mighty important that we keep a low profile and silent while we get the trap ready for this little ol' rat. Next, we slyly bait our trap and slip the noose 'round his neck when he ain't lookin'." Finally, David smacked his hands together which made everyone jump. "We snap the trap shut."

"How do we do that?" Jewel asked. "I want that no-a-count behind bars."

"Richard?" David said as he turned to his grandson.

"First, we have to gather all the evidence we can find without causing any suspicion. Then, we file a complaint, in your behalf, Miss Jewel. And, being that this is a violation of a state statute, the state's attorney will have him arrested."

"Well, let's do it then," Jewel responded immediately. "What can they do to him?"

"Quite a bit, actually. This here widow's law has some pretty tall teeth in it. Now, Miss Jewel, how many folks you reckon he does the farmin' for?"

"More than twelve, I think. Olabe, where's that list I made the other night?"

Olabe ran into the house and found the paper her mother was referring to, brought it out, and handed it to David.

"You've got to know that we probably won't get much money out of him. Folks like this usually only rent and lease land and equipment. Never have much of anything of value. But, as I said, every time he cheated one of you all, that's a separate charge. Now, let's look over the past five years. If he cheated all twelve of you over the last five years, why, that's sixty charges. Can you imagine that? Here's the best part of that ol' law. If found guilty, there's a minimum of $1,000 fine and up to five years in jail for each conviction. Now the way I see it is, that amounts to a fine of $60,000 and 300 years in jail. Of course, he won't get all that. Both sides will plea bargain and whittle it down some, but, if I was a bettin' man, I'd rest on a fine of $50,000 and probably twenty years in the slammer. Another interesting thing, though. We did find out that ol' Jimmy Wade pretends to be livin' like common folk down on that ol' dilapidated farm house outside of Ewell. I don't think he spends much time there, though. Turns out that he's got a big ol' house right on the Gulf, down 'round Gulf Shores."

"Let's do it," Jewel shouted. "Where's the pen? Just show me where to sign."

Jewel signed the papers where Richard showed her. Suddenly, her eyes filled with tears.

"It just grinds me to think about it all," Jewel sniffed and reached for her hankie

Olabe came over and put her arm around her mother's shoulders.

"It'll be alright, Mama. The main thing is that we're going to put a stop to it all."

"Yes, I know. It's not that he cheated so much from me, 'cause I'm older and should have known better. And, the good Lord has always provided me with abundance from my garden and orchard, so I've really not ever been in desperate need. But, when I think," Jewel's voice cracked and she fought off tears of anger. "When I think about them Thompson kids, and how badly they are in need, let alone their daddy, why forgive me Lord, but if I had a gun, I think I would take great pleasure in shooting that ol' boy and then stamp right on his grave."

"We understand, Miss Jewel," David said as he stood up and put his consoling arms around her. "We do understand and we are going to get this varmint."

They continued to talk for a while when Olabe happened to look at her watch.

"Look at the time, Mama. We told Rachael that we'd bring David and Richard over for supper."

"You all will go and meet the Thompson family, won't you?" Jewel asked as she walked towards the screen door. "We'll be taking a roast and sweet potatoes and a few other things with us."

"We certainly wouldn't miss some good ol' southern cooking for the world, now would we, Richard?"

They all went into the house. Jewel rushed around the kitchen packing bowls that were smoking hot into cardboard boxes. She opened the oven door and took out a huge pan with a big roast on it.

"Hmmmm," David sniffed the air. "Why, Miss Jewel. I wondered what was makin' the air smell so good 'round here. It surely does look wonderful."

Richard ran back and forth to the truck and packed the boxes inside the crew cab. Finally, everything was ready and they all got into the truck for the short trip to the Thompson farm.

When Olabe drove up to the little farm house, kids and people boiled out of everywhere. Two big dogs came bounding from the barn with three boys running after them.

Again, David wasted no time at all. He got right out and walked up onto the porch. He introduced himself. He shook Rachael's hand and walked over to where Raaf was sitting.

"Well, Mr. Thompson, certainly is a hot one, ain't it,"

"'Tis, at that," Raaf said and was instantly captivated by David's winning personality. "Sit down a spell right over there, so's you can cool off a little bit."

As soon as Liza Jane saw Olabe, she ran to her waiting arms. She jumped up and Olabe carried her as she always did, riding on her hip.

Olabe and Jewel brought Richard up onto the porch and introduced him to everyone. Richard's face especially tinged with scarlet when he was introduced to Elizabeth Ann.

"You all from Birmingham?" Elizabeth Ann's dark brown eye's sparkled.

Olabe couldn't decide whether Elizabeth Ann was flirting with Richard or just being friendly.

Everyone talked for a while. David asked Raaf about the farm and the crops.

"Bad year, this year. Just like quite a few back," Raaf sighed. "Seems like we don't get the rain when we need it. Then, when we do, it comes down too heavy to do much good."

"Have someone work the land?" David queried without anyone noticing.

"Same fella that Miss Jewel has. Jimmy Wade Betterund is his name. Been farmin' for most folk 'round here for years."

Soon, the three younger boys got bored with all the talking and wandered off to the barn to do those things that seem to entertain little boys.

Jewel assigned tasks to everyone else. She had Richard and David Thompson bring the boxes from the truck with the food in them into the house.

"How long before we'll be ready to eat, Rachael," Jewel asked holding the screen door for the boys.

"'Spect it will be at least nigh on to two hours or so."

"Well, now won't that just work out fine," David smiled. "By the way, Miss Elizabeth Ann, wasn't it?"

Elizabeth Ann nodded and seemed surprised that he had remember her name after hearing it only once.

"What 'bout you and your sister, Ellen May there, and your brother David, take a good walk around the farm with my grandson, there. He's a city boy, you know, and I think a good walk might improve his appetite."

Elizabeth Ann smiled a smile that told Olabe she had been flirting with Richard. No doubt about it. But, she was way too young for Richard. She would graduate from high school this year, but not only had he graduated from college, but law school as well.

Ellen May smiled and jumped up along with her brother, David.

"We could take you fishin' for a while, down at the pond," David Thompson said. "We all got cane poles in the barn."

It was agreed. Elizabeth Ann, Ellen May, David, and Richard trooped off to the barn to equip themselves for a trip to the pond.

Olabe leaned against the porch railing still holding Liza Jane. She was amazed at how skillful David Becker was at handling people, and did it without offending them or them ever knowing it at all. He had worked his magic with the young people which left the adults alone to discuss the matters at hand.

"Now, Raaf," David began. "Seems like we've found a little problem in the honesty of the fella doing your farming, and all."

"You mean Jimmy Wade Betterund?" Rachael said and came over behind Raaf's chair. It was apparent that she didn't like him for some reason.

"Yep. He's the one. Let me show you some facts and figures," David said as he shuffled through his briefcase.

He told them about Olabe's initial suspicion and how she happened to contact him. He told them about Richard's analysis of Jewel's records and the records of the mill. He told them about how much Jimmy Wade had cheated Jewel over the last five years.

"Now, Raaf. I also had Richard do some work on your records from the mill. Look at this sheet, here, and you'll see what your income should have been for the last five years. If you got your tax records handy, we can check on it for sure."

Rachael gasped.

"I always knew there was something wrong, Raaf. Remember? I've always said it." Rachael's eyes filled with tears. "We've gone with so little and had to struggle so much."

"Get those tax records, will you please, honey?" Raaf turned and asked Rachael. "I believe they're in the bedroom, there, under the bed."

David continued on. Olabe shifted Liza Jane to her other hip. Her blood was close to boiling. Rachael came back and handed the tax returns to David. He shuffled through them and wrote down some numbers.

"Without knowing the exact details, Raaf, appears that over the last five years, you were cheated out of about the same amount as Miss Jewel, there. Probably, more than $100,000."

"Blast him," Rachael shouted with vengeance in her voice. "I want that no-count, rascal killed."

Rachael's rath took everyone by surprise, but then David defused the situation. He broke into laughter. "Excuse me, Miss Rachael. Don't think we can quite do that, but sure think we can make this ol' boy pay the piper."

David told them his plan.

"Now, we'll need complete silence, as surprise is the key."

"You can count on us, Mr. Becker," Rachael said. "You just give me that paper to sign and a pen, and I'll do it."

"Just a little question, Rachael. Just to clarify it all. Do you and Raaf own this land in joint?"

"This land was part of my daddy's big farm, so my name is on the deed, along with Raaf's. Show me where to sign."

David pointed to the various lines for her signature. He smiled and put the papers back into his old battered briefcase just in time as the young people came running back up onto the porch.

"Should have seen him, Miss Olabe," Ellen May shouted. "He ain't never caught no fish before, or so he says. Anyway, what happens? He up and catches the biggest one. That's all. Show 'em, Richard."

Timidly, Richard held up a largemouth bass that surely weighed over five pounds. Big smiles formed across everyone's faces. Raaf and David congratulated Richard on his fine fishing skills and great catch.

"David and Richard?" Jewel instructed. "You all clean that ol' fish right away and we'll just fry him up and have him right along with the rest of our supper."

Raaf and David were the only ones left on the porch. They talked about crops and farming. David asked a few questions about Raaf's accident to which he openly talked about.

"So, Raaf, what do you all do about the pain?"

"Oh, just live through it mostly. On occasion, my David manages to bring me a small bottle of whiskey when he gets a little extra cash. Rachael hates that, so I have to keep it hidden and quiet, though."

"Well, nobody seems to be around right now," David smiled and opened his briefcase. "Care for a little nip before supper?"

"You all got a little whiskey in that case of yours?"

"Dump that water out of your glass there, Raaf," David smiled as he brought out a bottle with a black label. He poured a good helping in Raaf's glass and then his.

"That don't look like no whiskey I've ever seen." Raaf reached for the glass and sniffed. "Why, if I was a bettin' man, I'd have t' say, this here looks just like water. But, I'll bet it's moonshine."

David roared with laughter.

"Most any hills man can smell good shine a mile away." David held up his glass and they clinked their glasses together and each took a sip.

"Sweet Jesus," Raaf managed to get out. "Love that fire."

"And, aged just right. Probably less than a day or so."

"Where'd you all come by this fine shine, David?"

"Oh, I done some work defending the son of a man that lives a few miles outside of Birmingham one time. Guess he felt a little beholdin' to me, so every now and then, he up and sends me a quart or two."

The two men sat and enjoyed their "hills water" or "white lightning" to city folks.

"Come on in, you two. Supper's on the table," Rachael said as she came out onto the porch and yelled for the boys by the barn.

Raaf finished what little was left in his glass and then went through the strain and ritual of getting up. David had long since drained his and he sat his empty glass on the table. He helped Raaf get up and handed him his crutches.

"I'm a gonna leave this here bottle with you, Raaf. Maybe after supper we can pour it into something less conspicuous than this old whiskey bottle I've got it in."

Raaf smiled and said his son, David, could be trusted to handle the task. David held the screen door open while Raaf struggled to get inside the house. They were greeted with an almost overwhelming mixture of wonderful smells.

Raaf sat at one end of the long table and Rachael at the other. On Raaf's right was Elizabeth Ann, Richard, Ellen May, Obadiah, and William. On Raaf's left was David Becker, Jewel, David Thompson, Bart, and Olabe with Liza Jane on her lap. It was a close fit, but the table was large and everyone had just enough room.

Raaf held out his hands and quickly, everyone joined hands for the prayer.

"Lord," Raaf's voice sounded weak and tired. "Lord, I know you're terrible busy these days, but please Lord, I hope you can spare a little while to be with us humble servants here at supper today. Please bless all this wonderful food You provided for us, and all. Especially, Miss Jewel's sweet 'taters swimmin' in butter and pecans. And, to my loving wife, Rachael, for her wonderful biscuits and corn bread. We ask your blessing today dear Lord, and for giving us your loving son, Jesus. Amen."

There was a murmur of "Amen" said and then, chaos. People all talked at once, put food on their plates, and passed dishes. But, as plates filled, the noise settled down to silverware working on plates.

"Good gracious!" David Becker suddenly gasped with his mouth full. "These biscuits are truly manna from Heaven. I can truly say that I haven't tasted biscuits like this since I was a little boy growing up on the farm. Hmmmm, ummm, ummm. Now, who in the world made these wonderful things?"

Everyone laughed and Rachael's face turned red and she sheepishly looked down at her plate.

"Well. Miss Rachael, I must say your biscuits are fittin' for any king, includin' our Lord, God, and King above."

Ellen May reached out and picked up the big platter of biscuits and handed them towards David Becker with a big smile.

"Well, Miss Ellen May," David smiled and part of his charm was that he never forgot a person's name. "I believe I'm goin' to take two more. That way I won't have to bother you for at least another minute or two."

The bass had been rolled in cornmeal and fried in pork fat until it was crispy around the edges and the rest a golden brown. It was decided that it was to be divided up between Richard Becker, who actually caught the fish, David Thompson, who supplied the pole, Elizabeth Ann, who yelled out the encouragement, and of course, Ellen May, who dug the worms.

All of the food on the table was absolutely outstanding and wonderful. It was just good, down home, country cooking at it's very best. There was a huge roast beef, sweet potatoes, collard greens, black-eyed peas, biscuits, corn bread, and white gravy. For dessert, Jewel had made peach cobbler and a pecan and two apple pies. Today's fare was nothing less than first rate.

Conversation ebbed and flowed. As the noise level went down, suddenly, everyone's attention turned and watched Richard. For a little while he didn't seem to notice anything except shoveling food into his mouth. He was famished and had never tasted food so good as this, especially the bass he had caught. He was in his own little world.

"He looks like a big, ol' gopher," Obadiah suddenly spoke up so seriously, it would have made the Pope frown. "Mama? Do you think he might explode?"

Everyone exploded all right, but it was with laughter. Richard looked up as he began to show a nice tinge of scarlet all around his ears and neck.

"I don't think it's nice to tease a guest like that," Elizabeth Ann said as she came to Richard's rescue.

"Ah, it's all right," Richard mumbled as he wiped his mouth on his napkin. "I've never tasted food so wonderful as this. Besides, guess I was starved, too."

Conversation went back to normal. More food was consumed and more compliments were given out.

"It's surely been a long while since I've put away that much," David Becker said as he sat back in his chair. "No restaurant could ever come close to this feast, even the finest up there in Birmingham."

Elizabeth Ann and Ellen May jumped up and started to clear the table. David Thompson asked Richard if he wanted to come out to the barn and help feed and water the two cows and the mules, and of course, he did. The three younger boys had their chores, too. They had to gather eggs and feed the chickens. David Becker helped Raaf stand up and handed him his crutches. They went out and sat on the porch. Jewel supervised the two girls who immediately dove in to do the dishwashing. Rachael and Olabe sat at the table and enjoyed a second cup of coffee and chatted for a few minutes, before Rachael joined in with the cleanup crew. Olabe's job was to rock Liza Jane for a little while, and then get her ready for bed.

"You all want another little pain reliever, Raaf?" David said as he opened his case and took out the bottle.

"I surly do, David. I believe this really has helped."

"I always thought it helped a multitude of things."

Finally, it was time to go and everyone gathered by Olabe's truck. Richard and Jewel had already climbed into the back seat of the crew cab.

"Now, folks, remember, silence is golden," David said as he got into the passenger's seat, closed the door, and rolled down the window. "I'll contact Miss Olabe when everything is ready. All you have to do is wait."

Olabe turned out onto the road and headed for Ozark.

"Don't fret, now, Miss Olabe. Just wait for my call. If you don't answer right away, I'll leave a voice mail for you and you can call me back. I'll tell you when everything is ready and the authorities go after our good ol' boy. By the way, I'm going to apply for a restraining order for both you and Miss Jewel. Gonna get one for Raaf's family, too. That way, we've got some legal leverage, just in case he comes a callin' and gets a little pesky. If he does, don't be afraid to call 911, if you have to."

After dropping David and Richard off at the motel where they were staying in Ozark, they stopped at a fast food place to get coffee to drink for the short ride back home.

"I'm worried, Olabe."

"Why, Mama?"

"Now that Mr. Becker brought it up, I'm worried that ol' Jimmy Wade might come and pester us."

"Don't worry, Mama. In the first place, David told us that the last place he'll probably show up is at our house."

"But, what about that poor Thompson family? They've filed a complaint, too, you know."

"I know, Mama. That does worry me a little, too."

"'Specially, with Raaf being a cripple, and all."

Over the course of the next two days, Olabe was on needles and pins waiting. She was not a good waiter at all and, just wished things would move along.

It was Wednesday morning and Olabe had been up for about an hour. She and Jewel were sitting on the porch drinking a cup of coffee when they both were startled by Olabe's cell phone ringing in the truck.

"Good mornin', David's voice drawled. "I certainly hope I didn't wake you up with such an early call."

Olabe assured him that it was fine and that she and Jewel were sitting on the porch drinking their morning coffee."

"Well, that sure sounds good," David continued on with his ritual of friendliness that had the tendency of driving Olabe a little crazy. Sometimes, she wished he would just skip the "down-home" formalities and get right to the point. "Today is the day, Miss Olabe. Richard filed the papers late yesterday afternoon. I talked with the State's Attorney for a while yesterday. Remember, I told you about him? He and I went to school together. Anyway, he's going to send two Alabama State Troopers out this morning and pick up that ol' rascal. Course, he'll be out on bail this afternoon, but just wanted you all to know. Just in case he comes a callin', and all."

David again, warned Olabe and reminded her about the restraining order.

"Now, Miss Olabe. Don't be afraid of callin' 911, case you need some help."

Olabe told David that she and her mother would probably be fine, but she was worried about the Thompson family a little.

All throughout the day, Olabe kept one eye open. There weren't very many cars or trucks that went down the road that went by the farm any day, but today, there seemed to be quite a few. Olabe watched to make sure none turned and drove up the lane.

All day Thursday was a repeat of the day before and Olabe now began to feel a little relieved and that probably, Jimmy Wade was not coming.

Friday afternoon, Olabe and Jewel were working in the orchard when Olabe noticed a vehicle coming down the country road a long way off. It was making a huge dust plume, so it must have been traveling pretty fast, for an old dirt road, anyway.

Her heart pounded when she saw the vehicle slow down and turn into their lane. It was Jimmy Wade's pickup truck.

"Come on Mama," Olabe shouted and began to run. "Let's get up to the house."

Jewel hurried as best as she could behind her racing daughter. For some reason, when Olabe got to the house, she went inside, got her purse, brought it out and laid it on the table just as Jewel came up the two steps. They were both sitting in their rockers when the truck slammed to a stop being immediately overwhelmed by a huge dust cloud. A thin, lanky man leaped out, left the door open, and walked with a long, heavy gait up to the porch.

"Miss Jewel," Jimmy Wade Betterund wailed. "What in the world have you done? Why? You've knowed me since I was a little feller. Don't you remember? Haven't I taken care of you ever since your husband passed on? And, then you go and file charges on me for cheatin' you?"

Jewel surprised even Olabe with her firm and authoritative voice.

"Jimmy Wade, I should have known better than to trust you the way I did. Down deep, I guess I always thought there was something wrong, but just let it go. I was getting by alright. But, the thought of you taking advantage of the poor Thompson family. Well, that puts you beneath the lowest Alabama snake I've ever seen. You get off my property now. Do you hear? I don't ever want to see your sniveling face here ever again."

With that, Jewel went into the house and slammed the screen door behind her. Jimmy Wade stood silent for a few seconds with his mouth open. He had never seen Jewel outburst over anything before. She was always such a gentle and quiet lady.

"And, you, you cold-hearted bitch," Jimmy Wade snarled as he turned his attention to Olabe. His eyes had turned to the coldest steely gray she's ever seen. He was smoking with hatred. "You come down here, where things were quiet and peaceful, and turn it into a hell-hole of vomit. I'm warning you, missy, these here hills have a way of swallowing up trouble makers like you and nobody ever sees them again. Am I making myself clear? Now, you've got just one day to get your mama to drop them charges, or you won't see the light of day to the next weekend."

Jimmy Wade started towards Olabe. But, her confidence had returned with a vengeance. She had many years of experience in the dog-eat-dog music business and with people far more dangerous than Jimmy Wade. She also knew that most bullies, like him, were very cowardly, at heart.

"Are you threatening me?" she asked firmly and stood up to face her attacker. "It sure sounds like you are. You have two seconds to turn around and march back to your truck and get out of here."

"Or, you'll do what?" Jimmy Wade snarled as he came another step closer.

Olabe moved her purse which was covering a pearl handled silver pistol. She picked it up and pointed it in the general direction of her adversary.

"Whoa, there missy," Jimmy Wade shouted as he retreated a step. "You'd better put that thing down or you'll be in a heap of trouble. Lots of people get seriously injured by folks that don't know nothing about guns, and all."

"There's a problem, here, Jimmy Wade. The thing is, I'm trained, able, and willing to defend myself from an animal like you. And, to use your words, these hills have a way of swallowing up vermin and no one ever sees them again."

With that said, Olabe raised the gun, now pretty much in the general direction of Jimmy Wade, and, "BAM!"

Jimmy Wade was in shock. The bullet must have gone right through him. Suddenly, he felt that his groin area was getting wet. The thought that he was bleeding to death raced through his mind and his knees began to buckle and he started to grow weak.

"Did you kill him?" Jewel shouted as she ran out the door watching the cowardly Jimmy Wade now completely on the floor.

"No, Mama. I just shot that gopher over there that's been plaguing our garden for so long."

Slowly, Jimmy Wade realized that he wasn't shot after all and slowly got up.

"Oh, you're gonna pay for this, missy. Trying to kill me and all. You're gonna pay."

"Get out of here, you coward," Olabe shouted now pointing her gun for real. "I should make you clean up your pee off our porch. I'm warning you, Jimmy Wade. If you go over to the Thompson farm, for any reason, forget the restraining order that you've already violated. Because, if you even drive down that way, I'll come and hunt you down. Even if it takes the rest of my life to do it. Now, git!"

Jimmy Wade ran to the edge of the porch and tumbled down the steps. He picked himself up and virtually crawled to the open door of his truck.

"One last thing, Jimmy Wade," Olabe shouted. "When you drive back down the lane. Drive slow. I hate dust almost as much as I detest you, and I'll see your soul burn in hell!"

The truck motor started and Jimmy Wade drove away. Slowly.

*   *   *   *   *

The trial was held in Dothan and was a spectacular event. Newspapers all over southern Alabama carried the story which was front-page news for weeks.

The prosecution presented a long list of witnesses. Evidence was uncovered that Jimmy Wade had done the farm work for more that seventeen families and had cheated all of them for at least the past five years.

The jury was made up of five men; two white and three black, and seven women; four white and three black. When they were given the case, they deliberated for eighteen minutes and then took a vote. The vote tally was unanimous that Jimmy Wade Betterund was guilty.

During the sentence hearing Judge Mary Hastings Crills gave a long lecture and told Jimmy Wade that nothing would give her more pleasure than to put him away for life, except the law had a maximum sentence of twenty years. She pronounced that Jimmy Wade would receive the maximum and that he would not be eligible for parole until he had served at least ninety percent of his term.

The State confiscated all of Jimmy Wade's possessions and his wife filed for an immediate divorce.

CHAPTER 8
Opening a New Door

The whole area soon settled back into its old routine. Except now, there was a new promise. A farmer's cooperative was formed and Raaf was designated to be in charge of overseeing its regular operations. The overall supervision of the co-op, hiring and firing, scheduling, planting and harvesting teams and equipment, selling crops, paying the bills, and investing in a trust fund would be done by David Becker's grandson, Richard. Olabe provided enough seed money to get the co-op started and operational for the first year.

Jewel was elated to see such a deep, warm friendship develop between Olabe and Rachael. Olabe went over to Rachael's often and even took her shopping with her. They made many trips to Ozark and even down to Dothan a few times. Liza Jane became glued to Olabe whenever she came to see Rachael. She wanted to be held constantly, and of course, Olabe loved holding her. Jewel could see the "mothering instinct" in Olabe and it warmed her heart.

One early evening in the late summer, Olabe and Jewel were at the Thompson farm for supper and were inside the old farm house sitting at the long table. Rachael had just made tea for them and Olabe was holding Liza Jane, as usual. Elizabeth Ann and Ellen May were busy getting the dishes ready to wash while Bart, William, and Obadiah carried the plates from the table to the sink.

"Who plays the guitar?" Olabe asked as she noticed the instrument standing by the wall near the door to the boys' bedroom.

"Plays the guitar, my foot!" Elizabeth Ann snorted as she pushed a plate into the soapy water.

"Hurts our ears," Bart agreed.

"More like it makes us all sick to our stomachs," Obadiah was quick to elaborate.

"The good news is, there's hardly ever time enough for it to happen," Ellen May added as she wiped the dish just handed to her by Elizabeth Ann.

It was clear who the perpetrator was. It was the only person that hadn't rendered an opinion about the guitar playing. That was David. Besides, his neck and face were bright red and he smiled sheepishly.

"Aw, ain't so awful as all that," Raaf said as he came to the aid of his oldest son.

"'Tis, so, Daddy," Obadiah quickly attacked again.

"So, you play the guitar, David?" Olabe asked as she shifted Liza Jane to the other hip.

"Can't play nothin' much," David said softly and continued to look down as he studied the index finger on his left hand.

"Let me hear you try," Olabe smiled.

"Oh, Lord," Elizabeth Ann and Ellen May sighed together as they threw their hands up to their ears.

"Come on, David. Show me what you know," Olabe pressed onward.

"Well," David drawled as he stood up, walked over, and picked up the old instrument. He brought it over to the table by Olabe who was still holding Liza Jane playing "patty cake" with her. David strummed the strings a few times.

"See how awful 'tis, Miss Olabe?" William moaned.

"Ain't you sorry you asked him to play it and all," Bart joined in.

"Well, David, maybe I can help you a little," Olabe said as she picked up Liza Jane and sat her on the bench right next to her. "First thing, though, we've got to tune it. Now watch me."

Olabe plunked each string while she turned the respective little wheel located on the end of the arm of the old guitar.

"Hear that, David? See how each string sounds and how it sounds with the others?"

David nodded and was astounded. He had always wondered what those little wheels were for and now saw what they did. But, he still didn't know why you turned them.

"Now," Olabe continued, "here's the proper way to hold it. You try it," she said as she handed the guitar to David.

"Like this?"

"Very good, David. Now, put this finger right here," she said as she guided David's clumsy fingers. "Strum it now."

Everyone was shocked. The old instrument suddenly sounded wonderful. David's worried face grew into a wonderful smile that lit up the whole room.

"That's called a C chord," Olabe continued her lesson. "I'll tell you about all the chords later on. But, here's the important thing to remember. Each cord has a major, minor, dominate 7th, and augmented 5th sound. And, it's all done by just where you place your fingers. Here, let me show you."

Olabe moved David's fingers and had him strum the guitar as he listened to the differences. It only took David about five times going through the positions of the C chord before he could play all of them from memory. Next, Olabe showed him the F chord and, like the C chord, David mastered it rapidly.

"Too bad you weren't here all along," moaned William. "Just think of the wear on our ears you could have saved us from."

Everyone laughed. David kept strumming and learning. Olabe was pretty amazed and gratified at how quickly her student was progressing.

"Where did you get your guitar, David?" Olabe asked as she wrote some characters on an old scrap of paper Rachael had found for her.

"Oh, I was helpin' ol' man Fletcher clean out his attic one day. He lives a couple miles down the road, you know. Well, anyway, when he came to this ol' guitar, he done tol' me to throw it in the trash along with all the rest of the junk he didn't want no more. I asked him, if he don' want it, maybe he won't care if'n I took it." Well sir, he up and said it was alright with him. So, I drugged it home with me."

"It was a lucky find, David. This is a real good instrument," Olabe smiled. "Strumming is okay while you're learning how to play, but let's do something fun for a change. Elizabeth Ann? Ellen May? Can you two come over here?"

The two oldest daughters had just finished the dishes and were coming over to the table anyway. They stood behind Olabe and were curious.

"Remember the old Sunday School song; 'Jesus loves me, this I know?'"

Both girls nodded their heads that they knew the song.

"Fine. Now, David, while they sing the song, I'm going to point at each chord that I just wrote on this paper that you'll need to accompany them. Okay, girls. Go ahead and start."

Timidly, at first, both girls started singing the little church song. David struggled to make his fingers find the right position that coincided with the chord Olabe was pointing at on the paper. But, on the third time through, David no longer had to watch were Olabe was pointing and could play the chords from memory.

"Well, now. Don't that sound pretty," Raaf said as he hobbled over to stand behind his son. "I think we should all sing along. Come on over here Rachael and Miss Jewel."

They all sang. Jewel watched Olabe to see if her lips were moving and hoped desperately that they were. But, they were as still and silent as stone.

When the song was over, everyone cheered and wanted to sing it again. Olabe smiled and pulled Liza Jane back onto her lap. She put her arms around her and hugged her tight as Liza Jane snuggled in.

"David," Olabe said as she handed Liza Jane to Rachael as she and Jewel prepared to leave for the evening. "I think your progress tonight was truly remarkable. You've got some real talent."

He blushed and looked down. He was very grateful to Olabe, but all he could say was a very quiet, "thank you."

The next day, Jewel and Olabe were working in the garden. Jewel smiled to herself as she heard Olabe softly humming "Jesus loves me," to herself. Maybe, just maybe, Olabe was healing. She knew that God worked in mysterious ways, but she was now the witness of just how mysterious and circuitous it could be.

"Mama?" Olabe suddenly said on this hot, cloudy afternoon. She put her basket down that was only half full of the okra she was picking. "I'd like to give David guitar lessons. What do you think? Do you think Raaf would let him?"

"It's not the lettin' part, Olabe. Raaf is a proud man. Even though he's crippled, and all, he's still proud. I don't think there's any way that he would let you give David those lessons, unless they could pay you for it. And, there ain't no way those poor folks could afford that."

Olabe became quiet and went back to picking okra.

"Mama," Olabe smiled as she stood back up. "Come on. We're going over to talk to Raaf Thompson."

Jewel didn't know what had gotten into Olabe, but she knew that once she had made up her mind about something, nothing would change it.

"Hello, Raaf," Olabe said as she walked up onto the old porch and came over to where the crippled man slumped in his chair.

"Hello, Miss Olabe. And, hello, Miss Jewel. What all brung you folks out on a hot ol' afternoon, like this one?'

"We need your help, Raaf," Olabe announced firmly. "And, we need it today."

"Gracious, Miss Olabe. Course we'll all help. What you so all fired up, 'bout?"

"Well, Raaf. Here it is. Mama and I have been working our fingers down to the bone in her garden and orchard."

"Yes, I've always wondered how you two ladies could manage it," Raaf said thoughtfully as he stroked his beard.

"What we need is some help," Olabe went on with the same firmness in her voice. "We need some strong, male help. Someone with a strong back to help us for a while. We need a good picker to bring in our produce and fruit while Mama and I do the washing and canning."

"I sure do understand, and all. But, who do you all have in mind?"

"David."

"David? How long you figure you would need him? He does get some odd jobs, now and then, you know."

"We know, Raaf. He's free to take them whenever he can get them. But, right now we need him for at least a half day, every day for a while."

"Well, Miss Olabe. I think the only thing to do is to ask him. William?" Raaf shouted out to the young boy that was trying to catch a butterfly as it fluttered in erratic patterns around his mother's flower bed.

"Yah, Daddy?" William asked as he ran up to the porch railing.

"Would you all run down to the barn and fetch David? Tell him it's important, so's he'll come on the run."

William was off in a cloud of dust as he ran as fast as he could to the barn. In a few minutes, he and David trotted back up to the porch.

"Hello, Miss Jewel and Miss Olabe," David said politely as he came up onto the porch and stood by his father.

Olabe told David what she and her mother needed and, he quickly agreed.

"Oh, and one last thing, David. And, that's what to pay you."

"Shucks, Miss Olabe. You all don't need to pay me nothin'. Not the way you've helped us, and all."

"Wouldn't be right. Not right at all, David. Can't have you working for us for free. No, that surely wouldn't do." Olabe was a professional performer and now was the time she needed to act. She walked around quietly as though she was contemplating the world. "I've got it, David. How about if we pay you five dollars per half-day and an hour guitar lesson? I'm sorry it can't be more, but that's all Mama and I can afford, right now."

David looked like he was ready to explode. Five dollars for a half-days work, no matter what or how heavy the labor was, would be the most money he had ever earned. And, the best part was a free guitar lesson every day.

"Well, David?" Olabe pressed. "What do you think?"

"Is it alright, Daddy? I can still do my chores for you, and all."

Raaf broke into his biggest smile. He half knew what Olabe was doing, but on the other hand, knew the two women needed help. The guitar lesson, well, it was something David wanted, and only God knew how much he wanted something special for his son. David was a person that always did whatever he was asked to do and never complained. Maybe it was time he had a little something extra in his life.

"I think it's a great opportunity, son," Raaf said and was immediately inundated with the biggest hug he had received from David in a long time.

So, it was agreed. David would work for his father in the mornings. Then, in the afternoon, he would come over and work for Olabe and Jewel picking vegetables and fruit. This would be followed by a guitar lesson. It started that afternoon and continued all through the rest of the summer.

By fall, David had become a pretty accomplished guitar picker. Olabe had taught him well. Not only had she taught him by memorization, but she had also taught him how to read music. She knew almost right away that it wasn't her teaching so much, but it was his natural talent that was begging to get out that made David learn so quickly. He was a natural born guitarist, if there ever was one.

*   *   *   *

Liza Jane's silence still plagued Olabe. She had tried everything to get her to even make a sound, but all to no avail. One afternoon, she talked to Rachael about it.

"Has she ever talked?" Olabe asked as she held Liza Jane, as she always did whenever she came to their house.

"When she was small, and all, she made some sounds," Rachael said thoughtfully.

"Did she cry when she was a baby? I mean, did she actually make noise?"

"Yes. And, loudly."

"So, when did she become silent?"

"It was when she was not quite two. It was about the time the other kids had learned to talk. I was hoping and listening for Liza Jane to form her first words, but she never did."

"You mean, that when most kids start to talk, that was when she became silent?"

"Yes," Rachael said as tears welled up in her eyes.

"Did you ever take her to the doctor to see what was wrong?"

"Oh, we never had no money for doctorin', an' all. We had Doc Brown look at her once, when he was here to look at a sick cow."

When Olabe told her mother what Rachael had told her, Jewel scoffed.

"That ol' horse doctor. Doc Brown is a vet. Or, at least, that's what he called himself. No one ever really knew if he had much formal training or not."

"I've got an idea, Mama," Olabe said as she got up from the table and walked out to the truck. She picked up her cell phone and called David Becker.

"Hello?" a kind and slow, male drawl said into the phone.

"Hello, David. This is Olabe Mae."

"Why, Miss Olabe. How nice of you to call, and all."

"David, I'm afraid I need your help again."

"Help? You mean we didn't get everything done with that ol' snake we done got sent up to the penitentiary?"

"It's not that, David," Olabe said as she continued to explain her concern over Liza Jane. "And, David, all they've ever done, is to have her looked at by some old guy that was supposed to be a veterinarian. But, we're not even sure that he actually was even that."

David laughed softly. "Now, Miss Olabe. Don't be too concerned about that. Lots of them poor folks down 'round where you live have done that. Maybe, some of them ol' horse doctors are just as good as the regular ones, too."

"Maybe so, but do you know of any good pediatricians that might be able to help?"

"Well, Miss Olabe, give me a day or two and I'll have my people look into it for you. We'll see what we can find in Montgomery. Is that close enough?"

Olabe explained that she would find a way to get her to whatever specialist David could find. She thanked him for being so understanding and told him she would wait for his call.

Over the course of the next few days, Jewel became concerned that Olabe was slipping back into a depression because of her quiet spells. The fact of the matter was, Olabe was thinking of a way to get Liza Jane to Montgomery.

It was Friday evening and the weather had cooled a little. Jewel and Olabe were sitting out on the porch, each enjoying a cup of tea. The soft evening noises were suddenly interrupted by the electronic jingling of Olabe's cell phone lying on the dashboard. Olabe jumped up and made a mad dash for her truck

"Hello?" she said breathlessly.

"Good evening, Miss Olabe," David's soft, southern voice said. "I hope I'm not disturbin' your evening."

"Not at all, David. How are you?"

"By the sounds of things, the real question is, how are you? Sounds like you're takin' your last breath."

"Oh. Nothing serious. I just ran out to the truck. That's where I keep the phone to keep the battery charged."

David laughed and then got right down to the business at hand.

"Anyway, Miss Olabe. After talking to you a few days ago, I called my grandson, Richard, and told him about your problem. He told me that he had watched Liza Jane pretty closely back when he spent lots of time with you folks. It was then that I realized that one of my old friends that I had gone to the University of Alabama with was a pediatrician in Montgomery. Anyway, I got right busy looking him up. Well, after lots of talk about the ol' days, he told me he had retired from practice last year and was spending time playing golf and traveling around with his wife. I told him about a friend of mine that was havin' some real concern about the neighbor's little girl, and all. Course, all ol' Jack would say was 'hmmm'. He asked me a bunch of questions that I didn't know the answers to, so I had Richard talk to him for awhile. To make this story even longer, Miss Olabe, the bottom line was, he told me to tell you to give him a call."

David gave Olabe Jack Lambert's phone number which she immediately scrawled onto the dust on the dashboard with her finger.

Olabe thanked David from the bottom of her heart.

"Oh, that's alright, Miss Olabe. Just what else does an ol' country lawyer like me have to do with my time, anyway?"

The next day being Saturday made Olabe hesitate calling Jack, but her impatience got the best of her. It was not quite eight o'clock when she went out to the truck with a paper and pen and transferred Jack's phone number, written in dust, to something more permanent. Then, she couldn't wait any longer and keyed the number into her cell phone.

"Good morning," a soft, sweet sounding man's voice said into the phone.

Olabe spent little time on introductions and formalities and got right to the problem. She explained everything she knew about Liza Jane.

"Hmmm," came the response.

Olabe waited and didn't say anything. Just when she was about to say something, just to make sure they were still connected, she heard Jack speak.

"Well, Miss Olabe," he drawled over a considerable time. "I 'spect I've seen what you are describin' at least a hundred times. Maybe more. Course, with out examinin' the child, I sure could be way off base, you know."

"What is it, Dr. Lambert? Tell me. I've got to know."

"I suspect she's probably pretty deaf."

"What? You mean all that's wrong is she can't hear?"

"Seems so. But, remember, I could be way off."

"Why would she remain silent, just because of being deaf?"

"Kids are funny animals," he went on to explain. "'Cause she didn't hear much, it probably never crossed her mind that she could make noises. But, remember, only an examination can tell for sure."

Olabe was relieved and concerned at the same time.

"I can call one of my associates at the clinic that I worked at and they can arrange an appointment to look her over. They have an audiology department, too. Probably can tell what's wrong pretty quickly."

Olabe wrote down the number for the clinic and the names of the doctors Jack thought would be appropriate to examine Liza Jane. She thanked him numerous times.

"No thanks necessary, Miss Olabe. Glad this all came up. Renewed my friendship with old David, is what it all did. He and I are meeting for a friendly little round of golf this afternoon."

After she hung up, her mind was in a whirl. What should she do and how in the world was she going to get the approval of Rachael and Raaf? Finally, she went into the house and told her mother everything.

"So, Mama. What do you think?"

Jewel was relieved that it wasn't her daughter's depression that had come back after all. Rather, it was her concern over getting help for Liza Jane that was consuming her. Jewel tried her best to offer suggestions, but everything they talked about seemed to offer no good answers.

Finally, Olabe couldn't stand it any more and told her mother she was going over and talk directly to Rachael. Jewel smiled as she waved to her as the truck zoomed down the lane.

Olabe ran lots of thought patterns through her brain during the short drive to the Thompson farm.

When she drove into the driveway kids came out of everywhere to meet her. Raaf was siting on the porch waiting for his ride to work at the co-op. Rachael came out the door with Liza Jane right behind.

Everyone greeted Olabe and especially Liza Jane.

"Good morning, honey," she said right at her.

Liza Jane waved her little hand and came over with her hands up so Olabe could pick her up.

"You're getting too big to have Miss Olabe carry you, Liza Jane," Rachael said, but Liza Jane acted as if she was totally unaware of her mother's order.

Olabe picked her up and said right into her ear, "you're not too big, are you Liza Jane?"

Liza Jane didn't make a move at all. Olabe's brain was in turmoil. How was it that Liza Jane seemed to understand her when she was on the porch? Yet, she didn't seem to hear her when Olabe's lips were right next to her ear.

Olabe came up onto the porch and started talking to Raaf and Rachael. She told them the whole story and her talk with Dr. Jack Lambert. She told them that she would be happy to make the appointment at the clinic in Montgomery and take Rachael and Liza Jane up there. Rachael listened and wrung her hands as tears streamed down her cheeks. Raaf concentrated intently on Olabe's words.

"So, Miss Olabe," Raaf stammered and talked slowly. "You all think there's hope for Liza Jane to a goin' ta talkin'?"

"We won't know until the doctors look her over," Olabe said with just a hint of hope in her voice.

"Well, now we ain't takin' no charity, Miss Olabe. 'Specially, with me workin' at a real job, now. Course, I ain't saved up 'nuff money, yet, but, I will start with some from this comin' paycheck."

"Oh, Raaf," Olabe smiled. "Don't worry about that. I'll take care of it right now and you can pay me back as time goes along." Olabe hugged Liza Jane.

"That'll be fine. But, Miss Olabe, I want to make it formal and all. You know, sign papers."

At first, Olabe wanted to tell Raaf he certainly didn't need to sign anything. In fact, he didn't even need to pay her back. She could certainly afford it and wanted to get help for Liza Jane more than anything else in her life right now. But, she knew Raaf's feeling about charity and the importance of them being self-sufficient.

"That'll be fine, Raaf. Tell you what. I'll make the appointment right away. Then, Rachael and I will take her up to Montgomery to the doctors. When everything is done and I get the bills, we'll add them all up and write a paper so you can sign it. How's that?"

Raaf nodded it would be alright and thanked Olabe for her help. An old pickup truck rumbled up the driveway. It was a neighbor that worked at the co-op with Raaf and had come by to give him a ride.

Olabe ran out to her truck and picked up her cell phone. She called the clinic in Montgomery and made an appointment for Thursday at ten o'clock. She clicked the "call ended" button, put the phone back into its cradle, and came up on the porch all smiles.

She told Rachael the good news about the appointment and that she would be there early Thursday morning to pick them up.

Rachael smiled and thanked Olabe, but then, suddenly she frowned.

"What's the matter, Rachael? Is something wrong?"

"Oh, Olabe," she responded. "I ain't never been to no big city, and all. I know I've been down to Dothan with you a few times, but Montgomery is a big city."

"Well, there's nothing to worry about, Rachael. It's just like Dothan, only bigger."

"Miss Olabe," Rachael said as she looked down at her bare feet. "It ain't that so much. But, I ain't got but only one dress I made for church. Do you think that will be alright to wear?"

Suddenly, Olabe's eyes sparkled and a big smile crossed her face.

"Come on, Rachael. Get Elizabeth Ann and Ellen Mae, too."

Rachael looked confused, but called the two girls to come out of the house.

"Come on ladies," Olabe said ushering them all into her truck. "I know it's going to be a little crowded, but I think you can all squeeze into the back seat there. We're going dress shopping."

"But, Miss Olabe. We ain't got no money for dresses, and all."

"Rachael, this is a time for action. I'll just add it to your bill. I know Raaf will want you to look your best when we go up to Montgomery on Thursday."

Rachael and her two teenage daughters managed to get into the small back seat of the crew cab. Liza Jane sat on her mother's lap.

"Who all's goin' sit on the seat there in front with you, Miss Olabe?" Elizabeth Ann asked.

"Got to stop and pick up my mama," Olabe responded as she started the engine, turned around, and drove down the driveway.

The trip back home took just a few minutes and soon they were stopped by the side of the porch. Olabe went in and explained the situation to her mother.

"So, you see, Mama. You've got to come along to help get some things for Rachael. She'll listen to you, probably better then me."

"Well, I suppose I can go with you," Jewel said. "But, I've got to change my dress. I can't go to Ozark with this old garden rag I'm a wearin'."

It took Jewel just a few minute to change clothes. She came out and got into the front seat of the truck and they were off.

The trip to Ozark was only eighteen miles and took less than thirty minutes. Everyone chatted and had a good time. Olabe drove into the parking lot at Wal-Mart and found a place to park.

Elizabeth Ann and Ellen Mae stared. They had been to Ozark a few times, but never inside a huge store like this one. Liza Janes's eyes were as big as saucers as she rode on Olabe's hip.

"Now," Olabe announced. "Let's look for a dress for your mama."

Everyone scurried around looking at first one rack and then the next.

"Oh, Mama," Elizabeth Ann said as she held up a royal blue dress. "Don't you just love this color?"

Rachael nodded her approval, but held up a yellow print that had lots of little white flowers on it.

"There's a room right over there, Rachael. Go try it on," Olabe said and much to her amazement, Rachael looked shocked.

"You mean I can actually put it on without buying it first?"

"Sure. We have to make sure it fits and we want to make sure it's just the right color."

Ellen Mae held up another dress and said she thought it would look good on her mother. They handed three dresses to her to go try on.

"Ellen May," Olabe said. "Here, look at this one. Why don't you two girls each try on a dress for your mother? That way we can see three dresses on real people, at the same time."

Both girls looked delighted and quickly scurried away to the dressing rooms.

"Here, Mama," Olabe said as she handed her mother a dark green dress. "Would you try this on so Rachael can see what a darker color might look like?"

Jewel had been told to help all she could, so she thought this might help a little. She took the dress and walked toward the dressing rooms just as Rachael came out wearing the yellow dress.

"It's just a little tight 'round the bust line," Rachael said as she tugged a little at the material. "Sure nothin' I can't fix, though."

"Come on, Rachael," Olabe said. "Let's see if we can find something that fits you a little better."

Just then Elizabeth Ann came out of the dressing room in the royal blue dress. It fit her perfectly and made her dark brown hair shine against the blue color of the material.

"Well, Mama, how do you like this one?" Elizabeth Ann said as she twirled around which made Liza Jane clap her hands.

Soon, Ellen May and Jewel came out and showed Rachael how their respective dresses looked. Olabe was surprised and gratified that all four of the women had basically the same shape and took about the same size.

After lots of dresses were tried on, Rachael made her decision. She still wanted the yellow dress, even though she would have to make a few modifications. Olabe took the dress and placed it into their shopping cart. She also laid the royal blue dress that had looked so good on Elizabeth Ann along with a pink dress for Ellen May and the dark green dress for Jewel.

"Now, what about that green dress, Olabe," Jewel worried. "Rachael didn't pay much attention to it."

"Don't worry, Mama. It's not for her."

"What? Now, just a minute here," Jewel sputtered. "I've got a good dress hanging in the closet at home that you bought me and I surely don't need another one."

Everyone laughed.

"And, girls," Olabe smiled. "The other two are for both of you. Your graduation is coming up soon and you've got to look nice for that, don't you think?"

Elizabeth Ann and Ellen May were astonished. Neither had ever had a store-bought dress in their lives. Tears filled their eyes and they raced over and hugged Olabe.

"Now. Let's find a nice dress for Liza Jane. Then, it's time for finding some shoes."

Things were in pandemonium. The two younger girls must have tried on twenty pairs of shoes each before they found the right ones. Rachael settled on the second pair she tried. Liza Jane was much easier. She wanted a pink pair of running shoes and would not have anything else but them.

"Suppose you want me to try on some shoes, too," Jewel said still sputtering.

"Of course I do, Mama. You can't have a new dress without shoes, too."

It took better than two hours to find just the right things for all the women and little Liza Jane. It was one of the most fun times Olabe had been able to enjoy for a long time. Faint memories surged through her mind as she remembered how she had wanted to shop for her own children and herself, and even buy something for her husband. But, her fame had prevented all that. She had "people" that bought whatever she wanted. Here, she didn't stand out and nobody cared who she was.

After their excursion to Wal-Mart, Olabe decided to take everyone out for lunch. She stopped at a small, but nice restaurant called "Belle's" on the edge of Ozark on Highway 105. "Nether Elizabeth Ann nor Ellen May had ever been to a restaurant before and couldn't help themselves as they looked at everything.

"Oh. Elizabeth Ann," Ellen May exclaimed as she held a small bowl for her. "Hmmm. Try a taste of this."

They both agreed that the chocolate pudding was the absolute best tasting substance in the world. Liza Jane thought so, too, but she wasn't sharing her's with anyone and immediately spooned it all in.

It had been a wonderful day for all the women and everyone laughed and remembered things that had happened as Olabe drove the truck back to the Thompson farm.

The three young boys ran out of the barn when they saw the truck coming up the driveway, followed by David.

"Where you all been, Mama?" Bart shouted as he ran along side for a few seconds.

When Olabe stopped the truck, pandemonium broke loose as Elizabeth Ann and Ellen May exploded with where they had been.

"And, you should have seen the huge store that Miss Olabe took us all to," Ellen May expounded as everyone helped carry in the many bags and boxes. "We got things for you all, too."

Jewel watched and smiled as she felt the enthusiasm rub off on her and basked in the warm glow she felt at Olabe's sincere interest in it all. She sat out on the porch as the others went inside to distribute new jeans and shirts to the boys and show off what was in their parcels.

The girls put on their new dresses and shoes. They modeled them so that everyone could see them. The boys stripped right on the spot and put on their new clothes. David, being older and not as blatant as his younger brothers, went to their bedroom and changed into his new overalls and blue shirt.

"You should see Mama in her new dress, David," Elizabeth Ann said. "Try it on, Mama, so we can all see it."

Rachael needed little coaxing. She went into the tiny bedroom, took off her old, handmade dress, and put on her new one. She was just about ready to come to the main room when Raaf struggled to get the screen door open so he could get in with his crutches.

He came inside and suddenly stopped. Rachael came into the room.

"What the......?" Raaf stammered. He stood as best he could with his rounded shoulders supported by his old and very worn crutches. "Oh. Rachael, honey. I don't believe you've ever looked more beautiful."

Everyone rushed over to their father to show off their new wares. All Raaf could do was smile and struggle to stay standing. Finally, he managed to go back out onto the porch and dropped into his rocker.

"Well, Miss Jewel," he drawled slowly and laid his crutches on the floor next to his chair. "That daughter of yours, she's surely a wildcat, ain't she?"

Jewel nodded and smiled.

"Seems like she's always right there to jump in with both feet, at the drop of a hat."

Olabe came out to the porch and stood by Jewel while the others were busy changing back into their old clothes and hanging up the new ones.

"Miss Olabe," Raaf began, but lost his voice as his eyes filled with tears. "What in the world are we goin' to do with you? We all goin' have to start callin' you 'Wildcat' 'cause that for certain, be just what you are."

Suddenly it hit both Jewel and Olabe at the same time. That's what Olabe's father had called her back when she was a little girl because of her willingness to fight over anything.

"I remember being called that, a long time ago," Olabe finally said.

"Well, anyway, Miss Olabe. I don't know how I'm ever goin' to be able to repay you for what you've done for this family, and all."

"I love doing it, Raaf," being careful not to imply she was helping or giving charity. "I'll just add it to your bill."

"I'm 'fraid that ol' bill is a probably getting pretty tall these days," Raaf smiled as he moved his hips to get a little more comfortable. "Just so you know it, Miss Olabe. I dearly appreciate your kindness and thoughtfulness."

CHAPTER 9
Opening Up a New World

The next few days were a nightmare for Jewel because of Olabe's impatience. She paced back and forth on the porch in the evenings and sulked. But, what troubled her most was Olabe's silence. She was afraid that Olabe might be slipping back into depression again.

Actually, this was not the case at all. Olabe's brain was racing one hundred miles per hour as she planned and worried about what Liza Jane's diagnosis might be.

Finally, it was early Thursday morning and Olabe was at the Thompson's a little after seven. Rachael was waiting on the porch with Liza Jane.

The trip to Montgomery was long, but not difficult and took a little more than two hours. Liza Jane sat on the back seat in the crew cab and slept most of the way. Olabe found that the directions the clinic had given her when she made the appointment were easy to follow and took them right to the parking lot of the facility. It was now just twenty minutes to ten.

"May I help you, ma'am?" a pleasant woman asked from behind the white counter.

Olabe told her who they were and that their appointment was for ten. The woman smiled and handed Olabe a clipboard with a form on it. They went into the waiting room and sat down. Olabe asked Rachael questions and wrote down the answers.

"Mrs. Thompson?" a young nurse asked as she came walking over to where they were sitting.

They were led into the interior of the clinic and brought into an exam room. Olabe was carrying Liza Jane, as usual, and sat her on the large exam table.

"Good morning everyone," a man said wearing a white coat. "I'm Dr. Vance Parker."

Dr. Parker looked to be about fifty or so and was quite tall. He had intense blue, steely eyes, but was very friendly, especially to Liza Jane. He listened to her heart which caused her to wince at the cold stethoscope. He looked into her throat and felt the glands in her neck. He looked into her right ear using an otoscope.

"Hmmmm," he mumbled and then looked into the other ear.

Olabe's heart jumped with anxiety. Rachael was startled and grabbed Olabe's wrist.

"Well," Dr. Parker said as he leaned back and faced the two woman. "First of all, your child looks very healthy and normal. She has huge wax buildup in both ears, but I don't think that's quite all there is to it."

"Wax buildup?" Olabe asked. "That can be easily cleared can't it Dr. Parker?"

"Sure can. In fact, I'll get a nurse practitioner in here right away to take care of it. Then, we'll have you take Liza Jane down to our audiology people.

Dr. Parker had no more than stepped out of the exam room when the door opened and a rather large woman appeared. Her face was pumpkin shaped and she had laughing blue eyes. She wore a white smock that had "Nancy" embroidered on it.

"Well, hello, y'all," she smiled and went right over to Liza Jane.

Nancy was wonderful. She talked constantly and showed Liza Jane everything she intended to use.

Liza Jane frowned from time to time as the solution was squirted into her ears to soften the wax and then flush it out.

"Sure looks much better," Nancy announced as she patted Liza Jane's ears dry with a towel. "Now, let's get her down to audiology."

They followed Nancy out of the exam room, down the hallway, and waited with her at the elevator. When the door opened, they all stepped inside and Nancy had Liza Jane push the button marked "3" which made her smile. Nancy went up to the reception desk and put Liza Jane's chart down.

"We all got Miss Liza Jane here," she announced. "She's all wantin' to see Dr. Damon."

They were told to sit in the little waiting room, but before they even had a chance to get seated, a young woman came up to them and told them to follow her into another exam room. This room looked different from the regular medical exam rooms Olabe had seen before. This one had lots of equipment that almost reminded her of being in a recording studio. Dials and knobs, headphones and cables were everywhere.

"Well, hello there," a short, pudgy little man said as he rushed in with his white smock tails flapping. I'm Dr. Damon."

Dr. Damon wasted no time and set right to work. He looked into Liza Jane's ears. He put headphones on her as Liza Jane sat looking a little forlorn. Olabe felt little pangs of guilt and fought back the urge to rush over and scoop her up into her arms.

Suddenly, Liza Jane's eyes got as big as saucers. She looked around, and then up at the ceiling. She looked to the right and then to the left. Dr. Damon reached over and took the headphones off Liza Jane's head, but she reached up to get them back.

"Like that sound, eh?" he smiled and gave them back to her.

"Well, ladies. I think I know what's going on here."

Both Olabe and Rachael snapped to attention and asked "what" at the very same time.

"Well, first of all. What we have here is a little girl that's not completely deaf. She's pretty hard of hearing. But, we can help that."

"Why doesn't she make any sounds?" Olabe asked.

"It's probably never occurred to her," Dr. Damon smiled and got out a chart of the human auditory system. "She couldn't hear anything from the outside world, so she probably never thought there was any reason for her to even try. I've seen this happen in quite a number of kids."

"So, what can be done?" Olabe asked.

"First, we'll fit her with a hearing aide in each ear. That should make a pretty dramatic improvement. She may even naturally improve some over time. It does happen, but don't put much stock in it."

Two more technicians came in and they pushed a warm wax-like substance into each of Liza Jane's ears to make molds for the hearing aides. Liza Jane watched with big eyes, but was still fascinated with the headphones.

"Now, let's have Liza Jane back here next week about the same time and we'll see if we can open up the world of sound for her."

Olabe and Rachael thanked Dr. Damon and he just smiled and said he was glad to help, but not to expect miracles.

Olabe paid the bill with one of her credit cards and they went out to the truck. It was almost noon, so she drove to a fast-food place and went through the drive through, which truly amazed Rachael.

The trip home was better than the one coming. Olabe's stomach was not churning as before. There was now hope, at least. Liza Jane was totally exhausted and slept all the way back home.

Everyone listened as Rachael and Olabe told them about Liza Jane's examination and how each detail went. All seemed truly elated. Everyone except Liza Jane who sat quietly and played with two of her rag dolls. She seemed totally oblivious to the possibilities that could be waiting for her.

The next week dragged, but Olabe's mind wasn't so bothered this week, as last, and her gut didn't churn as badly, either.

Finally, it was Thursday and Olabe was at the Thompson house early in the morning for the long trip back up to Montgomery. Again, Liza Jane slept most of the way while Olabe and Rachael chatted. They talked about each of the children and how they were doing in school. They discussed Raaf's new job at the co-op, how much he seemed to like it, and was glad to be back to work. All the talk made the miles go by quickly and soon Olabe turned into the clinic's big parking lot.

After a few minutes of getting Liza Jane awake, they went into the huge glass building and straight to the audiology department. After a short wait, they were taken into one of the exam rooms.

"Good morning everyone," Dr. Damon said as he came into the room. "Hope everyone is well this fine day. And, how's Liza Jane?"

Liza Jane stared off into space, not looking at anyone.

"Why is it, Dr. Damon, that sometimes she seems to understand perfectly well what we say and then, other times, she acts like she's in her own little world," Olabe asked.

"I suspect she's learned to read lips. Let's test it out. Rachael, get her attention and ask her a simple question. Something like; are you hungry or are you cold?"

Rachael moved to intercept Liza Jane's line of vision and smiled at her little daughter. Liza Jane smiled back. Rachael asked her if she was hungry. Liza Jane shook her head up and down to indicate that she was.

Olabe, who was almost behind Liza Jane, asked her if she was cold. There wasn't even the slightest hint that she was even aware that Olabe had said anything.

"That settles it," Dr. Damon said as he came around the exam table with a little blue cardboard box. "It demonstrates that when she can see you, she understands by watching your lips move. But, when she can't see you, she is completely unaware that you are talking to her. Now, let's try and see how these fit."

Dr. Damon inserted a tiny hearing aide into each ear

"Let's see what happens now when I turn them on."

He moved the little switches to the "on" position and turned up the volume in each one of the hearing aides until he saw Liza Jane smile and started swaying back and forth.

"I think she's hearing the music from the ceiling speaker," Dr. Damon smiled. "Ask her the same questions and let's see how she reacts?"

"Liza Jane?" Rachael asked timidly. "Are you hungry?"

Liza Jane spun around so quickly, she almost fell right off the exam table. Her eyes were as big as saucers and she wore a big smile. Again, she shook her head up and down.

Both Rachael and Olabe rushed up and hugged her. Liza Jane squirmed back and pointed at Rachael.

"I think she wants to know who you are," Dr. Damon smiled widely.

"Mama," Rachael said slowly.

Liza Jane smiled and everyone talked excitedly together for a few seconds when suddenly, they were interrupted.

"Maaaa....ma," a tiny voice said.

The room exploded. Again, Rachael hugged Liza Jane. Olabe hugged Dr. Damon. Rachael hugged Olabe. Olabe hugged Liza Jane.

Liza Jane pointed at Olabe and said, "Maaa...ma."

Time stood still for a while as Olabe's mind digested what Liza Jane had just said. How she wished she was Liza Jane's mother, but she wasn't. A pang of guilt shot through her brain to even have thought such a thought.

"Oooo...la..beeee," Olabe smiled and pointed to herself fighting back welled up tears.

"Ooo...beee," Liza Jane said and again everyone was hugging.

"Just a word of warning," Dr. Damon said. "You'll have to be a little careful, at first, with the volume on these hearing aides. Remember, here's a child that has lived in almost total silence for most all of her life, and now, suddenly, her new world is a cacophony of sound. What I mean is, for a while, you may have to keep the levels down. Some kids even experience vertigo as a result of noise overload."

Liza Jane was pointing at everything now. As she heard the word, she immediately tried to pronounce it. Some were very clear and others, well, needed a little work. But, her curiosity was unquenchable.

Unlike before, when Liza Jane slept in the back seat, she was now pointing at everything. Her vocabulary was increasing at an exponential rate and by the time they drove into the Thompson's driveway, she was even connecting a few words together.

Kids poured out of the house and barn all talking and shouting at once. Each one couldn't wait to hear Liza Jane, and she certainly didn't disappoint any of them.

Olabe raced home, picked up Jewel, and brought her back so she could see this miracle first hand. Jewel was astounded when she heard Liza Jane try to pronounce her name.

"Ja...ja...lll," she smiled and Jewel rushed to hug her.

It was almost five o'clock and about time for Raaf to come home from work.

"Let's surprise Daddy," Rachael said as she scurried around getting things ready. An old truck drove up to the porch and Raaf struggled to get out. Rachael pointed out the window at him and said to Liza Jane, "Daddy."

Raaf slowly made his way up onto the porch and opened the screen door. Just when he moved to come in, Liza Jane ran up to him. She stopped with her big eyes shining and wore a huge smile.

"Daaa....dee," she said and held her arms up to be picked up.

Raaf stood stone still for a few seconds. He looked around the room at all the smiling faces. Tears streamed down Rachael's and Olabe's faces.

"Liza Jane. You talked," he whispered and his dark, ruddy face was wet with tears.

"Daa..dee," Liza Jane said again and held up her arms.

With superhuman strength and willpower, Raaf somehow managed to reach down, picked up his little daughter, and hugged her.

"Daaa..dee," Liza Jane said now, almost perfectly.

      *   *   *   *

Time passed and things got back to their old, regular routine. Liza Jane was now talking all the time. Even her pronunciation had improved so much that virtually no one could even tell she had any hearing problem.

One evening Olabe and Jewel had driven over to have supper with the Thompson family. Jewel had baked a huge ham and made corn pudding. Olabe helped make three peach pies. Rachael made her wonderful biscuits and Raaf had stopped on his way home from work at the Jarvis farm and got two pounds of butter. All-in-all, the meal was a feast and everyone ate their fill.

While Elizabeth Ann and Ellen May were clearing away the dishes, Bart, William, and Obadiah left the table and sat on the floor, near the big window, to inspect a new picture book that Olabe and Jewel brought for them.

"Play something for us," Rachael said to David who had just stood up to leave the table.

Soon, all the children where urging David to play. He held his guitar and picked the strings to tune the old instrument.

"What you all want to hear?" David asked as he strummed a few chords.

All shouted out their own special favorite at once. David smiled and started to play. It was like a short interlude of guitar chords. Then, he started to sing.

"Jesus loves me," he started out and everyone quieted down immediately.

Liza Jane's eyes were wide open. She was sitting on Olabe's lap and started to sway in time to the music.

"Jesus loves me, this I know," she sang so softly that only Olabe heard it at first. Olabe began to cry. "For the Bible tells me so." Her voice got stronger.

When the song was over, everyone rushed to Liza Jane. They hugged her and congratulated her on singing so well. She jumped down from Olabe's lap, turned around, and faced her. Her little finger pointed at the guitar, and then to Olabe.

"You play," she said. "You sing."

Olabe's mind closed in around her trying desperately to protect her. On the one hand, she had vowed to never pick up any instrument again and to never sing not even one syllable, ever. But, on the other hand, here was this innocent little miracle asking her to break those vows. After what seemed like an eternity of thinking to Olabe, but really only a few seconds, she reached out her hands to David. He brought the guitar over and handed it to her.

Olabe held the old instrument for a few seconds and then strummed a C chord. Instead of hearing some devil-noise, she heard the sweet sound that only a well-seasoned guitar could make. It seemed like an old, long lost friend. She played a few more chords.

Liza Jane was jumping up and down and pointing at Olabe.

"Sing song," she pleaded.

Olabe's mind rushed through the long since, closed book of music that she had played and memorized over the years. Suddenly, she found one.

"Puff, the magic dragon," she began to sing. "Lived by the sea."

Soon, everyone was singing along. Even ol' Raaf's deep, scratchy voice was heard. By the time Olabe had sung the chorus twice, Liza Jane had memorized it and sang along.

Olabe played it again. This time, she had Liza Jane sing the chorus by herself. Her tiny, very high soprano voice rang true and clear. The second time Olabe played the chorus, she sang harmony with Liza Jane which caused everyone to sit silently and listen.

Jewel stood by the wall and took it all in.

Truly there is a God, she thought. *I've been witness to not only one miracle of Liza Jane's hearing, but now, the second miracle of giving Olabe's voice back to her.*

They sang far into the evening. They sang hymns and gospel songs. Olabe even taught them a few of her country songs. Finally, the old guitar was, once again, on the floor, leaning up against the wall. Rachael had made coffee while Elizabeth Ann and Ellen May cut and dished up the pie. They all sat, ate, and talked.

Liza Jane was sitting on Olabe's lap, as usual. For some reason, Olabe looked down and saw this innocent little child, sound asleep, snuggled against her breasts. At first, Olabe struggled with a deep longing to be a mother again. She wanted to feel the need and warmth that only a child could bring. She regained control and fought off her tears as she hugged Liza Jane a little tighter.

"Guess we had better put her to bed," Rachael said as she reached down to pick Liza Jane up from Olabe's arms.

"I'll help," she said as she stood up and followed Rachael into the bedroom carrying her soundly sleeping little miracle.

When the two women came back out into the main room, Raaf was struggling to stand up.

"I want to make an announcement," he said clearly which caused everyone to quiet down and listen. "I know our little family has more blessings than any man could ever count." He paused and adjusted his stance as he hung onto the back of his chair for support. "If'n Miss Olabe would be so gracious to allow one more thing," he said and looked over at Olabe.

"Anything," she responded softly.

"Well. Miss Olabe and Miss Jewel. Don't you think it be time now that we all go to church on this comin' Sunday. That is, if'n Miss Olabe would drive us, and all."

The word "church" shot through Jewel's mind like a lightening bolt. Church. Oh, how she had wanted Olabe and her to go to church, but she had always refused.

She never hesitated a second to take her, but would never even step out of the truck when she got to the parking lot to drop her off.

The room went silent and everyone looked at Olabe. The silence went on for what seemed like an eternity to Jewel.

"Yes. Sure," Olabe whispered. "Yes, absolutely," she said in much stronger voice. "We can all fit in the truck, if of course, the boys don't mind riding in the box."

Pandemonium erupted. Everyone excitedly tried to talk at once.

"It's a third miracle, Lord," Jewel whispered as tears streamed down her face. "It's another miracle."

It was all agreed. Olabe and Jewel would come over to the Thompson farm on Sunday morning. The ladies would all squeeze into the crew cab and the boys would ride in the truck box.

The week passed and Jewel noticed a serene peace had come over Olabe. She didn't seem so driven and actually looked like she might even be a little satisfied with her life now.

When Olabe and Jewel arrived in front of the Thompson house, everyone was clean, polished, and waiting. It was a tight fit to get everyone in; Olabe drove, Jewel sat on the passenger's side, Rachael, Elizabeth Ann, and Ellen May squeezed into small back seat, and Liza Jane rode on Jewel's lap. David, Bart, William, and Obadiah jumped into the back.

"This is 'bout as far as I can get," Raaf said as he sat on the extended tailgate. "Tell Miss Olabe not to hit any big bumps."

The trip down to the little church outside of Skipperville didn't take long and Olabe drove quite slow so there wasn't any danger of pitching Raaf into a nearby tree. When they arrived at the parking lot there were already lots of people and cars. Olabe drove right up to the main door and stopped to discharge her passengers. She then drove off and found a place to park.

Rachael and Raaf were immediately inundated with old friends welcoming them back to church services and told them that they had been greatly missed. Jewel talked and laughed with some friends she had known since she was a little girl.

When they entered the little country church most of people were already seated. There was only room enough for all of them in the second pew from the front. David went in first, followed by Bart, William, and Obadiah. Raaf followed and sat down next to the aisle. The ladies moved onward to the first pew. Ellen May, Elizabeth Ann, and Rachael filed in and sat down. Olabe followed and sat holding Liza Jane. Jewel sat next to the aisle, a little self-conscious, but just happy to be anywhere inside the old church.

An older, white-haired lady was softly playing the piano. A slender, partially bald man, dressed in a long black robe made his way up to the pulpit.

"Good morning, friends," he said without looking up and shuffled his papers.

The crowd murmured, "good morning."

Finally, the old minister was satisfied with the arrangement of his announcements, sermon, today's bulletin, and other bits of paper with little notes jotted on them.

"How blessed we are today. Our little church is virtually filled to capacity," he said as he scanned around the sanctuary. "I see many familiar faces, and some that

I've seen only on rare occasion. And, a few that I've never seen. Regardless, welcome to you all."

The little choir led everyone as they sang the first hymn. It was one that most folks were not very familiar with and the singing sounded pretty thin. The song was followed by some scripture reading and then some announcements.

"The Women's Society will meet this coming Wednesday evening in the church basement," the lady behind the piano said as she stood facing the congregation. "Adult fellowship will be on Friday evening at Tom and Mavis Brown's. It's a potluck, so bring your best concoctions."

They turned their hymnals to page 184 and Olabe noticed right away that it was one of her favorites. The whole congregation knew it too. People stood and sang their hearts out and Olabe, Jewel, and the whole Thompson family were no exception. Even Liza Jane was singing.

Olabe started to harmonize with Liza Jane and little by little, people stopped singing and started listening. Soon, it was only Olabe and Liza Jane that were singing. It was truly beautiful. The morning sun poured down through the old stained glass windows making deep blues, reds, and greens flood across the people like the firmament of God was washing over them.

The old minister stood and motioned for everyone to be seated.

"Today," his deep voice resonated off the high ceiling and walls. "Today..." he stammered and shuffled his papers again. "Friends. I've decided to put aside the sermon I've worked diligently on this past week. Instead, I've decided to talk to you just plainly about the love God has for each and every one of you."

The sermon was not very long, but right to the hearts of the whole congregation. People nodded their heads in agreement.

"Love your neighbor as yourself," he continued.

The little church was silent as a grave and the only sound to be heard was the preacher's voice.

"In Jesus' name, we ask You to bless and keep us, always. Amen."

The lady started to play the piano again. People stood and turned around and followed each other down the aisle and out the door.

They lined up to talk to the minister and all told him how much they enjoyed his sermon.

"And, who do we have here, Miss Jewel?" the minister asked as he shook Jewel's hand.

"Why, Reverend, this is my youngest, Olabe."

"Well, well, well. My, my, how you've grown and all, Miss Olabe. Why, I remember you when you were just a little thing running around in Sunday School. This young-un your child?"

Olabe explained that Liza Jane was Rachael's and Raaf's who were right behind her.

He talked quite a while with Rachael and Raaf, thanking them for making such an effort to come here for services today.

Olabe took everyone out for lunch at the little diner in Skipperville. Full of the Spirit and full of food, Olabe took the Thompson family home and then drove home. They changed clothes and went out and puttered a while in their garden and picked up a few pecans off the ground.

"We find a few more and I'll be able to make a pie," Jewel said as she scanned the thin grass.

After supper and the dishes were washed, Olabe and Jewel took their cups of tea and went out onto the porch to enjoy the evening air. They sat for a long while, rocked, and sipped their tea. Finally, it was pretty dark. The evening bugs made their little sounds. A dog barked in the distance. The sky was filled with a whitewash of stars of the Milky Way.

"It was a wonderful day. Didn't you think so, Mama?"

"I truly did, Olabe. I truly did."

Again, there was a long silence.

"Was it just awful, Mama?" Olabe interrupted the silence.

"What? Was what awful, Olabe?"

"You know. When Daddy got killed."

Jewel's heart sunk. But, suddenly, new strength surged through her. She needed to tell Olabe what had happened all those years ago.

"It was awful."

"And, did you think you wanted to die, too?"

"I did."

"Does it ever end, Mama?"

"It took a long while, Olabe. I don't think it ever ends. It just lessens some, so you can somehow get through each day."

"Tell me about you and Daddy, Mama."

Jewel sat for a while and thought.

"Well. You know I was born right down the road there, along with a mess of brothers and sisters. We was pretty poor, but there were lots of folks worse off than we all were. My daddy, your grandfather, worked for the railroad and made pretty good money, as far as poor folks go.

"I went to school right over there in Clopton, just like you and your sister did. But, I only went through the eighth grade. Most folks didn't think much schoolin' was necessary, especially for girls. I 'member how proud my mama and daddy were when I graduated from the eighth grade. Daddy brought me a new dress all the way from Montgomery, just for the ceremony. It didn't fit, but Mama worked on it until it did.

"I used to see your daddy lots of times as he walked down the road past our house. He was lots older than I was, but even as a little girl, he always had time for me. I told my mama that I was going to marry that man. I think I was about six at the time, and he was twelve.

"Things have a way of working out. As we grew, we became friends. Then, real friends. We were almost inseparable. When we announced that we were going to get married, nobody was even surprised. They all just expected it. Your daddy was twenty and I was fourteen.

"We got married and I loved that man with all my heart. I wanted babies right away, but they didn't come. I was scared that something was wrong with me and I prayed and prayed. When I told my mother, she said most women would have been thankful not to be pregnant right away. Anyway, finally your sister, Rebecca June, came along and we were a real family.

"Your daddy was an electrician and gone lots of the time. But, he was always home on weekends. It wasn't long and you came along. You were as different from your older sister as night is to day. Rebecca was a little lady and loved wearing dresses and such. But you, you were a regular tomboy. You were the apple of your father's eye. You followed him everywhere. You used to ride around with him in his old truck as he went to farms and such on Saturdays doing welding and helping folks, to pick up extra money.

"Then, Rebecca grew up, got married, and moved away. But I still had you and your father. Oh, I know. Rebecca didn't disappear off the face of the earth, and all. She and her husband moved to California which is just about the end of the world, as far as I'm concerned.

"You grew up and followed your dream. I remember how you sang and practiced that ol' guitar, until I thought I would go crazy. But then, you too, went away. You got married, and all, and had your own family. Which, by the way, I've never asked you about and hope you'll find a way to tell me someday.

"But I still had your daddy. By that time, my mother and father and four of my brothers and sisters had passed on to their reward. It was just your two aunts; Mabel and Ella, your Uncle Frank, me and your father left. Two years later, Frank died from heart failure.

"Anyway. Your father was working down in Dothan on a new bank building. He was a wirin' on the big main electrical cabinet when someone outside the building turned on the main breaker. He was electrocuted instantly.

"I'll never forget watchin' that big black car as it drove into our driveway. I knew something was dreadfully wrong. The man that owned the company your daddy worked for stepped out, came over, and told me. He said lots of words about how sorry he was, and all, but all I ever heard was, 'there's been a bad accident.'"

"I cried until I could cry no more. I couldn't go to bed because I wanted to feel him laying right next to me, but it wasn't going to happen anymore. I felt that God had abandoned me.

"Both you and your sister were a long way off with your own families. You came for the funeral, and all, but left right afterward.

"I was then, truly alone. Oh, people came by for a while to make sure I was doing alright. But, after a while, that stopped and I was really alone. I wanted to die. I hoped to die. I wanted to go to bed and never wake up. I prayed to the God that betrayed me, to just let me die.

"But, God didn't let me die. He had other plans and one of them was to be here for you. He has shown me so much of His love over the time you've been here, I can't even begin to recall it all. To see you with Liza Jane, and all you've done for her. You're a great friend to Rachael and she surely needs that. You've helped all of their kids.

"My heart is no longer broken, Olabe. It's been filled to overflowing with love. Oh. I still long for your daddy and probably always will. It's just not constant now. I can rest knowing I will join him someday, but only when God says it's time."

Olabe came over behind her mother. She bent down and put her arms around her.

"I'm so sorry, Mama," she said as her heart was breaking.

Jewel patted Olabe's hands and told her it was alright.

But, everything wasn't alright. Olabe went back to her chair and stared into the darkness. She was silent. The only noise that could be heard was the creaking of the two rocking chairs.

"Mama?"

"Yes?"

"Did you tell Daddy that you loved him?"

"What?" Jewel asked as she turned toward Olabe.

"Did you tell him that you loved him on the morning that he didn't come back?"

"Yes, Olabe. I did. We always told each other how much we loved each other. Every day."

"Even if you were mad at each other?"

"Even if we were mad. When we told each other, all our problems seemed to melt away. At least for a little while."

Olabe went back over to her rocker and became silent again.

Jewel had never told anyone about her life before. It felt good. It felt safe with Olabe. It was the right time to say it. She smiled and took a little sip of her tea that was now only tepid-warm.

"Mama?" Olabe finally said softly.

"Yes, dear."

"I never got a chance to say it to Bill."

Jewel rocked silently and waited.

"I never got to hug my kids one last time, either."

Jewel didn't say anything.

"I was supposed to go watch Alexia and Robert play soccer before I had to go do a concert that night. They were going to pick me up with a helicopter, so time wasn't really a problem. Well, my manager called and said that they needed to come get me sooner. So, then I didn't have time to go to the soccer games, and I actually felt relieved that I didn't have to go. Isn't that awful? I didn't want to see my own kids play soccer games that were so important to them."

Jewel rocked and stayed silent. She didn't want to ask any questions or make any comments now that Olabe seemed to be opening her soul up to her.

Olabe stood up and walked to the porch railing and stared off into space. Jewel was afraid that she had lost her for the time being and that was all she was going to tell her. Then, she noticed that Olabe seemed to be crying and was desperately trying to regain control of herself.

"Anyway, Mama," Olabe finally managed to say so quietly that at first Jewel wasn't even sure she heard it. "I flew off to Atlanta and I never saw my two babies again."

Now, Olabe was sobbing. Jewel stood up and went over and put her arms around her all-grownup daughter that desperately needed comforting.

"How did it happen?" Jewel asked softly still holding Olabe.

"Oh, Mama. It was awful. Nobody told me until late that night and then, they told me over the phone."

Olabe's body shook as she sobbed while Jewel couldn't do anything to relieve the pain her child was feeling. She just held her tight.

"I guess two teenage boys were high on drugs and stole a car for a joy ride. They were driving way too fast and were following a big dump truck that was coming onward towards the direction that Bill was driving. There was a hill and the kids passed the truck. Just at the top of the hill they saw Bill and swerved to the right. Right in front of the truck. At the same second, Bill swerved to his right to miss the oncoming car. The truck smashed on his brakes and came into the opposite lane and hit Bill head-on. My husband, my two kids, and even my dog, Jackie, were taken from me instantly."

"My dear child," Jewel said doing her utmost to keep composed and provide help and stability to her struggling, hurting daughter. "What happened to the truck driver and the two boys?" she asked mainly to keep Olabe talking.

"The truck driver was taken to the hospital in serious condition. The truck clipped the very back end of the car which caused it to skid off into the ditch and roll a few times. Somehow, the two boys must have escaped serious injury, managed to get out, and took off running. I guess it took two days for the police to find and capture them. The last I heard, they pled "insanity" in a plea-bargain deal and were serving a one year probation sentence each. That's all I know and that's all I ever want to know about it. The only thing I know for sure is that my wonderful husband is gone. My two children are gone. And, my dear companion, Jackie, is gone. All were taken from me in a matter of a few split seconds.

"I don't even have any hatred for the two boy that caused it. Whatever punishment they gave them would not bring back my Bill, Robert, Alexia, nor Jackie."

Olabe crumpled into her mother's arms and both women sobbed. Jewel knew, first hand, what an awful shock it was to lose a loved one, and she understood it fully. What she couldn't fathom, was the magnitude of the mental trauma Olabe had suffered from losing everyone in her life at one time.

From that night onward, the women formed an almost mystical bond. A bond beyond a mother and her daughter. Having experienced terrible, earth-shattering tragedies, this seemed to provide both of them with the cement that made them see that they were brought together for a reason far beyond mere human comprehension.

CHAPTER 10
Singing For the World Again

Time passed and everyone settled into a regular routine. Life centered around the seasons. The local co-op farmed many of the small farms in the southern Alabama hills. But, instead of being scammed by Jimmy Wade Betterund, who virtually forced everyone to live in absolute poverty, the land owners now made a much better income. None were wealthy by any means, but now, at least, they were able to live above the poverty level.

Elizabeth Ann and Ellen May graduated from high school in the spring. This now made three of the Thompsons that had graduated from high school, counting David. Bart graduated from eighth grade and would be starting high school in the fall. William was promoted from the sixth to the seventh grade and Obadiah moved from the second grade to the third.

Ellen May got a job at the little general store in Clopton. The store reopened after being closed and boarded up for years. It was an almost instant success. She walked to work every day and worked Monday through Saturday. She only earned minimum wage, but she lived at home which made her expenses very low. Every week, when she got paid, she gave her check to her father so he could deposit it in the bank for her when he went down to Ozark to work at the co-op. She paid for lots of extras that, otherwise, the family would have never had.

She turned into an outgoing, very pretty girl which didn't go unnoticed by the local eligible men. A young man from Skipperville caught her eye and they started seeing each other after the evening church services on Wednesday night and the regular services on Sunday.

Elizabeth Ann turned out to be the most beautiful woman anywhere around. Her eyes and smile were mysterious and alluring. After graduation, she signed up at a business college in Ozark. While attending the Baptist church in Ozark, she became acquainted with their new minister and lots of folks thought that a relationship would start to bloom.

David continued to work the Thompson farm and hired out to the co-op whenever they needed extra help. He continued to play the guitar and was becoming quite an accomplished musician. He even put some of his poetry to music, which pleased Olabe greatly. She bought a guitar for herself and every Thursday and Saturday afternoon, she and David sat out on the Thompson porch and played and sang together.

Life was good. It was still a hard life with an enormous amount of physical work that had to be done by everyone. One of the high points was the church in Skipperville. Its membership exploded and now required two services every Sunday to accommodate the growing flock.

One Tuesday evening, Olabe and Jewel were enjoying their evening cup of tea on the porch.

"You know, Mama," Olabe said. "I've been thinking."

"Oh, dear. Sounds a little bit scary."

"You know the house needs lots of repairs."

"Yes, I know. But, what can you and I do? Neither one of us knows the first thing about hammering nails or sawing boards, and such."

"Not us, Mama. I mean to hire it done."

"But, Olabe, we don't make that kind of money. Granted, it's lots better now with the co-op, but still, we just get by."

"Don't worry about money, Mama. I've got more money that I could ever spend and I think it's high time we do some work around here. I think we should get electricity and a real refrigerator."

Electricity scared Jewel. After all, it had killed her husband and, she had heard cases of it burning houses down while people were asleep.

"Our ol' gas ice box has served us well. I don't see any reason to change it."

"It's not just that old refrigerator, Mama. Wouldn't it be nice to just be able to turn on a light at night instead of lighting a lamp? Wouldn't it be nice to not chop wood and feed that antique cook stove? And, in the wintertime, wouldn't it be nice to just turn up the thermostat and have the heat be automatic?"

All these changes were making Jewel's head spin. She didn't want to just turn on the light. She loved her old wood-burning cook stove. She didn't have the least idea what Olabe was talking about when she said, all you have to do is turn up the thermostat. But she knew she didn't like it. She didn't like it at all.

"Just think, Mama. We could even have a real, inside bathroom. You wouldn't have to run out to the outhouse on those cold winter nights. And, the best thing is, you'd be able to take a bath in a real tub."

Jewel sputtered and complained. Changes scared her and she wanted no part of it. But, she also knew that once Olabe had made up her mind, it would be like trying to stop a freight train, right in its tracks. Maybe, if she just didn't say anything, Olabe would forget it and move on to something else.

But, Olabe didn't forget it. Within a few days, she had people out from the electric company. She had two electrical contractors come and make estimates on wiring the house. Three different contractors showed up and gave bids to repair the house and build on a large bathroom. It all made Jewel dizzy.

Within the next month, the house repairs were completed, the foundation for the new addition was poured, the building structure built, and a well had been dug.

"I don't know how you can stand living in this awful mess," Jewel complained one evening as they sat in their rockers. "Seems like there isn't one place in this house that isn't torn up."

"Don't worry, Mama. It'll all be over soon, and just think, it will all be worth it."

"Well, I suppose. If you say so."

"Don't sulk, Mama. You're going to love it."

The next month, Olabe was a tigress. She pushed the contractors and even pointed out to one that his contract included a penalty clause, if he didn't make his completion date. The new addition was finished and the plumbers finished their work. The new bathroom was a dream come true. Even Jewel had to admit how much she enjoyed soaking in their new whirlpool tub, but she didn't like the huge size of the bathroom. She told Olabe that it violated her modesty and she felt as though she was on display, even though the drapes were closed on the large windows.

Olabe took Jewel to Dothan one Monday afternoon to look for a new refrigerator. It was a warm day and the air conditioning in the truck was a welcome relief.

"We're getting soft," Jewel said as she got out of the truck and was blasted by the hot Alabama heat. "Just think of all those years that we got along without any of these new fangled conveniences."

Olabe laughed and led the way into a large appliance store.

"May I be of service, ladies?" a middle-aged man dressed in a white, short sleeved shirt and dark blue pants asked. His stomach was a little too large for his pants and his belt strained to keep him all together. But, he was a warm and friendly person and very knowledgeable. "My name is Stan Handly. What can I do for you?"

Olabe told him they were looking for a large refrigerator.

"Okay, here's one that just might fit the bill," Stan said as he opened the door of a huge, side-by-side refrigerator with stainless steel doors. "Just look at all this room."

Olabe liked the size and the glass shelves. It reminded her of the one in her house outside of Nashville. Suddenly, a sad, depressing feeling stabbed through her whole being as she thought of that house. She had told her manager to just leave it, until she could decide what to do with it. She forced her mind back to what the salesman was saying.

"Of course, you can see that there is an ice dispenser right here in the door.

"What in the world is an ice dispenser?" Jewel asked as she couldn't hold back any longer.

"On a hot day, like this one, all you have to do is put your glass right here and push this lever," he said as he demonstrated. "Ice cubes will drop right in your glass of lemonade."

Jewel was astounded. All these new contraptions confused her mind. She knew she would never be able to work any of these modern things.

Olabe said they would take it and while they were walking towards the office to pay for it and work out the delivery date, Jewel tugged Olabe's arm.

"Did you see the price tag?" Jewel whispered. "It's more than your father and I paid for our house," and she was dead serious.

Olabe laughed which was very contagious. Soon, they were both laughing and Stan chuckled along with them. He didn't know why, but it didn't matter. He had just sold one of the biggest and most expensive refrigerators the store stocked.

The new refrigerator was delivered on Wednesday morning. The delivery crew really had their hands full trying to fit such a large unit through their front door. It required that both the refrigerator and freezer doors be removed and still it was an extremely tight fit. But, after a good hour of hard work, the two men had the new unit in place and put back together.

"This is sure an old antique," one of the delivery men said as he helped his partner get Jewel's old gas refrigerator through the front door, out onto the porch, and over to the truck to haul away.

"You all better be careful with that," Jewel said with a sorrowful look. "It's served us well for lots of years and I'm sure this new one certainly won't do as well."

"Probably won't," the man said as he took off his baseball cap and wiped his sweating forehead. "Probably won't."

Jewel had trouble getting used to all these new, modern conveniences. Going to the grocery store with Olabe was an exasperating experience. Never in her life had she seen so many choices for everything. Olabe bought so much that Jewel thought that she must be planning to feed a whole army. Jewel's total grocery shopping prior to going with Olabe to a supermarket had been the company store that Jimmy Wade Betterund had owned in Skipperville. And then, it was only for simple things like coffee, sugar, flour, and tea where you just told the clerk what you wanted. There was only two kinds of tea; leaf and bags. Now, there were so many brands and kinds, it made her head spin.

One Wednesday afternoon, Olabe and Jewel went back to the appliance store in Dothan. Olabe had decided that they needed a television. By the time they left the store, Olabe had ordered a huge, flat screen, high definition television and a satellite dish. It was all installed on the following Saturday. It took one of the deliverymen almost forty-five minutes to explain how to use the remote. Jewel declared that not only would she never use the thing, but that she would never watch it either.

By Friday of the next week, Jewel was hooked on two afternoon soaps and the Country Music channel. It didn't matter where they were or what they were doing, she absolutely had to be in front of the television when certain programs came on. She even learned how to operate the complicated remote control, so if Olabe happened to be over talking with Rachael, she didn't miss anything.

Jewel still loved to sit out on the porch with Olabe in the evening drinking tea together, but there were now occasions when she would suggest that they wait until a particular show was over. Olabe smiled, but never said anything.

One evening, Olabe was sitting on the porch watching the sun go down behind the hills when Jewel came running out of the house with the porch door slamming behind her.

"Olabe! Olabe! Come, quick," she shouted.

"What is it Mama?" Olabe responded and jumped up quickly as visions of something being on fire inside the house.

They went inside and Jewel pointed at the big-screen television.

"It's you," Jewel continued to shout and acted like a high school girl seeing her favorite rock star. "It's really you. You're on TV."

Olabe watched for a few seconds.

"It's an old rerun of the CMT Awards from four years ago. I was the master of ceremony, Mama."

Jewel sat down and was mesmerized. Here eyes were glued to the screen and shock rippled through her body when the program was interrupted by a block of commercials.

"You're a big star, Olabe. I knew you sang up there in Nashville, but I had no idea you were on television."

Olabe smiled and sat down with her mother to watch.

"And, now Miss Olabe Mae's latest number one hit of the year....." a voice shouted.

A beautiful, young woman dressed in a pure white outfit with many rhinestones floated out onto the stage and began to play her guitar. Her song had topped the charts for four weeks and her fans loved her.

"Boy, that was sure a long time ago," Olabe sighed. "Just look at my hair."

"Shhh," Jewel shushed her daughter. "What's wrong with your hair? I think it looks wonderful."

The show was an hour long and just showed the highlights of the actual awards program. Jewel stared and watched her daughter perform. When it was over, she was exhausted. Evidently, she clenched her fists so tightly during the whole program, that now, her hands and arms ached.

Olabe turned the television off and went back out to the porch while Jewel went into the kitchen and brewed some tea in an electric tea pot. She poured them each a cup and brought them out to the porch. She handed one of them to Olabe.

"You're a big star," Jewel said as she smiled widely. "I had no idea, Olabe."

Again, time passed, as it always does. The daily routine took over again, but slowly, there were more changes in Jewel's and Olabe's lives. At first, when the new refrigerator came to live in their newly remodeled and expanded house, trips to the grocery store were infrequent and they bought only a few essentials. Now, the trips were more frequent and the amount of food they bought seemed gigantic. But, Jewel adapted quickly. She now loved going to the supermarket. It was a wonderful experience. She looked, sampled, and selected items from an uncountable array of products.

It was Saturday afternoon and David had been working in Jewel's garden all morning with her. They were sitting at the little table on the porch and had just finished lunch when Olabe drove up in the truck.

"Hello, Miss Olabe," David said politely, as always. "You sure missed out on a good lunch, here, that Miss Jewel fixed. It was tuna salad, pickles, and chips. And, lookie here at this big ol' piece of peach pie she put out for me."

"What would you like, Olabe?" Jewel asked as she jumped up and was about ready to open the screen door. "Still have plenty of tuna salad, and such."

"That will be fine, Mama," Olabe said as she came up onto the porch, over to the table, and sat down. "I'm really hungry."

"Where did you go in such a hurry this morning," Jewel asked as she set a plate full of tuna salad and chips down in front of her.

"I had an appointment with Richard Becker, Mama. Down in Ozark."

"How's he doing these days? I haven't seen him since the trial, and all," Jewel said as she filled a glass full of lemonade for Olabe. "Suppose he's too busy to come up here for a visit, and all."

"Mama tells me that Elizabeth Ann is sweet on him," David said in a matter-of-fact voice as he shoveled another big bite of pie in his mouth.

"Thought she was going strong with that Baptist minister down there in Ozark," Jewel added and set a piece of pie down for Olabe.

"Well, according to Richard," Olabe said with a twinkle in her eyes, "They've got marriage plans coming up here pretty soon. Seems that the minister got transferred just about the time Richard bought the law practice from some old retiring lawyer in Ozark, not too far from where Elizabeth Ann lives. I always thought there was some real sparks between them when he was down here investigating Jimmy Wade Betterund for the trial. But, I guess nothing got started because Elizabeth Ann was too young and still in school."

"'T weren't that," David smiled. "She was interested all right. It was Mama that wouldn't let them two get together. I 'member her saying one time that he was a tall, good lookin', educated, big-town lawyer and would take advantage of a little country girl like Elizabeth Ann."

"Funny how things seem to have a way of working out, isn't it?" Olabe said as she ate the last chip on her plate and picked at her piece of pie with her fork.

"You just never know what God's plan is," Jewel said firmly. "He makes our plan for us and then, sets us loose to try and figure out what it all is. We run around from here to there, and many folks never find out what it all means."

After everyone had finished their pie, Jewel took the dishes inside to the sink and rinsed them off. She had less than three minutes to get the television on and tune in her first soap of the afternoon. Nothing could keep her from *As the World Turns* followed by *Bachelor's Children*.

Olabe went in the house and got her guitar. David took his out of the case, which was lying in the corner of the porch. They each tuned their instruments and them tuned their strings to each other. Finally, they were satisfied and Olabe started out playing one of their favorite gospel songs; *We'll Meet on Judgment Day*. It was a song that could really get your heart beating and your toe tapping. David especially liked the way Olabe's voice blended with his when they sang the chorus.

After singing two more gospel songs and three old country favorites, they took a little breather.

"You know, David, you are really becoming a fine guitar player. I think you're certainly as good as most of the pickers I've played with, and that's quite a few."

"Ah, Miss Olabe. You're just a saying that."

"No, I'm not. And, here's the thing. Not only can you play by ear, like lots of the so called players, but you can read music very well, and play in any key."

"Well, Miss Olabe, that ain't magic, and all. It's 'cause I've had the best teacher in the whole wide world."

The two talked for a while and David continued to softly pick strings and play chords.

"Miss Olabe?"

"Yes, David?"

"Would you mind if'n I asked you a big favor, and all?"

"Sure. Ask away."

"Well, it's kind of embarrassing."

Now, she was curious. She wondered if David had a crush on her? How could she let him down easy and not hurt his feelings. After all, she was thirty-seven and he was only nineteen.

"Would you mind listening to a little ol' song I made up?"

"What? A song you made up? Oh, David, I'd love to hear it."

David played his song and sang the lyrics from one of his poems. When he finished he noticed tears running down her cheeks.

"You alright, Miss Olabe?"

"Yes, David. I'm alright. It's beautiful. You've got a few rough edges here and there, but maybe I can help you smooth them out."

"I'd be grateful, Miss Olabe. I truly would."

"Okay. Let's look at the music first."

Olabe wrote the notes on music paper she'd bought for David a while back. She showed him how to change a few of the chords and their tenses to make the tune flow better. They both played it together. David picked the melody while Olabe strummed the chords. On their third time through, Olabe noticed that her mother was standing just inside the screen door watching them.

"Well, Mama," Olabe said as she and David came to the end. "Thought you were watching your soaps."

"How can I with you two making such wonderful music out here. That last one sounded like it came straight from Heaven."

Olabe helped David with the lyrics, and then the chorus. Finally, it was ready for it's first performance. They played and sang it together. Olabe just couldn't help it. Tears flowed while she sang.

"David, it's an absolutely wonderful song," Olabe said as she wiped her eyes.

Jewel hadn't heard their latest performance. She had gone back in to watch TV and was now glued to it.

David said it was probably time for him to go home and help his mother get things ready for supper. Without the help of Elizabeth Ann and Ellen May, David's help was now invaluable to Rachael. They got into the truck and Olabe drove him home.

All the way back home, Olabe's mind was on fire again. Thoughts of what to do raced through her brain. Then, the right idea popped into her head. She pulled into the driveway and stopped. She got out, ran up to the porch and picked up her guitar. She came back to the truck and got out her cell phone.

"Hello?" a man's voice said.

"Carl," Olabe responded. "This is Olabe."

They talked for a while making small talk.

"I've got something I'd like you to listen to, Carl."

"Sure, of course, Olabe. What is it?"

"Just listen for a few seconds."

Carl was used to his "stars" discovering untapped talent over the years, but Olabe had never done that. Yet, throughout his career, he had heard it all, both good, bad, and some even terrible. He wondered where this would fit in. Carl settled back in his huge, black leather chair in his study at home, overlooking the glorious Cumberland river valley.

Olabe laid the cell phone on the hood of the truck, picked up her guitar, and performed David's song. When she finished, she wiped away her tears and picked up the phone.

"Well, Carl. What do you think?"

Silence.

"Carl? Are you there?"

"I'm here, Olabe. I'm here. I just had to blow my nose. Great God. Where on God's green earth did you find that song? Did you write it? We've got to record it, you know. And, fast."

"A young man that lives next to us wrote it, Carl. Both the music and the lyrics. What do you think of it?"

Carl exploded in enthusiasm. He wanted to send a private jet down and pick Olabe up. He wanted to get it recorded and out into the marketplace. And, right away.

"First, Carl. What can you do about David?"

"Does he have an agent?"

"Not yet, but I thought maybe you could take him on."

"Well, Miss Olabe. You know I usually don't represent unknowns, but if I'm right about this song, I can make an exception. How about if I work on setting up a recording studio next week? I'll get a private jet down there and bring you and this David up here. And, Olabe. Why don't we cut a new CD while you're up here? We can feature this new song as its centerpiece. It'll be a smash hit. I just know it."

Olabe agreed and Carl told her to be thinking about the song list for the new CD and he would write up one, too.

Within a short time, Carl called Olabe back and told her everything was set. She and David were to be at the Dothan airport Tuesday morning at eight o'clock and would be flown to Nashville. He would have a limo waiting and they would be taken right to the Southern Belle Recording Studio. Olabe couldn't wait to tell David.

She drove straight to the Thompson farm. As usual, the flock of kids came rushing out onto the porch.

"Miss Olabe," Liza Jane called out as she ran across the porch in her nightgown and jumped into Olabe's waiting arms.

"David," Olabe began. "I've got some very exciting news for you."

She told him about her agent and that he wanted to record Olabe singing David's song. They were invited to go to Nashville to a recording studio and that he was to come along. David was dumbfounded. Everyone was excited for him and swarmed around congratulating and patting him on the back.

"Miss Olabe," Raaf said as he came over to her on his crutches. "You'll take good care of my boy up there in Nashville, and all, won't you?"

She assured him that she would look out for him, as she would one of her own.

Rachael wanted to know how long they would be gone.

Olabe told David that they would need to buy some clothes and some kind of suitcase. She said that she would take care of it all. She told David that she would be waiting at their door next Tuesday morning about six-thirty.

When she got back home, she found Jewel sitting on the porch in her rocker.

"Hello, Mama. Wait until you hear this."

Olabe told her mother about going to Nashville and recording David's song.

"I knew it was a good one when I heard you two out there working on it," Jewel said, but didn't know if she liked the idea of Olabe running off with that crowd again. The thought that maybe she wouldn't come back flashed across her mind.

Olabe was once again a whirlwind. Whenever she set her mind to something, she was dead set on making it happen. Monday morning, she and Jewel drove down to Ozark and bought some clothes for David and a nice suitcase. She even bought a few things for herself and, as always, sneaked in a few items for Jewel, when she wasn't looking.

That night, Olabe had two large suitcases lying on her bed, both open.

"How long you planning on being gone?" Jewel asked as she came into Olabe' bedroom.

"Probably four or five days, Mama. Carl wants me to record enough songs to make a CD."

"I'll worry about you the whole time."

"There's no reason to worry, Mama."

"Well. I will."

"Better not."

"Why not?"

"Because you're going with," Olabe said and smiled to herself.

Jewel was thunderstruck. She didn't know what to say. She tried, but the words wouldn't come out right.

"But, I ain't never been farther away than Montgomery. And, that was only one time. I just wouldn't know how to act."

"You'll do just fine, Mama. Come on now and pack this case. I got it for you."

Jewel sputtered as she was buffeted around as Olabe rushed here and there.

"But, I ain't never been on no airplane. They's scary, you know. Flying so high."

"There's nothing to it, Mama. You just get on, sit down, and before you know it, you're there."

On the one hand, Jewel knew it was an opportunity of a lifetime. Especially, being with her daughter and going to such a big city as Nashville. But, on the other hand, she was faced with all these new things, like airplanes, and such.

Tuesday morning came and Olabe and Jewel arrived at the Thompson farm right on time. David was ready and waiting. All the rest of the family were there to see him off. They said their good-byes, and soon, were racing down 431 towards Dothan.

Olabe dropped her mother and David off at the terminal building and then drove to the long-term parking lot.

"Well, everybody ready?" Olabe asked as she came through the door of the terminal. Jewel and David rushed over to her and stuck right to her like glue.

There were lots of people rushing around the terminal building. The overhead speaker announced that the flight to Atlanta was going to be about twenty minutes late boarding. One man ran past them on a dead-run as he sped toward the little coffee shop.

"Hello," a friendly looking gentleman dressed in an immaculate brown suit said. "Miss Mae?"

"Yes?" Olabe said as she looked up.

"Everything is ready for you folks. Here, let me put your luggage on this ol' cart."

They followed the man through some doors while another man pushed the cart with their luggage behind them. They went out a door that suddenly took them outside. The bright sun made them immediately shade their eyes. Right in front of them sat a brilliant, white business jet, with a red stripe painted from it's nose to the vertical tail fin. It had no markings on it except a number. The door near the front opened and a young woman stepped out and walked down the little stairway. She welcomed them in and helped Jewel up the steps.

Inside, it was if they had walked into someone's living room or study. There were a few leather seats near the windows and thick carpeting. There was even a plasma television on the forward bulkhead. The flight attendant helped everyone get seated and showed them how to buckle their seatbelts.

"If this is so all-fired safe, then why do we need these things to hold us in the chair?" Jewel sputtered.

Olabe smiled and sat down. She buckled her seatbelt and remembered back on how many countless flights she had made in airplanes like this one.

David was exploding with questions. He wanted to know everything.

"We're a movin'," he shouted. "I think were are a going backwards, though."

Jewel couldn't look out, even though they were still on the ground.

The jet sat there a few minutes while the tug vehicle was unhooked. Suddenly, a soft whistling sound came into the cabin which steadily got higher pitched and louder. When it was at a steady roar, another whistling sound started on the other side of the airplane. Jewel shut her eyes tight and held on to her chair for dear life.

Within a few minutes the jet rolled along the taxiway. It stopped short of the runway and waited.

"Wow," David shouted. "Look at that. A big airplane just landed right over there."

The little jet lurched forward and the engines roared. The acceleration was blinding and Jewel knew they would never make it to Nashville alive, so she prayed that her flight to Heaven would be quick.

Soon, the acceleration seemed to fade away as the airplane lifted and gained altitude.

"You may take off your seatbelts," the flight attendant said as she walked by each person.

Jewel still couldn't open her eyes. If she was still alive, there was no way she was going to unhook the only thing that was keeping her in her chair.

The flight attendant told everyone that her name was Carol. She asked Olabe if she would like something to drink. Olabe decided on coffee. She then asked Jewel who barely cracked an eye open.

"You mean we dare drink something on this thing?" Jewel asked in a croaking voice.

"Yes. We're now at our cruising altitude and it should be a very smooth ride up to Nashville this morning. How about a nice cup of hot coffee?"

"Young Man? What can I bring you to drink?" Carol asked as she stopped by David's seat.

Carol had to ask him twice and finally touch him on the shoulder to get David's attention. He was glued to the window.

"I'm sorry, and all," he said while his cheeks and neck turned a brilliant shade of crimson. "Guess I'd like to have one of them cola drinks. If'n you don't mind, o' course."

Carol went back to the little galley. In a short while, she came back carrying a tray with two cups of coffee, a glass full of ice, and a can of Coke.

"How long you reckon it's gonna take us to get to Nashville?" David asked Carol as she put the glass of ice into a holder and poured cola into it.

Jewel heard what David asked and perked up her ears. She was almost afraid that the answer was going to be in the neighborhood of all day or maybe even tomorrow. She didn't really want to know.

"Should be there in about an hour," Carol said as she handed Olabe a cup of steaming coffee. "Would you like cream or sugar?"

"Oue, Wee," David said in an astounded voice. "How fast we a going, anyway?"

"I think the captain told me our flight plan called for us to fly at 39,000 feet and we would be going at about 480 knots. That's little over 550 miles per hour."

David's eyes were as big as saucers and the numbers made Jewel's head swim. She didn't know how high 39,000 feet was, but she knew it was way too high to even imagine. In fact, they must be dustin' right up next to Heaven, itself.

The time went by quickly. Carol came up to the seats and told everyone to buckle their seatbelts as they were on the final approach to Nashville International Airport.

It seemed only seconds, but in fact it was more like fifteen minutes and they touched down, slowed down, and turned off onto a taxiway. Their pathway took them to a long row of steel buildings that looked like big warehouses instead of the busy passenger terminal building.

Finally, they stopped and the shrill whistles of the engines began to spool down. The door opened and a man dressed in a smart blue uniform with a cap with a black bill stepped aboard.

"Hello, my name is Travis and I'll be your driver this morning. If you will just step off the airplane and into the limo, I'll get your luggage."

As they walked out the door of the aircraft, Carol stood just outside bidding everyone goodbye and wishing them well. Just a few feet from the steps sat a long, stretch limo with darkened windows.

The limo was running and the air conditioning was on. They all got in and were no sooner seated when they heard the trunk shut and saw Travis walk around from the back and down the length of the long limo. He opened the driver's door and stepped in.

"Welcome to Nashville," he said over the intercom. "It sure is going to be a hot one today. It's almost ninety degrees and it's not even ten o'clock yet."

The trip from the airport to the recording studio took almost forty-five minutes, but it didn't seem to matter to Jewel nor David. Jewel was just glad to have her feet back onto the ground and David was almost speechless by all the tall buildings and the chaotic traffic.

Nashville seemed familiar to Olabe, but her memories of it being home to her had faded. She smiled as she watched David point out things for Jewel to see.

The limo turned into a huge parking lot next to a many story glass building. David said it looked like it touched the clouds which made Jewel afraid to even look.

"We've sure been waiting for you to get here," a smiling, completely bald man said as he held the door for everyone to get out. "Sure nice to see you again, Miss Olabe. And, this lovely lady must be your sister?"

"Oh, Carl," Olabe teased. "Everyone. This is Carl Strom. He's my agent and has been with me through thick and thin. This is my mother, Jewel. And, this is David. The one I told you about."

"Miss Jewel," Carl said as he took her hand and shook it gently. "I'm so happy to finally be able to meet you. I'm going to do everything in my power to make your stay here in Nashville, a truly wonderful time for you." Carl then turned and reached out his right hand to shake David's. "So. You're the great talent that Miss Olabe has been ranting and raving about. David, my name is Carl Strom. And, you and I have a little business to talk over tonight at supper."

Carl herded them all into the building, into the elevator, and up to the fifteenth floor. When they stepped out they were met by a glass wall that had the words Southern Belle Recording Studio painted in gold lettering on it. Carl ushered them right into a huge conference room. One wall of the room was glass, floor to ceiling. David rushed right over to look around, but Jewel cowered back at the farthest point.

"Miss Olabe, I've asked a few associates to come in for this little meeting to help us get our work done as quickly as we can. Now, I've taken the music you faxed to me and had it printed up for the musicians and backup singers. We've done three recordings with them already for you to sing with, but if it's not what you want, just let me know and I'll call them in for a live recording session with you."

Three men, dressed in business suits, came in and everyone sat down. A young lady with a steno pad sat near one end of the table and seemed to be writing what everyone said.

Now, Miss Olabe," Carl said. "I think we should work on your new song this afternoon and see if we can get it wrapped up. I suggest that we include four of your older, number one hits and then, some of your better known singles, too. What do you think?"

Olabe told Carl that she would like him to hear some of David's other songs, and just maybe there might be two or three that they could use. Carl agreed.

Lunch was brought in and both David and Jewel were astonished by the size and variety of the spread. Jewel whispered to Olabe and told her that she hoped she wasn't paying for it. Olabe laughed and told her she wasn't and that it was all part of the deal.

Carl then led them to one of the recording studios. David was mesmerized by the huge audio sound board with it's soft glow from the many lights. Two men with headphones sat in front of the controls and seemed to be listening to something.

"Here's what the first cut of the full orchestra sounds like." Carl said and pointed at one of the soundmen.

The room boomed with the sounds of the deep, full sounds of strings, woodwinds, and brass accompanied by a full array of percussion instruments. David could hardly believe that it was his song he was listening to.

"Sounds okay," Olabe said and smiled at David. "What do you think?"

David was speechless.

"How about singing along, Miss Olabe?" Carl said and motioned to two women sitting on stools in the huge, dimly lighted room right next to them separated by a huge window. The lights came up to full in the room. The walls seemed to be made of black foam or some sort of sound absorbing material. Olabe walked up to the door and opened it. She went in and said something to the two women which made them both smile. Olabe put on a pair of headphones and stood in front of a huge microphone that was suspended from the ceiling.

The music started. Olabe began to sing and the two backup singers sang with her. The music and lyrics were overwhelming, and in no time, both backup singers had tears streaming down their faces. When it was over, Olabe sat down on a stool and waited.

The soundmen were working with the controls on the console.

"Alright, Miss Olabe. Here's the playback," Carl said into a microphone by the console.

It was almost unbelievable. It virtually moved everyone in the sound room to tears, even David.

"What do you think, Miss Olabe?" Carl said when it was over.

"I thinks it's good, Carl. Let's do recordings with the two other cuts you have. Then, we can pick the one we like best."

They spent the next hour making recordings. All seemed to be superb and making a decision on which one was best was going to be a real decision.

Carl decided that they all needed to take a little break and sent out for some sodas. David got up and timidly went into where Olabe was sitting.

"Well, David, what do you think?"

"It's wonderful, Miss Olabe. Just wonderful. But, you know, maybe it's all too complicated."

"What do you mean, David? Too complicated."

"You know. Too much music."

Olabe thought for a few seconds and said, "I think I know what you mean. There's a guitar over there, David. Will you play along for me?"

Both soundmen were listening and immediately turned some of the controls.

"You know, Miss Olabe. I wrote this song to tell the way I feel about my mama, and I think it should be sung slower and simpler." David started to strum a few chords. Then, he began to play the music he had written.

Olabe sang and the two backup singers joined in. At first, one of the soundmen shook his head, until they came to the first chorus. During the second verse one of the backup singers got choked up and it was plain she was having a hard time singing along.

"What's going on?" Carl asked as he came back into the sound booth with a soft drink in his hand. "What are they doing?"

One of the soundmen shushed him and told him to just listen.

When it was over, Olabe and David came back into the sound room while the two backup singers wiped their eyes. Then, it happened. The playback came across the speakers.

It was David's voice, at first, telling Olabe about why he wrote the song and who it was for. Then, came the simple sound of a soft guitar and a clear, true country voice of a superstar. Even when one backup singer's voice cracked, it was recorded. It was a masterpiece. When it was over, everyone just stood, speechless. Everyone's eyes were filled to overflowing. No one said anything. Finally, Carl regained his composure.

"That's it," Carl said as he continued to wipe his eyes with his handkerchief. "The centerpiece of the CD will, first, be the full rendition with the full orchestra. Then, including David's explanation, the simple, clear song in its originality should follow. Guys?" Carl turned and asked the soundmen. "Can you work it up for us to hear?"

It took a few minutes, but the wait was certainly worth it. It was truly wonderful.

"It's a number one hit," Carl said to Olabe. "I just know it will be."

That night, they had a fine dinner at one of Nashville's famous hotels. Carl excused himself for continuing to talk business, but, he said, there were pressing matters. He explained his normal contract with David, and why he needed an agent. Olabe's past business experience was invaluable to David, and it kept Carl on his toes. By the time dinner was over, David had an agent, and Carl had a new, budding song writer, and, he was pretty darned sure, they all had a number one hit on their hands.

The next few days were hectic. Olabe spent hours in the recording studio working on new and old material to be on her new CD. Then, on the third day, they spent the whole time working on three of David's other songs. Two of them were for certain to be on the CD and the other one pretty sure, but it needed a little work on the chorus. By the end of the fourth day, it was a "wrap." All the songs had been recorded, in record time.

"Well, Olabe," Carl said as he and she sat in a little office adjoining the much bigger conference room. "I'd say, not only will this CD go platinum, but the centerpiece will go through the roof. All we have to do now is to get the cover designed and then it can go into production and distribution. I'll bet it'll be on the shelves by Christmas."

"Carl?" Olabe said. "I've been thinking about the cover. Take a look at these." She took out a folder of photos. "These are from my digital camera and are of David's mother, Rachael. She knew I was taking pictures, but I'm sure didn't realize they were of her. I especially like this one."

The picture was an image of Rachael standing in front of one of the windows in her house. The window was open and the curtains were gently moving. Her face beamed with love as she was watching Liza Jane playing on the porch, out of sight to the photo. Rachael's face showed lines of hard living and heavy concern, but glowed with love and fulfillment. All in all, it was a gorgeous picture.

"Good God, Olabe. It's wonderful. Do you think we can get her permission to use it?"

Olabe nodded and thought they could. She gave Carl the SD card from her digital camera that contained the image and told him she would take a release form back with her. She would get Rachael to sign it, if she wanted to, and then fax it back.

"Wonderful," Carl said as he got up and put his arms around her. "It's so great to be back working with you again. I just can't tell you how terrific it is. Your fans are clamoring for something new from you, Olabe. And this will really do the trick."

They all waved to Carl as they got back into the limo and the trip back to the airport.

The little jet was waiting for them and Carol welcomed them back on board.

When they got to their cruising altitude, Carol came up to everyone and asked if they had a good time in Nashville.

"Was wonderful," Jewel said in a relaxed voice, being an old hand at this flying stuff now. "But, there is no way in God's green earth that I would want to live there. There's so much traffic and people. Why, it all just made my head spin."

"What can I get you for supper?" she asked Miss Olabe first.

Olabe ordered a salad with chicken and Jewel decided on roast pork with dressing.

"Guess I'll just have a big ol' hamburger. If'n you all got one," David said as he adjusted his seat so he could see outside better.

"Oh. I'm sorry, sir. But, I'm afraid we don't have any hamburgers on board today. How about a nice big steak instead?" Her eyes twinkled.

When she brought the meals, everything was so elegantly served on china plates and steaming coffee. David, of course, had a Pepsi.

David had never had a steak in his life and couldn't believe how wonderful it was. Jewel said she watched him eat it, and he never took one breath from the time he started it until he finally laid his fork and knife down.

Soon, they were back on the ground at the Dothan airport. Olabe drove her truck up to the terminal building and picked up her tired, but happy passengers. She smiled to herself as she thought about the stories that David was going to tell everyone back home at the Thompson house.

CHAPTER 11
Singing For The World Again

David's stories about his experiences in Nashville held the family's fascination for a long time and was the subject of interest at many evening meals.

Olabe's new CD was released and it was an instant hit. Sales exploded and the first batch was virtually sold out before stores could even put them out on the counters. Entrepreneurs put them on eBay where prices soared to over $100 each. More and more CDs were produced and the marketplace continued to gobble them up as fast as they were released. Money poured in and huge checks were deposited into Olabe's Nashville bank accounts.

Carl Strom, Olabe's agent, called frequently and begged her to do another CD.

"Olabe." Carl's voice had a tint of urgency and begging in it. "I think you should do at least one more concert. You could call it a 'farewell concert,' if you want to. That way, if you ever decided to do another one, it would be an 'Olabe returns concert.' Just think of the impact it would have on your fans. They love you, you know."

"Carl. Carl. Carl. I don't want any part of that rat race anymore. I love my simple country life. Besides, your accountant told me that we're having a problem with cash flow."

"Yah. That's right, Olabe. The problem you're having with cash flow is; there's too much of it. The money is pouring in at an absolute astounding rate."

"So, Carl, let me get this straight. We're already making too much money, so now, you want me to do a concert and make even more?"

"Olabe, just think how much your fans would appreciate it, if you did one last concert."

"Yah, Carl. Think about the prices of the tickets. My fans are mainly lower to middle-income folks with disaster nipping right at their back door. None of them would be able to afford the tickets. You know they will be sold out in blocks to radio and television stations to the highest bidder. They'll auction off a few, and then give away some to businesses that buy huge blocks of advertising. I've seen it happen all over the country, Carl."

He remained silent for a few minutes. In fact, Olabe wondered if the battery had gone dead in her cell phone.

"I just might have it, Olabe," Carl said with new enthusiasm in his voice. "Here's my thought. We make it part of the deal that we own all the tickets. That is, we'll have one of your companies buy all the seats. And, I mean, all of the seats. Then, we'll set up an 800 number with a bank of telemarketers to answer the phones. We'll make restrictions that only two tickets can be purchased per person and we'll have the computer verify that each credit card was used only once. That would absolutely prevent businesses from buying up blocks of seats. It won't be popular among the elite and high powered people, but, after all, it will be your last concert before you retire. I'm pretty sure that we can work out that kind of a deal with the Phillips Arena just to get you there. What do you think about that?"

Olabe thought it over for a few seconds. She asked a few more questions and told Carl she had some special conditions for the front row that she wanted to talk about.

"I want the front row to be for our next door neighbors, the Thompson family. And, for my mother."

"Fine, Olabe. Fine," Carl said. He was used to different and odd requests from various stars he had represented over the years, but this was the first time Olabe had ever requested anything special.

"Also, Carl, there's a young man and his wife up in Huntsville that I want you to arrange a limo for them to take to Atlanta and bring them back. Also, I want you to take care of a top notch hotel room for them the night before the concert and the night of it. I want all meals to be paid for, too."

"Not a problem, Olabe. I can take care of it right away. Just give me his name."

"That's the problem. All I can remember is that his first name was Ron and his wife's name was Marlene. Oh, and Carl. I remember that he worked at a Rebel Fast Gas Station right off the Interstate."

Carl wrote down everything she told him. He shook his head, but of course, told her he would take care of it all. He immediately wrote on his note pad for one of his assistants to get on this problem immediately. There was no way he was going to disappoint Olabe. Especially now that she had agreed to do the concert.

Olabe also requested that her mother and the Thompson family ride from Dothan to Atlanta with her in a private jet. Carl agreed immediately.

* * * *

"Ron Jordan?" a man in sunglasses, green polo shirt, and tan pants with a buzz haircut asked as he approached the counter one afternoon in a Rebel Fast Gas Station near Huntsville. The man certainly looked like he could have easily been an agent for the CIA or FBI.

"Yes sir? You got gas out there?"

"No. I would like to see some identification please."

"ID? What for?" Ron asked in a shocked voice. "Look here at my name tag. See? It says 'Ron" right on it."

"Sorry, Ron. But, I need something more than that. Could I see your driver's license? By the way, is your wife's name, Marlene?"

"What's my wife got do to do with anything," Ron asked becoming very alarmed. "Has anything happened to her?"

"Nothing like that, Ron. Sorry to have surprised you. But, I have to know if you are the right person that I'm looking for. I've got something very special to give you."

Ron was skeptical. He had always worked the late night shift before and had seen just about every sort of drunk or crazy person there was. He had even been robbed once. He had just transferred to the day shift so he could be home more with his wife and daughter.

"Here's my license," Ron said as he pushed it across the counter and put his foot on a pedal switch to activate the silent alarm, if it became necessary.

"Yep, Ron. Photo looks like you. Your wife Marlene?"

"Yes. Now, what's this all about."

The man took his sun glasses off and opened a huge manila envelope. He told

Ron what was being given to him by none other than Miss Olabe Mae, herself. There were tickets to the concert in Atlanta and vouchers for meals. There was a detailed schedule along with special t-shirts and other memorabilia. Ron was flabbergasted and had to make a mad dash to the restroom to keep from wetting himself. He couldn't believe it and, when he called Marlene to tell her, he ended up shouting in the phone so much, that she couldn't understand him at all. It all had to wait until he finally got home from work and laid everything out onto their kitchen table.

* * * *

Early on the morning of the concert, Olabe and Jewel drove into the driveway at the Thompson farm. Everyone was waiting on the porch and came pouring off as soon as they saw the truck.

"Miss Olabe. Miss Olabe," Liza Jane shouted as she ran to the truck. Olabe stepped out, scooped her up, and held her while everyone piled in. "We gonna fly away on a big airplane. Whooooosh!"

The drive down to the Dothan airport didn't take long and everyone talked at once. Olabe drove into the drop-off area and unloaded her cargo. A man dressed in a dark blue uniform was waiting for them. She parked the truck and ran back to the terminal.

The private jet was bigger this time, but nowhere near the size of a large commercial aircraft. It was painted a light tan with gold stripes. There were two big engines in the rear, one on each side of the fuselage.

"Good morning," the flight attendant said as three men helped Raaf up the steps.

The rest of the group then followed and "oohed and ahed" at the sight of the luxurious interior of the private aircraft.

"Where's Carol?" David asked as he came up the steps.

"Carol?" the blonde haired, very slender flight attendant responded. "Is there a Carol that's supposed to go with us today?"

"No. Carol was on the plane Miss Olabe and I took up to Nashville once."

The attendant smiled and her blue eyes sparkled. "My name is Anna and I hope to make your trip today as pleasant for everyone as I can."

David blushed, quickly found a seat, and buckled his seat belt.

Olabe came on board carrying Liza Jane. She stopped by the two seats on the right side in the back, next to the galley. Liza Jane scooted over and sat by the window. She wanted to sit on Olabe's lap, but was alright with it as long as they sat right next to each other.

The engines started and the airplane slowly began to taxi. As they turned onto the runway, the pilot brought both engines up to full power and they roared down the long ribbon of cement like a roller coaster accelerating down the first big hill at an amusement park.

Liza Jane's eyes were huge as she watched the scenery race past her window. She put her hands over her ears to protect them from the whistle of the engines.

The flight over to Atlanta didn't even take an hour. The flight attendant told them that it was less than two hundred air miles. Soon, they were on the ground and herded into two waiting limos.

The limos stopped in front of a huge hotel. Bart, William, and Obadiah stood on the sidewalk and stared straight up and declared that the top of the building touched the clouds. They were taken to their rooms and got settled. Rachael declared they were in a palace. She put her arms around Raaf after the door was shut and told him how lucky they all were and how much she loved him.

Lunch was served in a private room in one of the hotel's restaurants and was truly a lovely experience for everyone. William said that his burger was the best he'd ever eaten, but Bart tried to trump the hamburger by telling everyone how good his mac and cheese was.

Olabe told everyone that she had to go to the arena for rehearsal and get ready for the concert tonight, but there would be some people along in a few minutes to take them on a sightseeing tour of Atlanta this afternoon. And, not to worry, because there would be plenty of time to get ready for the concert. There would be some people to get them into the limos and to take them to the Arena.

Liza Jane clung to Olabe like glue. She reached down, picked her up, and hugged her.

"I'll see you in a little while, honey. And, when you get to the zoo this afternoon, will you wave a special hello to a big ol' polar bear that lives there?"

Liza Jane said she would and Olabe put her down.

The polar bear had been one of her own daughter's favorite attractions whenever they were there. A pang of guilt shot through Olabe's heart as she remembered how many times they had come to Atlanta and she was too busy to go with her husband and two kids to see the zoo.

The afternoon went by rapidly and soon it was time to go back to the hotel and get ready for tonight.

The limo stopped right in front of the main entrance of the Phillips Arena and discharged its passengers. Two men were waiting for them and helped Raaf into a wheelchair. He resisted a little, but actually was glad for the convenience. They were ushered into an ocean of people. Each of the Thompsons and Jewel were given a ticket that had been embossed in plastic and had a black chord through a hole at the top. It was to be worn as a necklace and available to any of the security people. When they came to the main entrance to the auditorium, all William could say was, "Wow!"

"Right this way, please," a young man said dressed in a dark maroon jacket. They walked down the long aisle all the way to the very front row. "Starting right here," he pointed at the third seat from the aisle, "and all the way down that way for the next nine seats." He wheeled Raaf down to the farthest seat and helped him get out of the wheel chair and get seated.

There were two vacant seats, then, Jewel, Liza Jane, Rachael, Elizabeth Ann, Ellen May, Bart, William, Obadiah, David, and last, Raaf.

The stage was right in front of them and was barricaded by a massive drawn drape. Music played in the overhead speakers, but was mostly drowned out by the murmur of the crowd as they were entering through the doorways and shown where their seats were by the ushers. The auditorium was filling quickly as eight o'clock was approaching.

"Right here," the usher pointed with his flashlight and a young woman sat down next to Jewel and a young man sat next right on the aisle.

When the two got settled, they both seemed to be captivated by the size and magnitude of the facility and crowd.

"Oh, I'm sorry," the young woman said as she lightly bumped Jewel. "I'm so excited to be here, I guess I just forgot my manners."

Jewel smiled and wasn't annoyed at all.

"My name is Marlene, and this is my husband, Ron," the young woman said to Jewel.

"Well, hello," Jewel answered.

"Did Miss Olabe send tickets to you all, too?" Ron asked. "I guess she's just about the most wonderful person in the world, and all."

"She sort of did," Jewel answered politely and smiled to herself. These two seem so excited and she wondered how Olabe knew them.

It didn't take long before Ron and Marlene told Jewel the whole story.

"And, when Ron came home that night and told me that he had met Miss Olabe Mae, why, I just didn't believe him. Even after he showed me her autograph, I still didn't believe him. I thought maybe he had bought her autograph, 'cause he knows how much I love her, and all."

"But, then when they sent that guy with the tickets," Ron bubbled over. "She had to believe me then."

Jewel chuckled over their enthusiasm and bubbly personalities.

"How did you happen to run into Miss Olabe?" Marlene asked Jewel as she took a sip of her soda.

Jewel sat quietly for a few seconds, turned, and looked right at Marlene and Ron. "I'm her mother," she said with a big smile."

"No foolin'?" Marlene said wide-eyed. "My God, Ron. Lookie here. This is Miss Olabe's mama."

The two were awestruck.

The house lights dimmed and there was a noticeable sense of urgency as people raced for their seats. Floor lights flooded the deep purple stage curtains giving them an eerie glow. Suddenly, there was a huge drum roll as the house lights went to complete darkness. The curtains opened and the stage was bathed in brilliant white lights. Indoor fireworks sparkled and boomed.

"Ladies and Gentlemen. It gives us here in Atlanta, great pleasure to present........Miss Olabe Mae!"

The band exploded and the crowd stood and roared. Olabe flew out on suspended cables that made her float above the stage and was lighted by a huge spotlight that made her light blue outfit full of rhinestones sparkle. She had blue cowboy boots on along with a large, matching blue cowboy hat. As she floated to earth she gave the illusion that an angel had just landed that was straight from Heaven. Her stage personality was turned on full and her persona reigned over everyone.

Olabe sang her opening number which had been a number one hit a few years ago. The crowd loved it. The experienced band was loud and upbeat. Olabe's voice was amplified clear and beautiful as she sang the lyrics she was so famous for. When the first song ended, she went right into the next, and then, the next. The crowd roared with delight. Olabe's performance was spectacular and she was really in her realm.

Jewel sat speechless. She couldn't believe that it was real. She had never seen any sort of live performance before, by anyone. And, of course, nothing that could or ever would match this one.

After the third song was finished. Olabe waited for the applause to die down, which took almost five full minutes. She stood at center stage with the spotlight illuminating her.

"Hi everyone," her voice boomed out across the audience. "How you all doing tonight? I hope you're havin' fun."

The crowd exploded. People cheered and clapped. Some shouted that they loved her. A large number chanted the name of her new song that was so popular right now.

"Here's the thing," Olabe's voice boomed out again. "Tonight's going to be a great night for all of us. The ushers are passing out little booklets to all of you right now and we are going to bring up the house lights."

The lights came up and ushers were everywhere passing out the little pamphlets.

"These are the words to the songs for tonight. I want every one of you to sing along. No more of this mumblin'. No more making the excuse that you don't know the words. So, girls, make sure your guy sings every word. And, guys, don't let your girl off easy. Make her sing, too."

With that said the band played and Olabe sang. The crowd needed no coaxing and joined right in.

Time flew by and before anyone realized it, Olabe had performed more than two hours straight.

She came to the front of the stage and motioned for the house lights to go down. The bright spotlight was still on her, though.

"Ladies and Gentlemen. Thank you all so much for your faithful support through all of my career. I love you all."

"We love you," someone in the crowd shouted and a murmur of laughter fluttered across the auditorium.

"Anyway. There's someone here tonight that I'd like you all to meet," Olabe said as she pointed to a person in the front row and a second spotlight appeared and illuminated Jewel.

Ladies and Gentlemen. Please meet my mother."

Everyone craned their necks and looked around. Then, they could see Jewel in the huge flat-screen monitors on the walls. Jewel finally stood up and waved. The crowd waved and there was a huge amount of applause.

The second spotlight faded and Jewel sat back down, but she could feel the embarrassment still raging through her face. Marlene and Ron leaned over and congratulated her.

As the noise disappeared, Olabe smiled and said, "Thank you. There's another person that I would like you to meet. She's the angel that came into my heart when my heart was broken," Olabe's voice cracked and she fought back tears. "I needed her and she needed me, at just the right time."

Olabe couldn't hold back and tears streamed down her face. More than half of the audience joined her. They didn't know why, but when their beloved star cried, so did they.

"Anyway, her name is Liza Jane," the second light turned on and found her immediately. Liza Jane scrunched down in her seat.

"Liza Jane? Will you please come up here with me?"

Two ushers came over and boosted her up onto the stage.

"Can we get a microphone for her?" Olabe asked as she came over and hugged Liza Jane.

Two sound men rushed over and quickly pinned a wireless mike on Liza Jane's shirt and tested it.

"When I met this little girl a few year ago, she didn't speak nor hear. She lived in a world of silence. Then, through the miracles of medicine, and two hearing aids, she can now hear and speak very well."

People clapped. Rachael's eyes flowed a steady stream of tears as did Jewel's.

"Liza Jane? Would you sing with me?"

A soft, almost undetectable voice said, "yes," and the crowd clapped their approval.

"You start, honey."

"Amazing grace, how sweet the sound," Liza Jane's little voice boomed out across the audience.

Olabe harmonized with her. The band was silent because no one knew what was happening. None of this was part of the program they had rehearsed.

The two sang in perfect harmony and in complete acapella.

Carl Strom was standing behind one of the side curtains watching. He was in total shock, but his business wheels were turning at full speed.

"My God," he whispered out loud. "We've got to get that recorded."

When Olabe and Liza Jane finished, the crowd was silent for a few seconds. Tears dropped off the tip of Raaf's nose. Suddenly, the whole audience, as if they were a single person, stood and applauded.

Olabe helped Liza Jane bow which only brought out more thunderous cheering.

The two ushers helped Liza Jane down from the stage and she ran into Rachael's waiting arms, before she sat back down in her seat.

"I still have another little surprise for you all," Olabe chuckled.

The crowd loved it. It threw the anal stage-manger into fits. Carl stood in awe. Olabe's concerts had always been full of surprises, but this one was by far and away, her very best.

"Ladies and Gentlemen. Please meet David Thompson," the second spotlight scanned around and finally found a shocked David in the front row. People politely applauded, but didn't know just why.

"Oh, yes. By the way. David wrote the song that's number one right now." People were now really applauding. "My Sweet Alabama Mama."

David stood and was immediately helped up onto the stage. He was quickly wired for sound.

The audience just couldn't quiet down. Here was their star, on stage, with the writer of probably one of the most famous country songs ever, and they were about to perform it together, right now!

David was given a guitar by one of the stage-hands and another to Olabe. They strapped them on and plinked a few notes together. Then, David strummed a chord and the song began.

The song was beautiful and meaningful. It told the age old story of not appreciating your mother enough. Always loving her, but there was never time to actually say the words.

"I've traveled the world both wide and far," Olabe sang and David played. "But I'm home now, in the Alabama sun. But, not in time to tell you, my dear sweet Alabama Mama, lying so cold and still. All I can do is stand here and cry and only hope you know how much I love you still."

The audience was standing and everyone in the place was openly crying as they felt the pain in their own lives of not telling someone that they loved so dear, for not telling them that they loved them near often enough.

"Good night, everybody," Olabe shouted and waved her hands. David bowed.

Pandemonium exploded. The crowd screamed, applauded, shouted, and whistled. The curtain came shut and the house lights came up to full.

"Just sit here a few minutes," an usher said to the first row. "Wait until the crowd clears out a little. Then, we'll get you right out of here."

"Olabe. Olabe," Carl shouted and ran across the stage as the musicians were packing up and stage hands scurried everywhere. "We've got to record that song with you and that little....what was her name? Oh, yes. Liza Jane."

They all ate supper in Olabe's suite. Even Ron and Marlene were invited. The food was terrific and everyone recounted their favorite parts of the show.

"Weren't you just scared to death on that big ol' stage, Liza Jane?" Elizabeth Ann asked while Liza Jane played with a new doll.

Liza Jane shook her head, 'no.'

"I jest opened my mouth and the words came out."

Everyone laughed.

Finally, the party was over and everyone was exhausted. They all made their way back to their rooms to sleep and then travel home the next day.

   *   *   *   *

A few months passed and slowly things got back to normal. The stories of the great adventure had been told and retold many times. But, as with most experiences, life works its way back to normality. People go back to doing what they did before.

One late afternoon, in mid-July, Olabe and Jewel were working in the garden when they saw someone running up their driveway. It was David, and he looked totally exhausted. They dropped their tools and ran toward the house to meet him.

"Come quick," David gasped and bent over as he tried to catch his breath.

"What's the matter, David," Olabe asked and put her hand on his shoulder.

"It's Daddy. He came home from work, sick. And he's got worse. Mama don't know what to do."

Olabe ran for the truck and grabbed her cell phone. She immediately called 911. Jewel ran for the house and grabbed a bottle of whiskey.

When they got to the Thompson farm they found Rachael sitting on the front porch with Liza Jane in her lap and the three boys huddled around her.

"I 'spect he's done gone," Rachael said and broke into tears.

Jewel went into the house while Olabe tried to comfort her dear friend.

When Jewel came back out of the house, she whispered to Olabe. "I think he's gone, Olabe. I tried to give him a little whiskey, but it just ran out of his mouth. Can't feel no heart beat and his skin is gray and cold."

Just then, the paramedics drove in. They rushed in and worked on Raaf for a while. Finally, they came out on the porch.

"I'm 'fraid he's passed," the most senior paramedic said. He was a kindly man with white streaks in his black hair. His immaculately pressed blue shirt showed heavy signs of sweat. "We done everything we could, you know."

They took Raaf's body in a green body bag and put it in their vehicle. They drove away normally, without lights nor siren.

"Oh, Olabe," Rachael cried. "What am I going to do?"

An autopsy was performed and it was discovered that Raaf had suffered a massive heart attack and was probably gone within a few minutes of its onset.

The funeral was held in the little country church near Skipperville and was attended by everyone in a wide area around. Raaf and his family were well liked and both he and Rachael were from old, Alabama families with lots of kin. There was lots of flowers and a wonderful service. Raaf was laid to rest in the little cemetery behind the church, not far from Olabe's father's grave. The Women's Society provided a lunch in the church basement after the burial.

"What in the world will that poor family do?" Jewel lamented more to herself, but loud enough for Olabe to hear.

"I don't know, Mama. I truly don't know."

CHAPTER 12
Epilog

The months turned into years. Kids grew and went to school. They graduated and the life cycle went on.

David became the rock of the family and immediately found a job in Ozark. But, in time, and through lots of Olabe's help, he found his niche in life. He had real talent and Olabe recognized it. Carl Strom, Olabe's agent, signed him, and over the years, he became very successful. David moved to Nashville and wrote many songs for lots of country stars. But, he never forgot his Alabama roots and came back often. He found a lovely girl in Nashville. She worked for a local radio station and happened to interview David one time. It didn't take long and they started seeing each other. A relationship bloomed and they were married. They now had a little girl named Emma.

It was a Monday afternoon in late September and Olabe had driven over to the little school in Clopton to pick up Liza Jane and take her home. It was a warm and beautiful Alabama day with a sky so blue that its color could only be known to those that live there. Olabe dropped Liza Jane off at home and talked a few minutes to Rachael before going home.

When she drove up the lane, she just happened to look over at their huge garden and noticed what appeared to be a bunch of cloth down at the far end. She thought that the scare crow must have blow over and tumbled down near the fence. She parked the truck and came in the house expecting to find Jewel watching her favorite soap program. But the television was off and the house was silent. Olabe turned and walked out onto the porch.

"Mama?" she called.

No answer.

Where could she have gone, Olabe thought to herself.

Then, she remembered the bundle of cloth at the end of the garden. Olabe walked toward the garden with dread in her heart. The closer she got the faster she ran until she was standing right next to the yellow work dress her mother loved to wear with pink flowers on it. Olabe reached down and felt her mother's wrist for a pulse. Jewel's arm felt cold and looked gray.

"Mama," Olabe cried and crumpled down on the ground. She cried for a while, and then, just sat there holding her mother's hand.

Somehow, she managed to get herself together after a while and came up to the truck and called 911 on her cell phone. The paramedics came and pronounced Jewel dead at the scene.

The funeral was held three days later at the little country church near Skipperville. The local minister of the church officiated. People came from miles around, as Jewel was well known and liked by everyone. Ellen May closed the mini-mart in Skipperville for the day so she could attend the funeral and be with her family and friends. William came up from Mobile and, of course, David came down from Nashville. Olabe's sister Rebecca June sent a huge bouquet of flowers, but sent a short note that she would not be able to attend their mother's services.

Olabe was in a daze. It was almost like she was watching the whole proceedings from afar. The service and the short processional walk to the cemetery all seemed like a dream. During the luncheon, people, many of whom she had never met nor seen before, came by to tell her how much her mother had meant to them. She ate the food and drank the coffee without tasting anything. Her brain was in a fog.

The days that followed were pure hell. Her mind wanted desperately to slip into a deep depression, and would have, if it wasn't for Rachael. She came over and stayed with Olabe for almost a month and saw her dear friend through it all. Finally, Olabe was able to find herself and started putting the pieces of her life back together again.

More years came and went. Life goes on, as the old saying goes, and so did Olabe's. The next year, she decided not to raise a garden at all and told the co-op to take down the fence and just make it part of the tillable land. But, she couldn't give up gardening altogether and she had a small plot spaded up near the side of the house. She could still do her gardening, but certainly not on the massive scale she and her mother did before.

Elizabeth Ann finished her business courses and found a job at the Ozark hospital. She married David Becker's grandson, Richard. They live in Ozark and now have two children; Johanna, and Rudy.

Ellen May and her husband run a new Fast Gas and mini-mart in Clopton and Skipperville. They are in the process of building another one near Ozark, right on the intersection of Highways 123 and 27. They recently built a house just outside of Skipperville and they have a new baby girl named Annette.

Olabe and Rachael each mourned for a long time, but had each other for comfort and companionship.

Rachael even learned how to drive a car and David bought her a new, little Toyota wagon. She drove to Clopton almost every day and helped Ellen May with her new baby and even took a turn now and then working in the mini-mart at Clopton.

Bart graduated from high school and went right into the Marines. Now it had become his life's career and he was doing very well. He was stationed in Honolulu, Hawaii. He was home for almost a month last year between Thanksgiving and Christmas and looked lean and very healthy. He had a girlfriend that was born and raised in Hawaii and Rachael was planning a visit in March to meet her. Rachael asked Olabe if she would go to Hawaii with her. She said that she was afraid to go so far away from home by herself. Olabe decided to go.

William was the first one of the family to graduate from college. He went to the University of Alabama and studied engineering. He was hired just before graduation by General Electric and has since moved to a suburb of Mobile. William married a girl that he met in college and they were expecting their first child in about six weeks.

Obadiah was the unusual one. He finished high school with honors. But, instead of going right to college, he worked a year for the farmer's co-op. He then enrolled at the University of Tennessee at Chattanooga majoring in pre-med. He worked very hard and was on the dean's list of academic achievement every semester. During Obadiah's junior year, he transferred to Temple Baptist Seminary. He graduated with a masters in divinity and, was an ordained Baptist minister. He was sent to Echo, Alabama, where he lived and was working getting a church built. As of yet, Obadiah was not married.

Liza Jane was in the 6th grade and doing well. Her hearing had improved a good bit, just as her doctor had predicted. She was the light of Olabe's and Rachael's lives and they desperately attempted not to spoil her, but they did, whenever any chance appeared.

Two more years passed and Liza Jane graduated from the 8th grade and would start high school next year.

It had been a warm day and Olabe was glad she had the house air conditioned. She had worked on a long letter to her sister explaining her feelings and hoped they could at least be friends. Maybe not as close as some sisters were, but at least friends anyway. Olabe wrote that she would be glad to come to California for a short visit or would love to have her come back to Alabama to visit and talk.

"Life is short," Olabe wrote. "With Mama and Daddy gone, it's just you and me left. I'm sorry for any hurt feelings that I gave you and hope you'll forgive me for any wrong doings."

She signed it and sealed the envelope. Olabe hated the thought of going out in the hot afternoon sun, but was driven, for some reason, to get it in the afternoon mail down at Clopton before five o'clock.

The days went by and Olabe waited, but her sister didn't answer her letter. She was sitting on the porch one late afternoon contemplating the thought of calling Rebecca. After all, she had a phone installed in the house a few years back, so she wouldn't have to sit out in the truck, that was now really showing it's age, and talk on her cell phone.

Funny, she thought. *After all these years of having a phone in the house, it still seems natural to sit out in the truck and talk on my old cell phone.*

Olabe rocked and the old chair creaked its annoyance. She noticed a vehicle going slow along the road and then, turned and came up the lane towards her house.

The truck was old and probably was once painted a light blue color. It labored up the lane and stopped by Olabe's truck. The door slowly opened and an elderly man stepped out. His hair was pure white and uncut. His face was tanned and wrinkled by age and long hours in the sun. He wore an old tan shirt that was clean, but had long ago lost most of its color from countless washings. He wore old jeans that appeared loose on his thin frame. They were threadbare and patched, but clean. His shoulders were slumped and rounded. He had trouble walking and assisted himself with a cane.

"Miss Olabe?" he asked in a quiet, soft-spoken voice.

"Yes?"

"May I come up and sit a spell and talk?"

Olabe thought for a few seconds as her mind raced through her mental files trying to place the old man. Maybe he was one of the many shirt-tail relatives she had met at her mother's funeral.

"Sure. Come up. Do you need any help?"

"No. That's alright. I can make it. It just takes a little while."

The elderly man came up the steps and virtually slumped down in the other rocker.

"May have to have a little push, though, when it's time to go," he said and his old gray eyes sparkled.

Olabe smiled and said she could lend a hand when he needed help and wondered how in the world he managed to drive that old truck as crippled up as he was.

"Don't know if you remember me, and all, Miss Olabe. There's no reason, I suppose."

Again, Olabe's mind raced through her mental files. She hated that part of aging when she couldn't come up with a name or face when she wanted it, and it seemed to be happening to her more frequently than she thought comfortable.

"Well," the old man drawled. "I'm the ol' pirate you all sent to jail a long time ago." He rocked a little and looked down and a little forlorn.

"Jimmy Wade," Olabe suddenly said. "Jimmy Wade Betterund. Yes. I certainly remember you."

"Well, Miss Olabe. It's been almost twenty years since I was sent away. I was released for good a few months back.

"My wife left me and filed for divorce the day they took me to prison. Don't know whatever happened to her. I wrote her a few times, but the letters always came back marked as 'address unknown.'"

"I did my time, Miss Olabe, and had plenty of time to contemplate my wrong doings. I know I did wrong to so many good folks and don't know how I ever let myself do it.

"I wasn't raised that way. My folks was good people, and all. Just got greedy, I guess. It was all about the money.

"I just wanted to stop by and tell you all how sorry I am and would like to tell it to your mama, too, if she's at home."

"Mama died a few years back," Olabe managed to say through her shocked feelings.

"Oh. I'm sorry to hear that."

"She lived a good long life and is now with my daddy. Bless their souls."

"Amen to that.

They both let the words settle in for a few minutes and rocked in silence.

"Don't matter none, Miss Olabe. But, I don't hold no grudge at all. I was an awful human being and someone powerful needed to take me down, and you got here just in the nick of time."

Olabe noticed the old man's eyes were filled with tears and for some reason, she felt sorry for him.

"You alright, Jimmy Wade? I mean, do you have somewhere to live?"

"Oh, yes, Miss Olabe. I rent a little place down near Pinckard. It's a little place. Actually, it's a mobile home on two acres of pine trees. It's very spacious, at least compared to where I had been living. I still got my old truck and a little savings. That and the little Social Security I receive gets me by in fairly good style."

They talked for a while longer and Jimmy Wade asked about lots of the neighbors. Olabe told him about the ones still alive. He asked about the Thompson family and was truly saddened when he heard that Raaf had died.

Finally, the old man managed to stand up by himself. He thanked Olabe for talking with him. He turned and managed to get down the two steps to the ground. Olabe followed him.

"Jimmy Wade?" she said which caused him to turn around.

She hugged him and said, "Welcome back. And, just so you know, I don't hold any grudge nor bad feelings. In fact, why don't you start coming to the little church over in Skipperville. It might do you good."

He promised that he would think it over. He got into his truck, started the engine, and drove back down the lane. A little cloud of dust followed along behind.

Olabe went back on the porch and smiled to herself.

"God?" she said as she stared up into the early evening sky. "You sure have a sense of humor," and she broke out into laughter.

* * * *

Rebecca sat and reread Olabe's letter. A shot of pain and guilt stabbed through her heart. She and Olabe had never been close at all. Even as little girls, they fought over anything and everything. But, Rebecca remembered exactly the thing that broke any bond they may have ever had.

It was when Olabe's career had really taken off. The media showed her on every evening news cast and many newspapers featured her in their Entertainment sections. Olabe's fame was big news and her fan base exploded exponentially.

For some reason, Rebecca had hoped that Olabe would fall flat on her face when she went up to Nashville. She didn't want her to succeed, even a little bit. She wanted to be able to say, "see! Told you so." But, that petty jealousy wasn't the real breaker. That came at a time long after Rebecca had moved to California and was in the middle of a divorce. California had proven to be a very expensive place to live and she really needed money. One night as she watched the evening news she saw a clip on *Entertainment Tonight* where they told about Olabe and her family building a huge mansion estate outside of Nashville. Rebecca actually got sick to her stomach as she watched. She considered Olabe's fame and fortune an absolute slam in her face.

Once, she even wrote a letter to Olabe and asked her for a loan of $1,000. It took all her effort to just write the letter. In fact, she wrote it four times and tore each one up, until the fifth time, which she actually sent.

She remembered the letter she got back, which came by Special Delivery. It wasn't even from Olabe, herself, but rather a short note from her business manager. Oh, there was a check included, and not for $1,000. It was for $5,000 along with a typed note that said not to pay it back and just consider it a "helping hand between sisters."

Rebecca did cash the check, mainly because she absolutely needed to. She used some of the money very sparingly, but saved most of it. As her situation got better, she diligently saved money from each pay check until she had the full amount in her special saving account.

Rebecca remembered the day she put the Cashier's Check in the mail to Olabe. She included a little note that said, "Here's your gift back." She still often remembered the satisfaction it gave her. Not that Olabe cared in the least, she thought. Most likely her check went to her business manager and Olabe probably never knew anything about any of it; sending Rebecca the money and then, getting the money back. That was what was so frustrating about it all.

*   *   *   *

But, Olabe didn't give up. She decided to write to Rebecca once a week, which she did. She always included little fun remembrances from when they were young and told her little anecdotes that had occurred during the week.

A few days later, Olabe picked up the mail from her mailbox. There was a letter from Rebecca. She rushed up to the porch to her chair and breathlessly tore open the envelope.

> *Dear Olabe,*
>
> *Received your letter and your attempt at restitution. Rest assured that I'll be no part of it. When you left to follow your dream, it included nothing for your family. You may think my heart is cold, but it's all from the years I've had to think about it. Please don't come out here. Please don't try to call and for God's sake, please don't write again.*
>
> *R.*

Bombard her with kindness was Olabe's plan, and it continued for more than a year. Occasionally, she would get a very short and snippy response from Rebecca. Her favorite response seemed to be; "Stop wasting your precious stationary, especially your nickel tablet paper." This always made Olabe laugh as she remembered how the two of them, when they were little, absolutely had to have different cover pictures on their tablets to make sure they could tell them apart.

Little by little, Olabe wore Rebecca down. After eighteen months and over seventy letters, Rebecca let down her guard. Just a little at first, but more and more as time went on. She finally began answering each of Olabe's letters and even included some of her own funny little stories.

Maybe it was just that now the two sisters were getting older, but whatever the reason, Rebecca seemed to be mellowing.

During late July, Olabe wrote a short note to Rebecca that she was planning a trip to Sacramento in September and would love to meet her for a few days, or however much time Rebecca could spare.

It took forever for Rebecca to write back, but she finally did. She wrote that she would be happy to spend time with her and even invited her to stay at her apartment. Olabe smiled as she read the lines and was even a little shocked.

The plans were made and Olabe left on the 10th of September for California. She flew out of Dothan to Atlanta, Atlanta to San Francisco, and finally, San Francisco to Sacramento. It virtually took all day and Olabe was exhausted when she finally got off the plane in Sacramento. But, her hopes and excitement level were high. And, there waiting right at the gate was Rebecca. The two hugged and tears streaked down both of their faces. They hadn't seen each other in many years. Old grudges seemed to have disappeared and the two chatted continuously. Instead of staying the four days, that Olabe had planned, her visit grew into almost five weeks. Rebecca had recently retired which gave her all the free time she wanted to travel all over northern California and southern Oregon with Olabe. They even stayed at an elegant little motel right on the rugged Oregon coast for almost a week.

One afternoon after the two women had returned from their travels, they were sitting on Rebecca's deck enjoying a glass of a fine California red wine. It was a beautiful afternoon with a clear blue sky and the temperature was very mild. It was a day to make a person just happy to be alive.

"Rebecca?" Olabe said. "Are you happy?"

"Happy? Oh, I guess so. I don't know if anyone is ever truly happy. But, all in all, I guess so."

They both leaned back and enjoyed the wine for a while in the late afternoon sun.

Rebecca began to tell Olabe about her ex-husband and how, at first, she loved him and wanted to have children with him. He didn't want any kids and was, in actuality, married to his career. They grew more and more distant and then, she found herself being attracted to a younger man that she worked with. He was only two years younger than she, but seemed to enjoy life and had a sparkling sense of humor. At first, they were just working friends. But, as time went by, they started meeting after work for glasses of wine and fun conversation. As these things have a tendency to do, one thing led to another, and one night, they both let their guard down and ended up in bed at a motel. Rebecca told Olabe how guilty she felt and promised herself that she would never allow it to happen again. But, her husband was gone all the time and she was bored and alone. The one time turned in to two, and then more. One evening, she and this Tim were having dinner at a small, intimate restaurant when Rebecca happened to spot her husband and a skinny, slutty looking skank that had her arms and legs virtually wrapped around him. She watched them kiss deeply, and that did it. In a rage, she stamped over to their table and confronted her husband. Her husband admitted to having an affair, but that it meant nothing. Even the skanky girl joined in and said it was "just for the sex." Hearing that, Rebecca dumped the table over on them and slugged the girl right on the nose.

"She jumped up shouting that I broke her nose and would go to prison for it," Rebecca laughed.

Tim stood in total shock. It was then that she realized that she was doing absolutely the same thing, and it had to stop right there.

Rebecca said that she and her husband tried to reconcile, but the gap between them had grown too large and the only course of action was a divorce.

The divorce was long and drawn out, but somehow, she managed to get through it all.

Olabe listened to her sister and laughed with her, hugged her, and cried with her.

It was then Olabe's turn. She told Rebecca about how her career started and her sudden rise to fame. She told her about her husband, Bill, and what a wonderful, caring, and thoughtful man he was. She told Rebecca about her two children, Alexia and Robert, and even her dog, Jackie. With quivering voice, Olabe somehow managed to even tell her sister about the accident that took away her whole life and the depression and guilt she felt afterward.

"God, Olabe," Rebecca said softly. "I had no idea. It must have been awful."

Tears streamed down Olabe's face and Rebecca came over and put her arms around her.

They talked about their mother and her passing.

"Oh, God, Olabe. I hope you'll forgive me for being so stupid. I was wallowing in my own guilt and just couldn't bare the thought of facing you. But, I hope you know that I loved Mama dearly."

"I do, Rebecca. I do."

"And, Olabe, I want you to know that I loved the song you sang about our Alabama Mama. I know it was about our mother."

"Rebecca?" Olabe said as she filled both glasses again. "Why don't you come back to Alabama and live in Mama's old house with me? It's a soft and easy life there. Those hills have a way of healing your very soul. They certainly did heal mine."

Rebecca thought for a long time before she responded. Then, she said softly, "Olabe, California is now my home. I love it here and I have friends here. I want to live and die here. But, I would like to come back home and visit Mama and Daddy's graves, though."

Within three days, Olabe helped Rebecca pack her things and they headed for the airport and the soft red hills of Alabama.

Rebecca only stayed two weeks, but seemed to enjoy it very much. She especially loved Liza Jane and her interaction with Olabe.

She remembered Rachael, but had not seen her in so many years. She found Rachael very warm and friendly, but thought she looked much older than she actually was.

All too soon, Olabe took Rebecca to the Dothan airport for the trip back to California.

"Thanks for coming, Sis," Olabe said as she hugged her sister at the gate. "Let's keep this going and see each other lots."

"We will, Olabe. Oh, and Olabe, thank you for everything," Rebecca said as she went through the gate to board the waiting airplane.

Both women knew what she meant and they both knew they were much closer now. As close as only sisters can be.

*   *   *   *

It was a cloudy day and Olabe was up early. As part of her usual routine, she sat out on the porch and enjoyed an early morning cup of coffee. She had always loved the soft sounds of the world waking up all around her and the early light of dawn turning into full daylight.

It was a little after eight when Olabe drove down the lane, turned right on the road, and headed for Rachael Thompson's house.

"Morning," Olabe said as she got out of the truck and walked up towards the porch where Rachael was sitting sipping a cup of tea.

"Good morning. Want a cup? The tea kettle is still on the stove."

"No thanks. I'm on the way down to Ozark to get some plants to take up to Mama's and Daddy's graves. I thought that maybe you'd like to ride along."

"Any other day, I surely would," Rachael said and sat her cup on the little table. "But, today, I've got to run over to Clopton and take care of Ellen May's little one."

Olabe sat and talked a little while. Finally, she stood up, told her friend that she had probably better be getting along, and drove off toward Ozark.

It was cool out, but Olabe felt a little too warm, so she rolled down the window and let the wind blow in. The trip to Ozark was a pleasant drive. The scenery was familiar as she had made this trip many times before.

It was now almost eleven o'clock and Olabe felt a little hungry, so she decided to stop at a little restaurant on the outskirts of Ozark and have an early lunch.

"Think I'd like a bowl of chicken noodle soup and a grilled cheese sandwich," she ordered from a hard looking waitress that snapped her gum. She made no response that she heard anything that Olabe had ordered or, for that matter, she was even a live person.

Olabe watched a young woman and man sitting in a booth nearby drinking coffee. They were trying to be very discreet, but she noticed that they were holding hands. It was now rare, but still happened, when something would remind her of her husband Bill. Pangs of longing shot through her heart and she had to force back tears.

Her soup and sandwich came. Even though the soup was very good, she decided that she really wasn't very hungry, after all. She ate a little more and then, tried a few bites of her sandwich. It, too, was good, but, for some reason, she had lost her appetite.

The waitress came over to her table, didn't say a word, put the bill down, and walked away.

As Olabe stood up, her body creaked a little, but it was just the aging process she decided. Suddenly, she felt a fair amount of indigestion. She thought that it was probably the soup that was a little too greasy for her.

When she went to pay her bill, she picked up a roll of Tums, lemon flavor. The gum-snapper took her money, didn't say anything, and gave her change back. She turned and walked away without a smile or "thank you." Olabe sighed and walked out the door.

She drove into the parking lot of the big nursery she liked. As she got out of the truck she felt another surge of indigestion, so she reached for the little roll of Tums.

Olabe looked over lots of plants and flowers before she selected just the right ones. She stood in line for a while and then got to the cash register.

"You all find everything you wanted?" a sweet, young girl asked at the register.

"Yes. I think these will do just fine."

The girl told Olabe the total and she handed the clerk some bills. The clerk handed Olabe change and her receipt.

"You all want me to have one of the boys carry that flat, and all, to your vehicle?"

"Oh, no," Olabe said as she felt a strong hot-flash coming on and she was starting to sweat. "I can carry them."

She walked back to her truck and put the flat next to the big water can she'd put in before she left home, along with her gardening tools.

Olabe started the engine and drove out onto the highway and headed for Skipperville. She was burning up. Sweat was pouring down her back and chest. She opened the window and turned on the air conditioner. Still, she felt too warm.

As she turned into the parking lot of the little country church just outside of Skipperville, the sun came out. Olabe's hot-flash let up some as she put on her big gardening hat and carried her tools to her parents' grave site. She made two more trips back to the truck to get the water can and then, to get the plants.

"Hello, Mama," Olabe said softly as she knelt down by her mother's grave. "Hello, Daddy."

Even through the sun was out, the temperature was moderate, which made working around the graves very pleasant. She hummed some of her favorite hymns as she worked. She pulled weeds and trimmed the grass. Then, she got her shovel and dug trenches for the plants she had bought.

Suddenly, Olabe looked up. There. Over by the fence. There was a young woman standing there along with a young man. Two little girls ran around playing. Olabe smiled and went back to work finishing her planting. She looked up again. Shock struck her very soul.

"Mama?" she somehow managed to say. "Mama, is that you?"

Then, she heard children playing on the other side of the cemetery. It looked like......was it? How could it be. It was her husband, Bill, and he was waving to her. She must be going crazy. Maybe it was the heat. The two kids saw her and came running towards her along with their black dog.

"Alexia? Robert? Jackie?"

Renwick:
Olabe Mae (Bostwell) Renwick died suddenly yesterday morning. She was the daughter of Henry and Jewel Bostwell. She married William Renwick and had two children; Robert and Alexia. She is survived by a sister, Rebecca June Martin. She was preceded in death by her mother, father, husband, son, and daughter. Services will be private.

The only obituary appeared in the Ozark newspaper, per Olabe's directive in her will.

Mourners gathered at the grave site behind the little country church near Skipperville and Obadiah came from Echo to officiate at the services.

"Friends," Obadiah said in his minister's voice. "We're gathered here together to say farewell to a dear friend. She touched the hearts of so many of us," Obadiah's voice cracked and it took him a few seconds to compose himself. "She always knew what to do, and did it. She never asked for anything in return, except our friendship."

Liza Jane hugged her mother. Both of them were sobbing.

"Miss Olabe helped every member of our family in so many ways, it makes me want to recount them all right now. But, according to Miss Olabe's request, she did not want any lengthy laments of her passing."

Obadiah stepped forward, picked up a soft yellow alabaster urn, and took the cover off. He poured the contents into a small hole dug in the earth next to Jewel's grave marker.

"Ashes to ashes and dust to dust. Miss Olabe, I commit your remains to the earth of your birth. May the soft red hills you loved so much, that nurtured you as a child, that welcomed you when you came back home, that healed your pain when you hurt so much, may they now accept you back home as your soul goes home to Jesus. May the soft red hills of your Alabama home, bring you final peace."

The End